ISABELLA

ELENA M. REYES

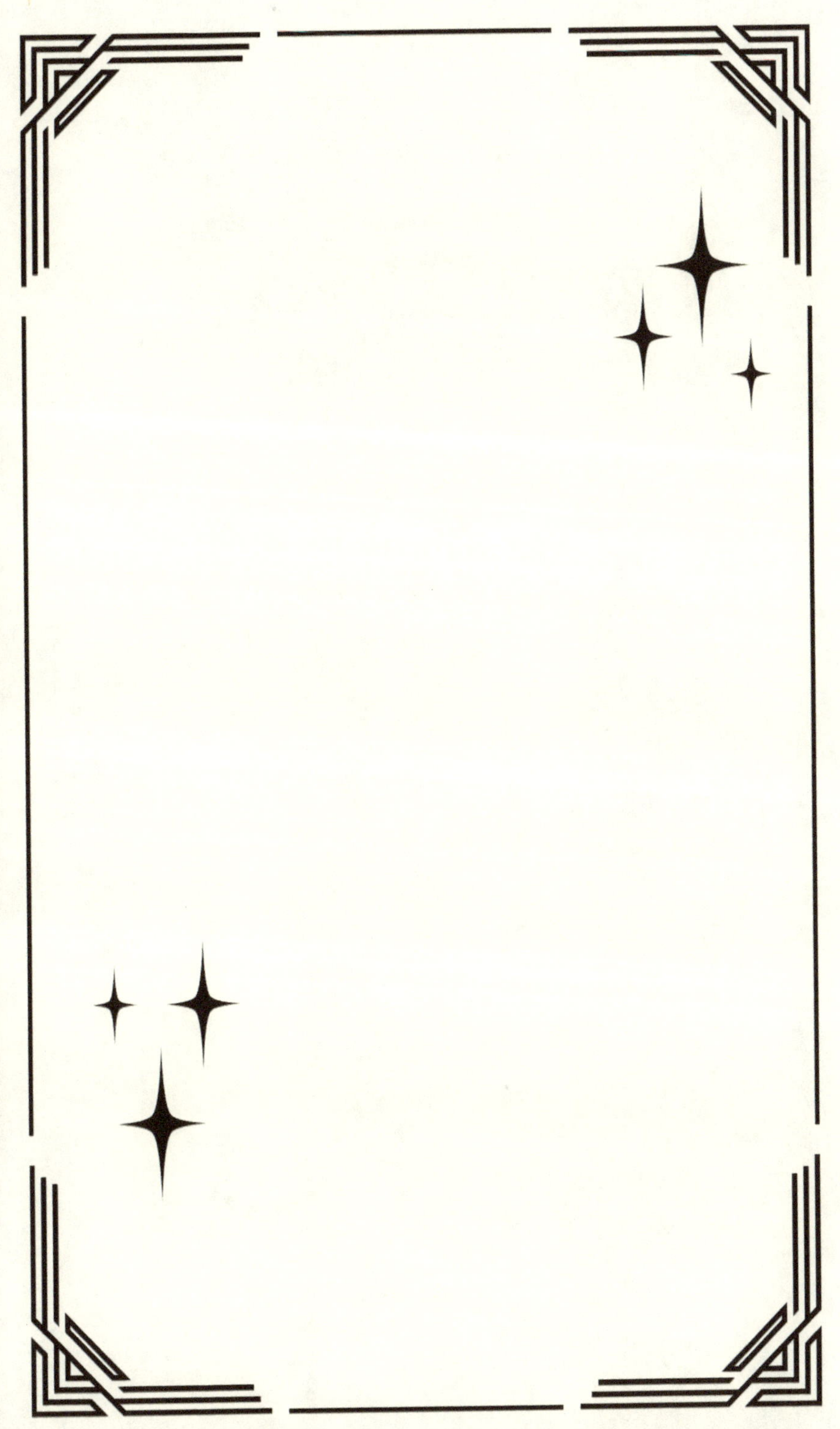

SUMMARY

Isabella
I've lied to those I love the most.
I'm the keeper of all secrets, but I've broken that trust. I don't know if they'll ever forgive me, but what I've done, I've done out of love and loyalty.
To my family. To my mate.
To the little one, I dream of every night . . .

Xadiel
Everyone has secrets.
Some are harder to hide than others, and yet, I see the strain in her eyes. I feel the hopelessness in her soul but have kept my promise to let fate run its course. Even when the animal within demands to take control—to fight and be her protector—when it's against herself she needs saving from.
But then she disappears. Is taken.
I'M A BEAST.
UNTAMED.
WILD.
And I'm coming for what's mine.

Check out the Spotify Playlist for HALF TRUTHS: NOW.
Each song took me on a heartfelt journey as I wrote this emotional,
fated mates DUET.

HALF TRUTHS NOW Playlist

ACKNOWLEDGMENTS

This one's for those who believe in soul mates.

Who love a brooding alpha: a man with an edge of violence.

And are PNR-loving whores like me, who live for a good
HEA with a BEAST. #HePurrs.

HAPPY READING, MY BEAUTIFUL BABES!!!

Also, a huge THANK YOU to my team:

Ana Rita, C.M. Steele, Marti Lynch, Emina Ros:
I LOVE YOU WITH ALL MY HEART. I couldn't do this without
your help, push, & tough love.

And lastly, to my husband:
You will always be my boyfriend. My muse.

XOXO
Elena

GLOSSARY

Mind link communications are in ***bold italic***.

Alpha King: Ruler of all werewolf packs. Also referred to as alpha of alphas

Luna: His Queen & Mate

Beta: Second-in-command, but under the Luna

Gamma: Third-in-command, also under the Luna

Pack: Community of werewolves; family

Heat: When a female wolf or the mate of one is most fertile. They have a fervent desire to have sex and can only become pregnant during this time. The males have a similar compulsion, a response called a **rut,** and this is triggered by his mate's needs. This usually lasts about 5 days.

Slick: Female's wetness. Much like her scent, this calls to the male and taste sweet and it's released in copious amounts. Used as lubrication to make taking his knot easier.

Pup: What werewolves call their offspring.

TRIGGER WARNINGS:

This book contains dark elements that some readers might find triggering. This man is brutal and unapologetic, please read at your own discretion.

Contains:

Explicit Violence (GORE)
Death & Torture
Biting/Mating Mark
Some Primal Play
Obsessive Anti-Hero
Knotting
Children Kidnapped (No Harm At All)
Threatening of FMC
Abuse of FMC by Villain (Not Sexual)
Some Blood Play/Licking During Sex (Bite or Cut)
Misogyny

Isabella

PROLOGUE

Silence surrounds me.

It slithers across my flushed skin and pricks at my other senses while my footfalls fill the night's air with their soft, thumping rhythm. They merge with my exhales—with the harsh rise and fall of my chest as I fight to take in deep breaths, my body throbbing with the need to keep moving forward.

I'm running, yet I don't know where I'm going.

I'm compelled to put one foot in front of the other and never stop until the tightness in my chest lessens.

Moreover, I don't question it. Don't want to. The forest is tranquil tonight, and I absorb the stillness—what most of humanity covets the most—yet runs from in the same breath.

Serenity. Comfort. Rest.

This feeling blankets you in warmth while stripping you bare, and while humans and creatures alike crave the blank sound of noth-

ing, it's their thoughts they run from. Because you can't hide from the voices in your head; for right or wrong, they force you to accept reality and admit faults.

Yet, I welcome the soundless noise like an old friend.

It's not unpleasant, just simply different. A calling only I seem to hear tonight.

Leaves crunch beneath my bare feet while a twig or two hurt the soles, but I don't stop to inspect the damage. Instead, I'm smiling as I dodge one branch and then another, moving slightly to the right to avoid a stump, and the closer I get to the tree line's edge, the moonlight peeks through the trees, bathing me in its soft glow.

And the closer I get to my destination, the giddier I become, giggles slipping through my parted lips while nature cocoons me with its love. While the earthy essence that drew me deep into the forest becomes stronger. Becomes more defined with its cedar notes and tantalizing note of mint that I can almost taste in the soft breeze.

My nipples pebble and thighs clench; the fiery lick of sudden need leaves me almost breathless, and I have no choice but to pause and find support against a tree. Tingles run up and down my spine, my chest heaving as a thrumming pulse grows between my thighs, leaving me weak.

Every nerve ending in my body is sensitive. Feels alive. Starved for touch.

I want to bathe in that scent and merge it with my DNA, becoming one. I also want to throw my hands up and twirl under the stars, thanking the deities above for this gift.

Because there's magic vibrating all around us.

We breathe it. We feel it. It's tethering us to this world—inside us —and right now, I don't want to stop this heady emotion building inside my chest from forming. I'm already attached to it and accept it.

My heart knows what it is. Recognizes what this sensation means.

In the distance, the deep rumble of a wild animal makes me pause, yet I don't experience fear. If anything, the sound causes plea-

surable goosebumps to rise across my skin. The predator's song is comforting with its deep base and cadence.

"Oh gods," I moan low as another shiver runs down my spine—a tremor that quickly becomes a caress the closer I get. Mine. All mine.

Because Mother has told us stories of her special day, of what to expect and how to greet your beloved, but nothing could've prepared me for the sudden influx of desire currently overtaking my senses. It's heady and rages like a storm; I'm caught in an avalanche with nothing but this invisible string around my chest holding me upright.

So close. Just within reach.

Pushing off the trunk, I take a few steps toward the next cluster of trees. They're thicker than those I've passed, their limbs hiding what's beyond. Deeper, the growl beckons me closer, and I take in a deep breath, clutching at my chest while that connecting string gives a sharp tug.

So hard that I almost lose my balance.

"Help me." The words leave me in a whisper, yet there's also a powerful surge of strength that pushes me forward. One step at a time, I'm being pulled toward the scent and owner—the rough rumbles—until I break through the thickest cluster and...

I stop in my tracks.

Unable to do anything but breathe, because staring back at me is a beast bigger than anything I'd seen. Or heard of.

It's a wolf, there's no doubt about that, but the sheer size alone makes me want to run. Not from it, but I'm compelled to move closer. To touch that thick, shiny fur the color of midnight and run my fingers through it. To nuzzle and then bare my neck.

"My mate," he snarls, the words dark and garbled while his golden eyes, with black swirls at the center, staring at me with an intensity that makes me shiver. His head tilts a bit to the side while my heart accelerates, thighs squeezing tight as I watch his large, fat tongue swipe across a sharp fang.

Yet I don't perceive him as a threat. If anything, the possessive glint in his eyes is soothing.

"Hello, my mate." My response and confirmation; one that brings a small wolfish grin to his maw, and my heart thumps wildly inside my chest. It feels right. To be in his mere presence gifts me a warmth I didn't know I'd been missing.

He moves closer, slowly and with his head low, as to appear non-threatening, but it doesn't sit well with me. Not the nearness, but the fact he'd think I'd be anything but thrilled to meet him sends an uncomfortable sensation through my chest and I rush toward him, meeting him halfway.

There's no shyness from me. No trepidation as this large beast, taller than me in this form, nuzzles his head against my neck while a low rumble comes from his chest. The sound calms me at once, a soothing lullaby that resonates through every nerve ending, and I hum with satisfaction.

He likes this, too. The beast puffs out his chest before licking across my collarbone in a kiss.

"Such a sweet guy," I coo at him, and he huffs, the act tickling my skin. It also causes me to giggle and move back just enough to meet his stare; I'm thrown once again by how magnificent he is.

Tall and strong, easily over two feet taller than me—and this is on all fours.

Golden eyes with swirls of black; a beautiful combination that calls to me.

Soft fur that shines in the moonlight.

The scent of cedar with a hint of mint that I find irresistible.

Every aspect of this wolf embeds deep, tattooing itself within every molecule of my DNA, and I can't deny him. Even without meeting the man and seeing his handsome face, I know I'll never belong to another.

Without conscious thought, I lean forward and close my eyes, placing my forehead against his lowered muzzle. I inhale deeply while that rumble deepens, while his exhalation warms my skin, and we stay this way without giving importance to time or commitment.

Quiet and without needing to fill the silence because we're content to just be. My fingers slowly stroke his fur, petting and enjoying the softness, but then bones begin to break and shift, his midnight pelt receding as a hint of skin breaks through.

My breathing accelerates.

It's want and wonder and hunger. It's excitement and acceptance and—

"I'm coming for what's mine."

"Where did you go in that mind of yours, ma sorcière?" two male voices speak in unison, yet I hear each clearly. Can make out the honest love coming from one, while the other reeks of jealousy. Hate. "Answer me, Isabella. Don't make me hurt you."

Alpha
XADIEL

The female lying before me is perfection.

She's the literal definition of beauty.

And more importantly, she's my one and only weakness.

It's been that way since the day I watched my mate bathe underneath the stars a hundred years ago. I lost more than my heart then as rivulets of water flowed down her naked back, each drop caressing where my lips ached to trace, even as I fought the connection. But then again, I never stood a chance when it came to Isabella. That moment and every single one that followed, I've been tied to her—worshipping at her temple—while she looks at me with nothing but love and adoration.

Her heart is pure and doesn't hold grudges. Her soul recognizes mine and accepts me as I am, and yet, it's moments like these where I'm humbled the most.

Isabella's asleep and lying on her stomach, so trusting and relaxed, while I stand guard and protect my most priceless possession. She is my life. My everything. And right now, unbeknownst to her, she's teasing the bloody fuck out of me.

Her right leg is slightly raised, exposing the delicious flesh of her inner thighs while a soft cotton sheet is strewn across her arse. Nothing else. She's bare and soft; her sinuous curves await my touch while she trustingly dreams under a full moon and the protection of her male.

Soft lighting filters through the airy, sheer curtains Isabella insists we keep in every home we own. And right now, I agree with my wife, loving the way the moon sweeps across her tiny figure while she shifts and resettles. Minute in action, yet the result is heady and sexy—coquettish in the way the cotton moves a little lower— how it exposes a tiny bit of her arsecheek.

"Motherfuck," I growl low in approval. It's a sound that builds inside my chest as I take her in just like this from the edge of our bed. I'm naked and hard, cock pulsing as beads of pre-come mark our bed frame, the pearl-like drops sliding down until they land on the cheeky pair of lace knickers she'd worn earlier tonight.

I'd ripped those off with my teeth. Little Moon knew I would, too.

In this room, no clothing is allowed. In our private space, I want access to her flesh.

Another shift, this one ending with a sigh. Each breath she takes causes my balls to grow heavy while my chest rises and falls, filling every crevice inside me with her mouthwatering jasmine scent.

I haven't slept all night. I'm unable to rest.

My beast rumbles inside me—has been for the last twelve hours— and is near thrashing with a violent need to mount his mate. It's not a rut. Not that I've experienced one, but knowing every facet of a wolf's life— male and female—is part of being king. I've studied our traditions, the gifts and curses that come with being a shifter, and this is different.

It's more. Rooted deeper within my genetic makeup.

Visceral. Raw. Unapologetic.

She's also not going into heat, but this filthy yearning is shaking me to the core. The perfect mark on her neck, and the tattoo of my wolf on her thigh—they're just a small part of what binds us together. Our goddess doesn't make mistakes in her pairings, and my mate was built for me.

Our merging did more than bring us together; it slightly altered her genetically to have some of my wolf traits. My scent is embedded with hers. Some of my blood flows through her veins. However, the more prominent changes have been dormant for a century; a promise she made with my blessing to the God of Death has kept them under lock, but even with the rebirth of Gabriella, there's been nothing.

No added physical strength.

No enhanced sense of smell.

Not so much as a sharp talon.

One day I'll be blessed to feel her claws break the flesh of my back.

"Xadiel," she whimpers in response to the heavy vibrations coming from my chest, a rumbling sound meant to soothe her. At once, Isabella's hand reaches out toward my side, patting the mattress but finding my pillow instead. Small fingers grip the case before pulling it closer, tightly against her side, while a whine escapes her lips. I'm not there and her brows furrow, lips sticking out in a tiny pout. "Alpha?"

One word, and I shiver.

I'm famished. Bloody crave her slick heat.

Every muscle in my body contracts. My primal instincts—the hunter—is alert and taking in every subtle breath from my prey. Each twitch while I swallow hard.

"I'm right here, love." My voice comes out deeper, the animal within merging his growl with my timbre. This ardor grows with each tick of the clock, a palpable burning in my veins that I welcome while her body reacts.

Goosebumps. A deep shiver.

Her thighs spread and the sheet bunches over the curve of her arse, giving me the perfect view of her pretty slit. Bare and pink, my heightened sight blesses me with a clear view of her wetness clinging to her swollen flesh. How her tiny hole flexes in search of my cock.

"Not close enough." Another needy sound. A call for her mate.

"Is that right?"

"Come to me, my king."

My fangs drop and my cock throbs at the command, while the knot at the base pulses in time with her heartbeat. Each *thump thump thump* is a siren's song pulling me closer by an invisible thread that connects us.

She is mine.

I am hers.

And nothing else fucking matters.

I've spent the last century worshipping what I almost lost, a thought that still leaves a bitter taste in my mouth. The self-reproach will never leave, but then she whimpers again, this time swiveling her hips against the mattress. The act and mewls are so motherfucking sweet—comforting me—while flashes of our life together clash with the present.

Our beginning. Her strength and convictions.

The rise of a guilt that will never truly wane.

But then her love for me vibrates through our bond, and I answer. The force is steady and unbreakable; I'm purring our sacred song while the scent of her arousal spreads through every crevice of the room. The rhythmic hum fills our space and my mate smiles, her lips curling a bit while I place a knee atop the mattress. It dips under me, distributing my weight as I slowly crawl over her tiny figure.

I'm a beast at seven feet tall in human form. I dwarf her petite body.

But she likes it. Loves how I tower over her in every form.

"What do you need, Little Moon?" I ask, fangs skimming the back of her neck while I rip away the sheet, tossing it somewhere to her left. A shiver rocks her at the act, anticipation meeting excitement, and it's a fire heightened when I nip the flesh at her nape, as I trace from her hips to the area just below the side of her breast with the tip of a black-tipped claw. "Tell me, my queen. How can I serve you?"

"All I need is you, Xadiel. Nothing else." Breathy, her tone is the same one she uses when I bring her to the edge on my tongue, and the reaction is instantaneous. A sharp jerk of my cock over her skin, a trail of my pre-come from the back of her knee to her inner right thigh. Then another. The need to mark every inch of Isabella with my seed is near uncontrollable, and I rock against her, rubbing the pearl-like fluid into her soft skin. "Please. Inside me."

There's a pitch in her tone that's different this time.

Her scent is also just a little bit sweeter. Calling out to my wolf.

Are her dormant traits—

My thoughts are cut off by a small gyration of her hips. The way she looks at me from over her shoulder. Blue eyes meet mine, heavy-lidded while her stare is heated. An almost challenge to deny her.

"So demanding." My fangs break the skin at the base of her neck, dragging lower while she squirms and tries to arch. I never take my eyes off Isabella. "But you've always been this way. Spoiled by me."

"Xadiel, I'm—"

"My perfect little witch. Always such a good girl for her mate." Tracing my canines lower, I exhale and watch as goosebumps rise. How a soft sheen of sweat forms, glistening in the moonlit room, the longer I make her wait. I'm scenting her. Taking her deep into my lungs while my purr becomes animalistic growls.

A declaration from her mate that I own her.

Each rise of my chest vibrates against her, causing the most delicious sensations against me before I trace my tongue down her spine and over the curve of her arse. *Fuck,* she's delicious. A bloody aphrodisiac.

"Present for your mate, female. Show me what's mine."

"Always yours, my male."

The second I move to kneel beside her, she lifts her arse and spreads, and I growl in approval.

Because there she is. Trusting and sweet and decadent; I love this woman with all that I am, and she gives so freely. Isabella Evergreen is my treasure.

With the tip of a claw, I caress her right arsecheek before palming it. It's round and firm and my teeth ache with the need to bite, but instead, I land a sharp slap to the flesh. It jiggles at the force, the sting causing her to cry out, and the sound is *so* fucking sweet.

I land another precise slap. Then another.

Alternating between each globe until her skin is heated and a lovely shade of rose. And while she whimpers, pushing back for more, I slip from the bed and kneel a few inches from her tiny feet. While she sways her arse from side to side, a clear invitation, I lick a fang.

Then I wait; nostrils flare while my mouth waters.

Thirty seconds of total silence.

"What are you...*oh fuck*!" One sharp tug and I yank her to the edge of the bed, her cunt pressed against my tongue. The single touch causes my mate to scream, hands gripping the sheets while I trace from ass to clit, sucking her trembling bundle of nerves between my lips before dragging a fang over the sensitive hood. "*Oh, Gods*."

"That's right, baby. I am your God." Another swipe of my tongue, right over her entrance, and I exhale roughly against the slick flesh. Rumbles build; the animal's rattling inside my chest as another rush of wetness coats my tongue and I take a hold of her hips, claws pricking her skin. There's a small whimper from Isabella. I can feel her blood on my fingertips, but I can't stop.

Instead, I growl over her lips. Rub my chin against her juices.

"Xadiel, please." Another whine. Desperate.

"Mine." Our truth. My obsession.

Pinning her in place, I drink every drop, lapping at her like the starved beast I've become. She's so soft under my tongue—quivering—but I don't take pause. No. I suck and nip, flicking in rapid succession where she's most sensitive, before slipping my tongue inside her flexing hole.

Now, I growl.

Loud and completely gone to my baser instincts.

This is an addiction, and I'm her willing servant. A century hasn't waned my desire for her. If anything, this has been our foreplay. Each day I want her more. It will never be enough.

"Yes. Yours." My mate's wet and soft and undulating, unsuccessfully fighting my hold—trying to ride my face from this position—but I take my time. Fucking her for a few seconds with rapid strokes before dragging the flat of my tongue up her slit; I suck on her clit with open-mouthed kisses and lave the tender flesh while she whimpers, "Take me, my king."

"Patience, my queen. Let me enjoy you." A huff comes from her, but I silence it with a quick nuzzle to her cleft before my eye catches something I've missed.

This won't do.

And while I've turned my female into a beautiful, horny mess—waiting and whining for my cock—my attention is on another proof of my ownership. One of the many I've left across her body in the last century. There's still the hint of a bite mark there. The faded shape of my teeth.

Unlike my mating tattoo or the wolf on her thigh, this one didn't change after it healed. Instead, it lightens with time, becoming slightly darker than her natural tone until I fix it.

Retracting the claws of my right hand, I release her hip and bring my fingers to her pussy and gently tap a rhythm onto the pink flesh. It's a tiny *splat splat splat* over her wetness while my nose caresses the shape of my fangs—tongue tracing each.

I'll spend an eternity marring her flesh.

She's watching me from over her shoulder. Lips in a pout. "Do it, Xadiel. I need it."

"And I love you." I sink my teeth in, tearing through flesh while my tongue traces the bit of wetness on her thigh below the bite. Her blood and slick; nothing tastes better. It's heady and decadent, a cock-throbbing ecstasy, and I lap at the wound while sinking two fingers deep inside her pussy.

"Fuck, baby," Isa utters in a long and drawn-out moan as her walls grip me, tightening as the taste of her blood and need blossoms on my tongue. It's an aphrodisiac; a mystical drug for a wolf as the essence of his soulmate melds with both the man and the wolf. "Don't stop...please don't stop."

"Come for me, love. Give your male what he needs."

She's everywhere. In me. All around me.

I'm consumed while my female shakes, mouth open in a silent scream while goosebumps rise and her nipples pebble. They throb in time with her heartbeat, the pulse between her thighs matching their cadence as I finger fuck her through the first orgasm of the night. While my knot expands, nearly painfully so, but for now I ignore it.

My spend is hers.

I will never rob her of pulling the seed from my balls.

Each pump draws out the waves cresting, the evidence of her release dripping down my hand and onto the sheet while her blue eyes never leave mine. Open and free, Isabella gifts me her trust and devotion. It sings through our bond, causing my cock to jerk hard, and I breathe through each electrical jolt.

I'm close to my own release, and yet I watch her through proud hooded eyes as a pretty, sated smile curves at her lips before I retract my teeth.

"So fucking beautiful."

"I love you, Xadiel."

"And I bloody live for you." My mark is red but already healing. Her juices soak my hand and our bed, but she's not covered in me.

My come. "Remember that, Little Moon. You will always be my world."

Before she can respond, I pull my fingers out and flip her onto her back. She squeals, an adorable giggle that dies off as I move us to the center of our bed and take my rightful place between her spread thighs. Now, I'm met with a mewl full of yearning and the soft, sweeping touch of her magic down my spine.

It's been quiet all this time, and I've missed it. Hunger for it.

Just like the first time at our lake, Little Moon's tethers stroke and pet, causing goosebumps to spread while I rub the bulbous tip of my cock up and down her slit. A little deeper each pass. Pausing at her entrance a little longer while her hands claw at my arms.

"I need you inside me, Xadiel. Fill me...*Gods*!" It's a scream, ripped from her throat as I slam into just above my swollen knot in one forceful thrust. Every nerve ending in my body is alight with fire as her walls squeeze tight. She thrums within my veins, and my roar shakes the walls around us. "Move, baby. Need you to move."

Yet I'm riveted by the filthy sight of her stretched around me. So obscene it nearly looks painful, but the salacious grin on her face tells me otherwise. That I please her. That she craves her beast.

An inferno licks at my heels as I watch her squirm and dance, wiggling beneath me to find friction. There's so much rightness to this moment, the electrical pulses currently riding me everywhere we touch, that I can't hold back.

"Breathe for me, Little Moon." That's my only warning. With one hand, I gather both her legs and push them back toward her chest, pinning her in place before pulling out so just the tip sits outside her entrance. Her hole flutters, kissing the head of my cock twice before I thrust in and set a pace that doesn't leave her much choice but to dig her fingernails into my shoulders and try to hold on.

I'm bent over her, lips hovering while taking her every exhale into my lungs. I fuck her with a punishing pace, keeping Isa cradled close as I slip a hand behind her neck, careful to not nick her with my claws, and angle her head back. My fingers sit across my mating mark. The bond sings as she closes her eyes; I'm riding her hard, and each punch of my hips strokes her cervix.

She loves it. Her cries and the sound of her wetness each time I enter is the most beautiful sound in my world. "Gods, I always need you. No one else, my alpha."

"You were made for me, Isabella." My other hand reaches between us, and I place a single finger on her bundle of nerves. I don't move it, just press down while licking across her mouth. "Mine to cherish, honor, and fuck like the perfect little toy you are."

"I'm so—"

"Again, love. Squeeze me like that again," I demand. She does, and the effect has me throbbing. I'm thickening inside her while my knot pounds against her labia, stretching her a little more so my female only feels pleasure. Never pain from being locked to me. "Gods, you're a gift. My heart."

Another thrust and her lips part; I kiss her while my grip on the back of her neck tightens. Her walls flutter, then contract, making it hard to pull out, but I piston my hips harder. Faster. Leaving her gasping for breath as I twine my tongue with hers.

And Isa kisses me back with just as much urgency, teeth clashing and biting. She's animalistic in her desperation, chasing the orgasm building, and on the next punishing stroke, my knot slips in. My female shatters immediately, biting down on my bottom lip and drawing blood as I swell to my full size.

And between the sting of her tiny teeth and the milking of her walls, I'm unable to hold back. We're locked in with the head of my cock against her cervix—pulsing—filling her to the brim with my seed. Each spurt of come pulls a deep shiver from her, robbing my treasure of breath, and she clings to me.

Helpless. Trusting. Mine.

"My alpha," she whispers low. Dreamily and completely sated.

"And you're my good girl. Take my knot so prettily." Moving us a bit so she's more comfortable, I cradle my world close to my heart while my dick vibrates within her channel. It's slow, a rhythmic throb meant to soothe her, as does the purr inside my chest. They lull Isabella into a sleepy state after a few minutes, so warm and languid. Even the tiny snore she emits when I lazily flex within her walls is adorable.

There's nothing in the world that can compare to this, how she loves me—gives herself to me—and I'm a greedy arsehole for committing this sin.

For her, I've become obsessed.

Unapologetically protective.

And when the day comes, I'll dethrone the devil himself to make her smile.

Isabella

I've been awake for a few minutes now, enjoying the silence.

This small window of time before the sun rises, when every member of our pack is asleep in their homes and a few select guards are stationed throughout the surrounding forest. Close, but far enough to give their alpha and luna some privacy. They walk the perimeters in wolf form to protect this family, because much like a coven, werewolves aren't solely connected by blood bonds.

This goes deeper. It's so much stronger.

They will kill to protect each other without a single doubt, something very few creatures will do. You don't rise against your alpha without punishment either, and it's a lesson that still haunts the corridors of our home back in England.

Every wolf in attendance that day watched the royal family exact revenge on those they trusted most: his aunt and the former beta. No mercy. No second chance. They were disgraced, ripped apart, and then the heads staked on a pike to display outside the royal pack's border lines.

A warning. A promise.

Harsh, yes, but I will never judge. Not when my kind has done so much worse.

Moreover, it's something wolves whisper about with pride.

He killed for me. He picked me above all else.

And a man or beast that will do so is fit to be king. I am his home, and they are a part of me.

Alpha King Xadiel Evergreen would give his life to protect those he cares for.

My male. The man that just a few hours ago left me sated and full of his seed, yet in the same breath, I'm needy.

Because I will never *not* need him.

Even now as I watch him sleep beside me, snuggled close and with his arm thrown across my midsection, the temptation to taste him is strong. I want his weight and girth on my tongue. To feel the delicious stretch of his knot again.

For a century, I've been more than blessed.

Like this, he's handsome and even boyish. Calm and resting, a serene expression while his sharp jaw gives one tiny pulse. A quick one, but when I flick my eyes to him, they're closed and nothing else moves.

For a beat, I watch my alpha. Take in the slow flair of his nostrils and rising chest, no sound or movement. He's asleep, and for a second longer I want to enjoy him just like this.

Unaware. Sexy. Mine.

At a hundred and ninety, this man doesn't look a day over thirty. His body is stronger and more chiseled than when we met, his hunger for me just as ferocious.

Clenching my hands, I lower my eyes to his pecs and then down his abdomen where an eight-pack is half hidden by a bedsheet. It sits just below his belly button, keeping from my gaze the deep V of his hips and his semi-hard cock.

He's always like this in the morning.

Always ready to claim me.

My mouth waters and I swallow hard, biting the inside of my cheek to keep in the whine fighting to break free—a call to my mate. This alpha male will always belong to this witch.

Maybe I can—

"Good morning." Rumbly and deep, Xadiel's voice causes a shiver to rush through me, the jolt fiery and strong, while my heart thumps harshly inside my chest. "What has you so wet, my female? I can scent your need."

My eyes flash to Xadiel, and the salacious smirk on his face makes my thighs clench. Makes goosebumps to rise across my skin.

"Morning, my love," I say with a calmness I don't feel, yet I maintain my composure. Refuse to let him know that I'd been lost in my desires and failed to realize those hypnotizing golden eyes were watching me. How he bites his bottom lip. "How long have you been awake?"

"Long enough." Another low growl, this one accompanied by the throb of his fully erect cock. It tents the sheet, jerking under my stare, and there's no mistaking the scent of my wetness in the air surrounding us. How it coats my upper thighs and the unmistakable shift of my lower body as I try to rub them together.

Try, because he's watching me. Eyes dark, the golden color slowly being overtaken by black while his nostrils flare.

I know I'm tempting him. My nonchalance grates the animal within.

Ravage me, my wolf. "What's that supposed to…*oh!*"

One intake of breath and he's above me, thighs spreading mine apart and cradling himself between them. I'm caged in beneath his delicious strength. Xadiel's naked and hard, pressed tightly against me so there isn't an inch of space—warming my bare flesh that tingles where we touch.

Like little electrical pulses underneath the skin. They unfurl and ignite, causing goosebumps to span across my skin while the scent of my desire fills the room. I'm clenching and needy, trying to undulate against his thickness with the limited space between us, but he remains still.

Too poised.

This is the stance of a predator. Just watching. His nostrils flare and low purrs build, yet he's unmovable as I try to get the friction I need and that he's denying me.

That is until a small tremor runs through me. Just that small taste of pleasure and he snaps his hips, sliding the bulbous tip through my lips and up to my clit with a hard stroke. Just one.

Because the second he kisses my bundle of nerves, I come for him like an obedient mate.

Can't stop the whiny mewl that leaves me nor the way I arch, back off the bed and molded to his chest while my orgasm tightens its grip. The way I respond to him, even the smallest of touches, is nearly painful, yet I welcome the bite. How owned I am.

Because I own him too.

Feel his pride and love every waking moment.

"Much better," he croons, flexing over where I'm most sensitive. It keeps me on edge, wringing every bit of pleasure from me while I can't do anything but take it. And when the last of the waves subside, I feel it. Him. The heat of his spend as it drips down my pussy and to my ass. "Can never have enough of you, Little Moon."

"Yet you denied me the stretch of your knot?" The reply is full of sass, but he finds it humorous. There's a slight curl of his upper lip on the right, exposing the tip of a sharp fang. There's also the flash of all-black eyes. The beast's warning me to behave, but I've never been one to follow rules.

Slipping a hand between us, I run the tips of two fingers across the head of his cock and through the mess he made, then bring it to my lips. I suck them, savoring the taste of him at its purest, while he grows hard once again. I moan, parting my lips and sliding my tongue across each digit, not leaving behind a single drop while Xadiel gives me a warning snarl.

Darker. Hungrier.

My beast is playful and strikes just as fast.

His teeth break the skin above my right nipple, digging in, and that bite of pain quickly merges with the last of my orgasm. Lashing, it strikes across every nerve ending and I come again, smaller yet just as powerful.

"Xadiel," I whimper, holding his face to my chest, not wanting this feeling to end. And he purrs at that, keeping his fangs inside for another minute before retracting them slowly. He licks the tender area after, cleaning my blood and sealing his mark, and every swipe across heightens the ever-present tingles that force another deep and harsh clench from my core.

"So perfect, my mate." Nuzzling the teeth marks, my alpha peppers tiny kisses across my breast until reaching my nipple, which he nips, sharp and fast before shifting so we're face to face again, lips hovering. "So sweet."

"I love you too, my king."

"Bloody fuck, sweetheart. You're making this difficult on me."

"Could be harder..." I trail off, a giggle slipping through when his eyes narrow.

"There's nothing in this world I want more than to watch you choke on my cock before I split you in two, Mrs. Evergreen."

Those words cause a hot rush of desire to run through me. For my pussy to clench. "Please."

"Can't." His mouth sweeps across mine in a teasing manner, a gentle back and forth while his eyes begin to crinkle at the corner in amusement. *Gods, he's handsome.* "We have somewhere to be this morning, Luna. Or did you forget?"

That stops me, and I tilt my head to the side and away from his teasing lips. "Where?"

"Breakfast." Xadiel tries to peck me again, but at my evading response, he raises a challenging brow. "Give me your mouth."

"No."

"No?"

"Yes." At my smirk, my mate bares his teeth while I preen at the attention. "Explain what you mean by break...*hey!*" Quicker than my next blink, I'm tossed over his strong shoulder while a large, warm hand lands on the back of my thigh. His grip is tight, nails digging in a bit, and I find myself smiling. We've played this game before, and it usually ends with me bent over any flat surface. "A simple explanation would've sufficed, Xadiel."

His grunt makes my lips twitch. I'm also caught between my never-ending desire for this brute of a man and trying to remember our schedule for the day. However, it's a lost cause when a second later his fingers stretch and skim the outside of my soaked lips.

"I can feel your smirk, Isa." Not that I'm hiding it. My grin widens as we enter the en suite bath, and he walks us straight into the shower. This I fight. "Warned you to behave."

"Don't you dare." My shriek does nothing to dissuade him, especially when another rush of my arousal soaks his digits. When I'm giggling. "Payback, Xadiel. Remember that."

"Not scared, my love." He steps further inside and reaches for the nozzle, but I'm faster this time. While he was busy answering me, I mouthed the words *calor* and the room fills with steam before the first jet of water falls over our skin. It's warm and feels good and my male snorts, slowly lowering me to the ground. Thick, he throbs between us while those devilish eyes glow with mirth. "Couldn't help yourself, could you?"

"No." I turn, and he follows me—never more than a few inches apart—shifting until his seven-foot frame blocks out the multiple shower heads. They're strong and massaging and as I raise onto my tiptoes and pull his face down to mine, nipping his chin, I whisper *frigus.*

"You little brat," he grits out, shooting his arms out to grip my waist and lift me. And I'm left with no choice but to wrap my legs around his waist and choke on a moan; I'm impaled on his cock with the now icy water running down my back. "Always so bloody tempting. My weakness."

I'm in his hold. Under his control.

Being bounced at a rapid pace, every upward drive is punishing, almost painful, but the sweet relief that follows is heady. Addictive. More so because I can't gyrate or arch or so much as breathe—Xadiel's hold on me is constrictive, and I love it. Welcome the pistoning of his hips, the way his balls slap against my asscheeks while his mouth fuses to mine.

This time he kisses me fully, parting my lips with his tongue and licking across mine. He tastes me fully, biting and savoring as his purring heightens every sensation. I can only take what he gifts me, how each thrust pushes against my cervix, but then the angle changes.

Xadiel drops one of my legs, leaving me in a vertical split; I'm hanging off the ground and held by his arms around my waist while the other grips the back of my neck. He's not moving, his chest rising and falling fast while he's bottomed out and devouring my lips.

It's rough and a claiming; his sharp fangs are now dropped, and they nick my bottom lip. Not that he lets a single sanguine bead go to waste. My male growls while licking and sealing the tiny cuts. They sting, but he soothes each with the tip of his tongue before devouring my mouth, slanting his over mine once more and stealing the very air from my lungs.

And when I shiver in his hold—when I clench so violently around his girth—I'm slightly pushed back by that hand now around the front of my throat. Just held in place. Dominated and kept from seeking out his mouth, and a second later it's clear why.

I'm fucked. Literally.

My mate rides me hard and brutally, each punch of his hips sending me spiraling high while I can't do anything but cry out. Beg. Dig my nails into his forearms as I'm catapulted head-first into a state of blissful heat that consumes me.

"Louder, Little Moon. Praise your king."

"Oh *fuck*," I grit from between clenching teeth as a finger skims from where we're joined to my asscheeks. Back and forth, he does this a few times with a feather-light touch until I tremble, and at that first shake, my male adds pressure until the rough skin of his thumb is against my rim. Then he strokes, firm circles against the tight hole, and I melt into his touch. "Xadiel, I'm—"

"Love me, sweetheart. Come for your male." One firm push and that finger slips inside to the first knuckle, snapping a sharp lash across my senses that sets off pleasure-filled pulses throughout my body. This orgasm is different than the one last night or a little while ago; it's a fiery lick that grows in intensity, leaving me a whimpering mess in his arms. "Good girl. Such a perfect mate."

"Love you," I say, voice low and raw while clinging to him as he nuzzles my forehead. Xadiel doesn't move. Instead, he lets my walls milk him, groaning above me when I tighten and release. It only takes three hard flutters for him to come, but I feel each rope— welcome the sense of peace that settles over me as my alpha fills me to the point I overflow and a little dribbles out.

This time Xadiel didn't knot me, his swollen bulge sitting right outside my lips, but the intensity is just as delicious. What I needed. Just him.

It takes a while for the aftershocks to slow; my legs are now around his waist while Xadiel holds me close, my face in his neck while I breathe him in. He's doing much the same to me, scenting and massaging my tired limbs as the now warm water slides down our bodies. We don't talk for a while, but then I hear it.

Low and rumbly; he's laughing. It starts slow, just a subtle chuckle until his shoulders begin to shake, and my entire frame is moved by the action. I pull back just far enough to meet his eyes. Mine are narrowed while his are full of mirth, near squinting from the full-on laugh.

"Are you done?"

"No." Xadiel's smile is wide, and his semi-hard cock gives a jerk inside me. He's not pulling out, and I'm not complaining— almost moan at the feeling—but then he laughs again. "You're insatiable."

My shrug is unrepentant and cool while I fight back the urge to squeeze him. "You created this monster. All your fault."

"Is that the best you can do to defend yourself, Isabella?" Bringing his face closer to mine, he bites my bottom lip, leaving a tiny cut behind. It hurts a little, but he's quick to lick and soothe, an action I feel where I'm still stretched around him…and I clench. An action that causes a flash of pride and renewed unadulterated hunger in those gorgeous golden orbs. "Blame me?"

"Yes." No shame. Just a simple fact.

"Good. Because I adore your playfully naughty streak."

Isabella

An hour later, we're entering the private dining room inside the pack house where all of the ranked and unmated wolves live. Our home isn't far but private; a grand two-story cabin built by my mate and the pack, as was everything else within our borders. We do not need to leave our land or the surrounding forest.

From homes to schools to retail, everything is provided by my male.

Moreover, to humans, this is private property owned by a billionaire who doesn't allow trespassers. No one outside the members and my family knows about the city we incorporated here. Of the business we own; a commercial real estate developing company with ties to properties all along the West Coast of the US, Alaska, and back home in England.

For more than a century Xadiel's been at the head, matching the fast pace of the ever-changing needs humanity has for growth. Because times have changed. We've witnessed the rise and domination of technology and the advancements in medicine. From the small mom-and-pop shops to the monopolization of large corporations and then the rise of online shopping.

And with it, we evolve too.

Adapt. Thrive. Dominate like the apex predators we are.

Heads bow as we pass hand in hand while my cheeks bloom pink. I'm pleasantly sore, happy, and my stomach grumbles in hunger—something that makes every ear in the room twitch before those in attendance stand.

They smile, unable to hide it; our beta and gamma, along with the elite guards, each place a hand over their hearts in a deep show of respect. Happiness exudes from these wolves, and their auras shine bright at the sight of us. They also gift an honest pledge to the king and queen of werewolves that we acknowledge with a nod as we make our way to our seats at the end of the largest table.

You're a bad influence on the alpha, Isa. It's your fault we're late and my mate is unfed.

Xadiel's words through the mind link, while playful, hold a slight edge of reprimand. My being anything but fully cared for doesn't sit well with him. Never has. It angers his wolf, big old softy that he is for me.

And I disagree, Your Majesty. The culpability of my addiction lies at your feet.

At my response, his chest expands, and a satisfied grumble comes from his chest. Cocky and pleased.

My apologies, Little Moon.

There's no hiding the way I react to the nickname. Even after all this time, I preen at the term of endearment while my smile widens. There's also the added sweetness to my scent that's solely for him. How my heart rate spikes, which each werewolf notices.

Not that I hide it. Everyone inside these walls is someone we trust—our most loyal and their families—and they've been asked to join us for a true English breakfast before half of them leave on a mission. They're heading to Italy and then England in two days, visiting both royal houses for the same reason.

The fae are slowly making an appearance.

The news of Gabriella's rebirth has spread.

And my deal with the God of Death is now complete.

What was once hidden is now in plain sight; the grimoire my father left me is ancient magic, the spells within older than his father, and they hold a connection to the gods. Both life and death. There are notes within those pages and explanations, but more importantly, they hold the key to ending this all.

The path to happiness is paved by tears.

It's also been so long since any of us have been back home, having relocated from the UK to Alaska to fulfill a promise, and not once has this pack complained. Instead, they serve the crown—protect their brethren wolves—and trust my word without asking the question so many would.

My alpha needs an heir. They long for the Evergreen royal lands.

And I understand as it's been years since I've physically embraced my Wiccan coven.

Since I hugged Leo goodbye.

Twenty-one years since my sister's rebirth, nine months since she's been changed, and now it's time to face the inevitable path we must take individually. Each has a cross to bear. Wounds to withstand. Because heartache is a part of life, no one is safe from its grasp, but I'll endure every bruise—shed tears of blood—with their well-being in my heart because the ending will bring me my prince.

So mote it be.

That's better, my wolf. Though you owe me a kiss in apology.

"Please sit and enjoy your meal." Xadiel's voice carries across the room and reverberates, ignoring my demand, but then his hand on my back slips low, skimming the swell of my right asscheek. I'm given a squeeze and then a tap, causing me to bite my bottom lip and keep in an inappropriate whimper. Not that it's needed, because a second later the pups in attendance yelp at the alpha bark that sneaks through, no matter how hard their godfather tries to keep it low. It's playful, though, and the twin cherubic wolves—the blessings given to our beta couple six years ago—startle before the giggling begins.

Loud and squeaky and mischievous, their innocent amusement is contagious and my heart melts at the sound. No one is immune, not even my male, but while he gives Emmett and Eve a mock growl, every part of me clenches for a different reason.

With love and then pain. With sorrow.

My womb hurts and my soul cries out for what I yearn for more than anything in this world: our pup. That tiny part of Xadiel and me, our beautiful creation I forfeited to tether Gabriella's soul to this world. He wasn't growing inside me yet, but after being marked, my first heat would've arrived within a month.

I can't playfully shush him. Can't kiss his chubby cheek or tickle his tummy.

And nothing hurts more than the fact my little one isn't here—an angel I dream about often. He'll be our future leader. Powerful and just.

"Yes, Alpha," everyone replies in unison, pulling me from my thoughts, moving quickly to retake their seats and eat, while Xadiel's heated stare is on me. He's watching me carefully now while understanding comes through our bond. It's like a gentle caress, a soothing tug that has me looking up, meeting his eyes.

So much love and understanding in them; Xadiel never begrudged me for the decision I made the day my sister died. Instead, I've been given his trust and devotion, then and now.

Even at times when his longing for us to start a family couldn't be hidden, trickling through our bond and settling in my heart. Not once was there a reproach. Not a single second of anger.

Leaning over, he nips my bottom lip. "You too, my luna. I'll serve your plate." ***And after they leave, I'll worship your cunt until the moon rises and cast her warmth over us. Only then will I mount you and let my beast have his fill.***

At once I blush, so thankful for the distraction. For his ability to know what I always need—how to pull me from the depth of sadness that fills my heart when I think of our son.

It's not forever, Isabella. You know he'll be in our arms soon.

"Thank you, my love." ***Promise?***

"Always. It's my pleasure to care for what's mine." Pulling out my chair, Xadiel seats me and then struts over to the eastern wall where a table is brimming with fry-up breakfast items; from sausage to beans to mushroom—grilled tomatoes, and blood pudding for those who love it. There's also one cook at the station, just to make the eggs while the rest is ready to be plated and kept warm on heated trays.

We serve ourselves here, and no one is exempt from that rule.

Not visitors, and much less their rulers.

In our pack and every alpha governed under our ruling; we don't allow omegas to be used as servants. No one is abused or considered weak; we respect those that willfully give what they can and never take advantage of their status within our kingdom.

Your rank is based on what you do within the pack. Each job is important, not an obligation, and is needed to run a happy and safe environment. Especially for those too young or too old to protect themselves.

"How was your morning, Luna," the beta female says a few seconds later and I turn my attention to her, catching a cheeky grin. "We missed you during our run, but I figured you were *tied* up in a private meeting and didn't want to disturb you."

"Thank you, Faith." I snort, yet become a bit flushed when every she-wolf looks over. "And yes, something like that. Very occupied."

"Completely understand, Luna. Cain has this penchant for using silk ropes—"

"Why is my beta looking like the seared tomato I'm about to eat?" Xadiel asks, placing two full plates in front of his seat, and then frowns. "That won't work." His eyes flick from me to the food and back again before tugging me up. One second, I'm to his right, and the next, I'm nestled on his lap while a few clap for us. "Much better."

Flustered, our beta waved it off. "It's nothing, Alpha. My mate's just telling a boring story about—"

"Then let her tell it." Raising a brow, he dares his beta to refute him. Meanwhile, Faith looks close to cracking up, and my lips twitch. Even Xadiel's tone holds a hint of a chuckle. "What embarrassing thing did Cain do now?"

Wrong question, and I know it.

Over the years, Faith has grown in her confidence as the beta female. She also loves to tease me, reminding me so much of my sister and the unique bond we had. It's made things better and yet worse at the same time, but I love her. Truly do, even if I know what's about to leave her mouth is meant to embarrass her better half *and* me.

"We were discussing the benefits of using ropes to play—"

"I'm not so sure. My chair looks *so comfy*." I cut her off and try as I might, the heat on my face blooms brighter. There's also the way he hardens beneath me at the sight. The small thrust of his hips when I lean over to grab the carafe of coffee and my creamers already set out; he senses my want. **Behave.**

Not that he pays any attention to the mind link or my attempt at a taunt. Instead, he waits for me to take hold of the next pitcher— orange juice this time—while pretending to steady me with a hand on my hip.

My fingers wrap around the glass handle tightly, lifting it just a bit to move it over when he pulls me down hard. The action startles me a bit and makes me look clumsy, when in fact, I'm biting back a whimper while the handle breaks in my grip. Intact and without cutting me, the two detach and the jug teeters, the cold juice sloshing over the rim and staining the white tablecloth. For a moment I'm frozen with soaked fingers, held by the pleasurable shock, and Xadiel doesn't make it easy on me, either. He holds me over him and flexes, forcing me to feel every solid inch of him throb, and my reaction is instantaneous.

A shiver crests over me, causing me to let out a startled gasp that makes me want to bite him.

I'm still sensitive after hours of being pleasured. Tender, yet I clench down hard on nothing; I'm empty and now craving his knot.

There's also a bit of embarrassment, and it's not for what the pack's thinking. Once we bonded—sealed our lives together with his bite—I used my magic to alter one thing. Our people can sense and scent my mood, every single one, but not my arousal. Every aspect is blocked.

That was something I couldn't live with, and Xadiel agreed without argument.

They know and see how in love we are. They're also aware of what I did; I announced it without an ounce of shame and they too, understood. Because I might be married to a wolf, and come from a close-knit coven, but the sanctity of a soulmate's union is private and should be respected as such.

However, this is something my darling mate takes advantage of whenever he can.

He's a possessive man. Always staking his claim.

"Are you all right, my love?" Xadiel asks, his tone full of concern, but when I meet his eyes, they're darker. They flash completely black for a moment, his wolf's prideful rumble coming through his innocent question. "Are you hurt?"

We both know I'm not and I shake my head, watching from the corner of my eye as Beta Cain blots the small spillage while his mate leans over and hands a wet towel to Xadiel. Where she got it, I have no clue, but a second later he's cleaning my hand before kissing the tip of my knuckles.

Through the bond, I feel his amusement. He's so pleased with himself.

This is his payback for the shower.

You're going to pay for that, Alpha Wolf. Be prepared.

Do your worst, Little Moon.

"I'm fine. It just slipped," I say, voice steady while my thighs clench, the action covered by the large table and cloth. Tender and swollen, I feel the rush of wetness coat my thighs, and his shuddering breath against my neck tells me he's aware. "Maybe I should move over—"

"No." Absolute. Resounding. The king has spoken and everyone bares their necks, yet I catch the small smirks on the faces of Faith and a few other she-wolves closest to us. *I'm going to shock him for this.* "Now please eat, sweetheart. Your food's getting cold."

The sharp retort sits on my tongue, but before I can, he brings a piece of cornetto to my lips. I'm surprised by this; the Italian version of a croissant isn't on anyone else's plate. It's warm and filled with chocolate, and I can't stop the pleased hum from slipping through as it melts on my tongue.

More so when I take a second to look down and see what my male has done. While he's having his English fry-up, my plate is filled with different kinds of breads, jams, and freshly churned butter. There are also two delicious-looking pastries with a berry filling and my mouth waters at the sight, my heart giving a happy thump.

This is cheating, Xadiel.

I know.

After feeding me another bite, he picks up his fork and feeds himself a bit of egg and bacon. Satisfaction radiates from him, and his still-hard cock jerks beneath me. Taking care of me—surprising me—has always brought him happiness.

Does the same to me, so I show my appreciation with a small tug on the bond. It's playful and coquettish, and I watch raptly how the corner of his mouth quirks. He's speaking, but I'm not paying much attention. Instead, I melt against the vibrations in his chest. How his woodsy with a hint of mint scent envelops me.

"…everything set up for their departure, Luna?" That snaps me out of my thoughts, and I look over at Cain. He asked the question.

"Yes." Clearing my throat, I pick up the glass with my now-served juice and take a sip. "I've already confirmed their arrival with King Moore, and accommodations for our guards have been made. I'll be opening the portal in forty-eight hours, giving those traveling and their families a bit more time together. They'll be greeted by Augusto fifteen minutes outside the royal coven."

For a few weeks now, rabid wolves have been sighted near the Wiccan royal lands. They don't come close, just patrol the borders back and forth with vacant, lifeless eyes. They won't stop, either. The grouping of ten hasn't slept or taken a moment of respite, which in and of itself is concerning.

That, and the decaying stench of dark fae magic exudes from their flesh.

Leo called us a few days after the rogues were spotted, and not long after Xadiel's father did the same. Neither party has attempted to communicate with the other. No demands or questions. For now, they've just been keeping track of them, but it's time to make a move.

"Thank you, my luna," Xadiel answers, giving my hip a small squeeze. "After breakfast, those traveling to Italy please head to my office for a quick briefing. After, you're free until it's time to go. I appreciate your help on this matter and the sacrifices you make for our pack."

"It's an honor, Alpha," every member replies in unison, their right hands placed over their chests.

The topic of conversation changes after that and the mood lightens. Voices mix, some about the chance to visit family left in England, while others talk about the upcoming pack run on the next full moon.

However, as they mingle and eat, I can't help thinking once again...

The path to happiness is paved by tears.

Isabella

Pouch in hand, I walk a circle near the edge of a cliff overlooking the cold Pacific waters below us. It's rainy, the light sprinkling crossing over the treetops as it makes its way to where we stand before mixing with the heavy, salted mist of the sea. Then there's the sadness that fills our pack—saying goodbye is never easy.

Even if it is for a short time.

Half of the elite are ready to leave with our gamma, their mates here to bid them farewell—wives and pups that I'm now responsible for. A job I take pride in.

These wolves are a part of my soul.

The shimmery powder brightens as it falls to the wet, grassy ground, shining like diamonds while Xadiel and I give the guards a bit of privacy. He's a few steps from me, arms crossed over his chest, while my wolfen mate flashes dark in his gaze. I know he's worried—they both are—and it's because of the small bit of pain I'm in.

Something I can handle. A headache doesn't stop me.

Yet explaining that to my male and beast is an impossibility—I lost the war.

"*Aperta*." Low, the command is understood and the magic around us gives a sharp pull in acknowledgment. I'm coming close to the beginning and completing the circular shape, which causes the ground to shake. It trembles as my small headache intensifies and becomes a constant throb at the base of my skull, which I ignore.

It never fails. Will only last a few minutes.

"I got you." Xadiel's rumble against my back is like a balm. The sound soothes me while those thick arms wrap around my midsection, offering me both his support and love. He's always there for me.

Thank you, my love. "Please steady yourselves," I say out loud, dropping the last bit of powder from my fingertips and finishing the ring. "This will be over soon."

Without delay, they do as I ask while a large oval appears at the center. Like a two-way mirror, the structure reflects us for a second but then becomes foggy as a blueish haze overtakes the view. It throws me off and I step back while bringing both hands up, prepared to defend and protect, but then a scent—light and crisp—filters through the opening.

"What is it, Isabella?"

"Strong magic." At my words, a warning growl leaves the back of Xadiel's throat and our pack mates shift, their brown and grey wolves bursting forth. Stances close, they form a straight line a few feet from us while their muzzles curl into a snarl.

The sounds leaving them are clear. A challenge to the unknown threat.

And while this entity feels powerful—more so than anything I've encountered in years—a second later, I understand why. Again, the wolves show their teeth, clicking at the unknown while my alpha waits. Head tilted to the side, his muscles expand and fur grows, the thick pelt rising on his arms and chest while the claws on his hands and feet tear the nail beds.

He's careful not to nick my skin, but the white jersey-knit sweater doesn't fare well, the rips inviting the frigid cold through. Goosebumps rise. A small shiver crests.

A looming shadow appears at the portal, still unclear who, and I'm moved behind the wall of my beast. The shirt and shoes he was wearing are now torn and trash, while gouges appear in the ground where he moved to stand in front of me.

Yet, I'm not worried. Protective and sweet, but it's unnecessary as the scent becomes stronger and their essence says *hello*.

They're familiar. A part of me.

"Leo," I breathe out with a smile. Xadiel's head snaps back to look at me and I nod, letting him know it's okay. The others follow, staying in their animal form, not that I pay them much mind when a second later I'm rushing toward the tall man now standing a few feet from me.

Grown up and with his copper hair in a ponytail, my brother—now king—catches me and holds me tight. I'm lifted off the ground so we're at eye level; blue eyes a few shades darker than mine crinkle at the corner and then close, his forehead falling to mine. The power that lives within sings. It flows between us and melds, embracing and sharing its love.

It's been so long, and I can't help the tears that fall from my eyes or the chuckle. "Why didn't you tell me, Brother? We texted last night."

"It's called a surprise, Isa." Gone is the childish tone, and in its place is a deep baritone almost identical to our father's. As is the chuckle he releases while setting me down, stepping back just enough to make eye contact. *Gods,* he looks so much like our father. The sharp jaw, mischievous eyes, and even the small cut at the dimpled chin that happens when they shave.

It all makes me smile while my chest clenches. It's happiness and missing them, while I'm proud of who he is.

I know he's a great leader. Honest and fair, and while I've missed many milestones in his life, I've never been too far. Keeping an eye on him or visiting in our dreams—Augusto also reports to me directly on his progress. And when he turned twenty-one all those years ago, we celebrated in literal purgatory with Gabriella.

She didn't know who we were to her, not wanting to scar or damage her emotionally, but Thanatos granted us the privilege to be with her during his birthday. We did that on special occasions as often as we could, just like we held ceremonies in our parents' honor every year until pack Evergreen moved to Alaska.

He knows why we did. I never regretted it.

We need Gabriella here. Alive.

"The best surprise, *Your Majesty*."

His groan makes Xadiel chuckle and we both snap our faces toward my mate. They too share a close bond, brotherly and pure. I also notice then he's retracted his claws and the fur has receded, leaving behind his deliciously tan upper torso and tattoos exposed, which he covers a few seconds later with a shirt someone hands over. His pants are also on, a little ripped, but I'm pleased by him being covered.

He's for my eyes only.

"She's never going to stop that, is she?"

"No way, kid."

Another groan and then a laugh, Leo bends just low enough to kiss my forehead before walking past me to embrace my mate. The sight makes me so happy. Through the years, Leo depended on Xadiel for counsel on things that only another king could understand. Because our uncle's betrayal cut deep, but more than that, it left the future Wiccan ruler without anyone to rely on for advice.

Roberto was never the king, but as the brother to one, he knew the ins and outs. He helped my father many times and trained quite a few young warlocks when coming into their magic.

It's why his betrayal stung. They hid it well—he and King Larue —yet my father knew, and of that, I have no doubt. Father let him walk this path because it would place every key into the right lock, and changing the past would've come at a cost that would've destroyed many.

Vampires, werewolves, and witches. Humans too.

No one was safe, and my heart breaks for Aunt Silla who's mourned her mate every day since then. He allowed her to be hurt— that female fae might have stabbed her, but her spouse didn't lift a finger to stop it. *My sight might've been compromised, but I should've listened to my intuition.*

No one deserved what he did, yet Xadiel filled that place in Leo's life without being asked to while Augusto took over his lessons.

One taught him how to rule. To not be afraid of making hard decisions while also listening to the needs of his people.

The other helped him welcome and control his powers. To never abuse his gifts.

Being able to control his body, to be seen or not, could be a blessing or a detriment. An ability such as this one could be used to gain power or kill without detection, the latter of which will help him in the future when the time comes. Leo must never abuse this. His mate will need him.

"Luna Isabella," another male voice says suddenly, catching me off guard. My eyes move away from my mate and brother—both tall and imposing—and meet those of someone I consider family. Someone who's also holding a small bakery box in his hands.

From where I stand, the sweet scent of pastries infiltrates my senses. Takes me down memory lane. This saccharine aroma reminds me of my mom's baking. Of the ladies in the coven gifting the Moore children our favorite desserts, always nurturing our love for confectionary treats.

A deep pang of longing hits me then, and I walk over to our coven's head guard. There's a grin on his face, while his aura is full of respect and love. Our hug is short and respectful but says so much.

This is a man my father trusted and who's never stopped caring for the prior king's children.

Our safety. Our happiness.

Taking one of his hands in mine, I give it a squeeze. "Augusto, it's been so long."

"Too long, Princess." The title change is not meant as a disrespect, but an acknowledgment of who I am by birth. Because of my parents. Because of the commitment and sacrifices made by my siblings and me to take care of our people. "Your joy is beautiful. It radiates from you, and it brings this old warlock peace, my child. We're all so proud of you—all of you."

"And I'm forever in your debt. What you've done for Leo—"

"Family and duty, Isabella. It's my honor to serve the crown." Holding his hand out, Augusto gives me a warm smile. "By blood and pact."

I place my palm against his and my lips open to respond when a chorus reverberates around me. *"We are one."* Their response is united and true; I feel their loyalty. I breathe in Xadiel's love for me.

"Thank you."

"And I love you." Xadiel's warmth meets my back as Leo moves back into my line of sight. He shares a look with Augusto. I can't decipher it, and a second later it doesn't matter.

Bombolone appears in my line of sight, and I can't stop the squeal from slipping.

"Are they for me, or are you teasing?" I ask no one in particular, but it's Leo who chuckles. My eyes flick from his to the donuts, their decadence calling to me, and I take a step forward. "Answer me, King Moore."

"They're a gift."

Another laugh, this one from my mate. "Never come between your sister and sweets, Leo. I've learned the hard way."

"Is that so?"

"She bit me."

Snapping my fingers, I tilt my head back and raise a brow at my brother. "A gift…?"

"Yes." Leo takes the box from Augusto and attempts to grab one, but I yank them away before he has the chance to so much as graze them. "Gods, we have an addiction."

"The point, kiddo?"

"I'm no longer a kid, Sister."

"To me and Gabriella, you'll always be our little brother, but that has nothing to do with this package. Who sent it, Leo? What's going on?"

Exhaling roughly, he nods at Augusto who after baring his neck, looks at our gamma and nods. One by one, our wolves follow him toward the portal and walk through after giving us a final acknowledgment. The portal holds steady. The magic used drains me a bit, but I can't move past the sudden flash of sadness in my brother's eyes.

"It's Aunt Silla, Isa. She needs to speak with you."

<hr>

"Are you ready, Luna?" a she-wolf to my left asks, grinning from ear to ear. As a matter of fact, all the women are smirking. Each is displaying a knowing expression on their face, while I have no clue what to expect.

No one utters a single one as we stand outside a spa twenty minutes from the pack house, in a large mall privately owned by the Evergreen Corp. It's one of the many amenities Xadiel's built for our community; a luxury that we keep exclusive—no one outside of those allowed on our lands can visit. By werewolves, for werewolves, with a few specialty shops centered around the needs of other mystical creatures.

One store, in particular, is just for me. My own metaphysical space where I import and export to and from the Moore coven. *So much has changed, yet stays the same.*

Also, as their leaders, we not only create jobs to sustain their living but also to give opportunities to those who want to start up their own businesses. Like this one, run by an older woman and her daughter.

The latter of which has been getting close to our gamma's son.

I think they're mates. So does the rest of the pack.

"I am ready, yet I have no clue what I'm walking into."

"Good. Alpha wants to surprise you," Faith says, throwing her arm over my shoulders before tugging me inside. At once, the calming scent of lavender with a touch of eucalyptus infiltrates my senses and I inhale deeply. The combination is soothing. It helps my mind slow down, yet I can't get Leo's parting words out of my head.

It's Aunt Silla. She needs to speak with you.

Moreover, it's been that way since he placed a kiss on my forehead and stepped through the portal. Over and over again. On an endless loop. The meaning behind the words is evident as is the heaviness of the note inside the back pocket of my jeans, which I've yet to read.

Because the signals have become more pronounced recently.

The near zombie-like rogue sightings. I'm expecting a visitor. And now this note.

What's worse, one day soon I'll have to leave.

"What's wrong, Isabella?" Xadiel moves in front of me and cups my face, immediately warming my skin against the cold breeze coming off the thrashing waters. The temperatures in Alaska can be rough, extremely cold and wet, but the man looking at me with nothing but love in those beautiful golden orbs is better than any fireplace or heated blanket on this planet.

He's also astute. He knows what I need and never fails to show me I'm his priority, just like he can read my concern.

What's more, I'm lucky he doesn't push. That he grants me the time I need to understand what I see and then trusts my judgment.

"Just thinking about what Leo said."

"Why is your aunt wanting to speak with you a surprise? It's time she faces you, my love."

"But that's just it, Xadiel. She avoided me all these years. Hid like a coward." Turning my face into his palm, I kiss and then nuzzle it. *"No matter how many times I've tried to reach out, Silla denied me. The last time, she left the coven for a week to not be in the same house as me."*

"Does she deserve any leeway for helping take care of Leo?"

"Was she there out of love, or buying time?" I counter, exposing my thoughts to him. I've always kept track of her, checking her future, but have come up empty. Whenever I get a glimpse of her, it's clear and unmuffled, which makes it worse because I see no deceit.

Yet the future depends so much on our next thought.

My gut says not to forget.

Fool me once, shame on me. Twice, and I'm an idiot undeserving of my gifts.

"Trust yourself, Little Moon. You won't fail."

"It's her husband I don't trust." Closing my eyes, I exhale slowly. Take in his scent; a woodsy aphrodisiac that always brings me down from the ledge. Because I worry. Live knowing that everything will come to a head one day soon. *"He betrayed his family—almost got his mate killed—and not once has he shown any semblance of remorse. Didn't check on her. Didn't care about us."*

Xadiel bends down a bit and places his forehead against mine. His exhale is warm on my lips. *"Did you see something? What can I do to make this right?"*

"I haven't. Nothing that tells me what they're up to."

"Okay." This time he places a soft kiss at each corner of my mouth before nipping me. His sharp teeth cut, a tiny wound he seals with a quick swipe of the tongue before sliding it against mine. The kiss is slow and sweet. Reverent and all-consuming. And right when my chest begins to burn from lack of oxygen, my mate pecks me three times before lightly hovering over mine. *"Then there's nothing to worry about at the moment. You're brilliant and a blessing to everyone you meet, Isabella. Trust yourself, baby. If the time ever comes, you'll see it. We'll stop them."*

"Yeah?"

"Yeah."

His confidence in me makes me preen and causes butterflies to take flight in my stomach. "And how do you propose I take my mind off things? Do you have any suggestions?"

"I do." Tone huskier. A low growl, and I react by dragging a finger down his chest, stopping at the waistband of his trousers. "Behave."

"Do tell, Alpha," I say instead, dipping the digit inside to the second knuckle and then running it from side to side. "Please."

"You..." his hand grabs mine and places the palm over his cock at the same time his fang pierces my bottom lip "...my lovely little mate..." now I receive an Eskimo kiss "...have an appointment at Mood & Moon Spa where you'll be pampered and catered to until your male comes to pick you up in a few hours. Then, I'm going to take you on a date before eating your sweet little cunt under the stars. How does that sound?"

"Like you remembered," I breathe out, swooning at the dark, pleasure-filled promise. It's not at all what I expected, but it's better. It removes every negative thought in my body and fills my soul with pure joy—excitement replaces the trepidation I've been fighting against.

"I could never forget. My life began that day."

"Luna?" a female voice says, pulling me away from my thoughts and into the present. Ember, the owner, is a few steps from me and smiling. She also has a robe in her hand with my initials on the pocket that looks identical to the one I have at home. A gift from Xadiel. "Your private room and the manicurist are ready. Alpha has already chosen the color to match the clothes for this evening. You'll receive those after your massage and then blowout."

"Is that so?" Can't help but match her grin. I'm excited about the gift and tonight... *especially, tonight.*

"Yes, Luna. We've been instructed to spoil you today, and it's our honor to do so."

Alpha XADIEL

King *Xadiel, we have a situation at the western border.*

A patrol guard on duty sends the alert as I'm signing the buyer's contract on a piece of land in Seattle after sending Little Moon off with some of the she-wolves whose spouses left on assignment. I'm in my home office planning, putting the finishing touches on a surprise for my queen—my gift for our moonlit date.

The property is about a thirty-minute car ride from Theodore and Gabriella's home on an empty lot where an old industrial building once sat, surrounded by a few abandoned auto body shops. There's also a vast forest with plenty of wilderness for my wolf to run—explore and hunt—as this residence is meant for us to use while visiting family.

Little Moon both needs and deserves this, and the world is an easier place to navigate now with so many travel options. Not that we need them. By wolf form or with the aid of Isa's magic, we can balance our time between our people and the needs of my mate. My girl could visit her sister; begin to let go of the misplaced guilt she wrongly carries since Gabriella's death because my mate holds the weight of the world on her slim shoulders.

Always willing to sacrifice herself.

She worries and watches over everyone.

Loves and gives unselfishly without asking for anything in return.

And her beauty is deeper than the blue of her eyes or the sultry red of her hair.

It's her heart. It's simply her.

On my way, I say, opening the connection to my beta who remains silent, but his presence is there. A familiar crackle. **What happened?**

Pushing my chair back, I crack my neck before heading toward the French doors that lead to a small patio area just outside this room. This was Isabella's idea. A place where we can have our morning coffee or late-night snacks while she perches on my lap and lets me feed her.

The need to care for my mate is ingrained into every fiber of my being, but her willingness to indulge this wolf makes me love her all the more. However, at the sight of our oversized chair and the blanket she must've forgotten two days ago, my heart clenches.

I've kept certain things from my female.

She's concerned enough for our people—wolf and witch—back in our respective homelands. That, and the multiple sightings of this new breed of beast that we know so little about…

Knowing they're here, too.

"Isabella doesn't need the added stress." Not until I have answers or a solution to give her. Something has changed since her sister's rebirth; I've noticed both her exhaustion and trepidation. How there's sadness in her eyes when she thinks no one's looking, yet I see.

Her. Everything.

I also haven't forgotten who our enemies are.

The threats made and the sacrifices that followed.

Trespassers, Alpha. Two of them, but one isn't like those in Anchorage. He's coherent and demanding to speak with you. Says he's here to deliver a message.

Where on the border? I growl at the audacity of this rogue, to command my presence, and the anger-filled sound causes my beta to unleash one of his own. It travels through the link and the natural reaction to submit is automatic; the guard's connection to me bows to the dominance, and I grit my teeth to hold back the level of authority I emit. *Answer me. I need your exact location.*

My apologies. Two others arrived to help. We're at the last patrol station before reaching the storage warehouse by the docks.

On that side of the territory, I keep the pack's boats, heavy machinery, and fishing equipment. There's nothing of importance there. Nothing you can easily steal. No homes nearby.

Contain, but do not kill. Understood?

Yes, my king.

Just as wild rogues have been spotted on Italian and English soil, three have appeared in Anchorage. They're just like the others. Zombified and wandering, they track through campgrounds while aimlessly heading toward the untouched wilderness. That, or ransacking the trash of the nearest supermarket.

They haven't attempted to make physical contact with any humans. Instead, they skirt around—scrounging and drawing attention—but so far have stayed harmless. And I've left it alone for one reason:

To see what they do.

Because give someone enough rope, and eventually they'll create their own noose. These beasts are either on drugs or someone is using them to draw my attention, and my money is on the latter.

Are these the same ones roaming in Anchorage, or are there more?

I'm neither blind nor deaf and understand more than most how anger can motivate someone. Then, there's the gift of my mate's sight, blessing me with a sixth sense of my own.

I don't see the future but can hear a warning whisper in the breeze.

Foreboding has a color, and I can read the hues.

And I will protect what is mine. Will kill for her.

Tearing off on a run, I head north and shift midair after jumping over the thick trunk of a fallen red cedar a mile from our home. It's been there for years, a casualty of a training exercise with the elite and Cain, the latter being the catalyst for the destruction of five trees.

And this one is the last of the damaged logs. The weather-worn and decaying trunk is musky, filling the area with a deep, earthy smell as it breaks down the organic material and melds with the earth. Most people wouldn't be able to detect the difference, especially in a rainy forest like this one, but wolves pick up the subtle changes and notes.

Just like I hear him well before he appears.

Another set of paws comes up from my right; I'm not surprised to find my second-in-command, his sandy blond wolf heading in the same direction. His lips are curled, the bow of his head the only greeting as we plow through the dense vegetation. Our pace is set by my wolf; he's not holding back and propels forward while tearing through the grassy undergrowth beneath my black-tipped claws.

He's angry. Insulted by their attempt to enter our land; I let him take over completely.

Branches snap off my flank, combing through my thick pelt as I make a small right turn at the grouping of giant intertwined trees Isa likes to visit. My nostrils flare then as her scent still lingers—faintly —but that's not what causes my tongue to lick across my fang.

Two hundred yards, and a rumble builds in my chest.

One that makes Cain's hackles raise while I follow a new trail. The closer we get to the first patrol station on this side of the property, a different scent infiltrates my senses.

Rotting and a touch of death, not the filth associated with your regular wild rogues.

Beta Cain sneezes as the breeze sweeps past us, scrubbing at his nose with the bottom of his paw in response. Yet I don't.

My guards said the western side, but there's someone else here. I'm inhaling their stench, the sewage scent burning my nose.

This is familiar. The same as Bartolo all those years—

We're not alone, Xadiel.

Turning my head slightly toward Cain, I nod. Now that we're closer, I catch four heartbeats. They're spread out and hiding behind clusters of trees in a circle, trying to ambush us a few minutes from the first patrol check-in station in this area.

Surrounded. You take the two on your left and I'll—

I'm cut off by the sudden slam of a body into my flank, causing me to stumble a bit, but I'm quick to regain my balance. The male is dirty and has eyes a disgusting shade of puce, but he's unfazed by my wolfen size and snaps his teeth at me. His aggression is rabid and uncoordinated, swiping his nails at my face but they're brittle and some completely broken, doing little to no damage.

In the background, I hear Cain fighting. The snarls and thunderous clashing of bodies crashing fill the silence of the forest while the light-brown wolf tries to charge at me again.

I sidestep him, though, swiping my own black-tipped paw from its shoulder to its ribs. Fur and flesh give way under the sharp claw, causing the rogue to whimper and shuffle back as blood spills from the wound. A pitiful yip leaves its muzzle. Its cry hurts my heart.

I hate having to hurt a fellow wolf, but some cannot be saved.

I will kill to save Little Moon and my pack, even if it's against my own kind.

This one is gone, though. You can see it in his eyes: the malice and something else, a little darker yet empty at the same time while the unforgettable stench of death clings to his matted fur. At one point, this was a brother—someone's son—but a deviated path led him here.

He's weak and ill-prepared for this, it's clear to see, and the sound of his distress causes a wolf hidden within the trees to my right to howl. It doesn't come out, and I'm bloody amused by the threat he ensues with the sound.

And my response is to snap my jaw at his arsehole companion.

Without any real effort, I take a firm grip of his neck and swing my head from side to side, thrashing the wolf in my grasp. My teeth rip into its hide; I taste his blood, and it's acrid—of another creature.

Like the fae, but before I can fully digest this, the other mutt steps out of the trees.

Foaming at the mouth, the grey beast with filthy white paws growls at me. Angry. A warning I do not heed, and with a quick tightening of my jaw, I crush his friend's neck before tossing his brethren at his feet.

A second later, another sharp crack of bone slips through the silence, and I know Cain also disposed of one. His growl is taunting the other trespasser.

Two down. Two to go.

I almost wolfishly grin at Cain's amusement. Almost. ***Wanker.***

I'm bloody hurt, Alpha.

Sure you are.

Glaring at me, the grey wolf steps closer while I sit on my haunches and wait. Don't move a single muscle as once again, fighting occurs a few steps from my back. It's closer and louder, and I tilt my head while this rogue puffs his chest and his fur bristles.

He's larger than his dead companion, and more alert too.

The difference between the two is startlingly clear as his eyes turn black and his lips peel back, exposing sharp fangs. Another dissimilarity is the health of his teeth. Those of the now-dead rogue were yellow and decaying—there was sickness in his eyes as their color was that of a seeping, infected wound—but the scent is the same.

Wolf mixed with fae blood. It's clear to me now.

A thunderous growl leaves my chest; the demand is bloody clear. Shift.

His response is a challenging step forward while meeting my eyes head-on. Bad move.

Disrespect is something I will never tolerate.

The snapping of bones fills the air, but this time they're mine. My body realigns but doesn't complete the turn, and my beast stands on two legs with his clawed feet digging into the ground. I'm bigger than he is, towering over his frame, and release one final howl in demand. *Shift now.*

Instead, the arsehole tries to do as I did. Fights and struggles to control a mid-shift, but only pants in agony after two failed attempts. I will give him credit for not giving up, though. Exhausted and shaky, he drops to all fours and centers his grip before catapulting with his jaw open toward my stomach. His teeth barely graze my underbelly before I swat him off, and the strength used sends his body into the nearest tree.

The trunk yields under the impact, cracking in half, and then falls in the opposite direction, filling the night with what anyone could mistake as thunder. Like a strong electrical shock lashing against the solid ground during a brutal storm.

A pain-filled whimper follows, and I notice his left hind foot is at an awkward angle. From where I stand, I can tell it's broken and a jagged edge pokes out, but that doesn't keep him down for long. Shaking the impact off, he lowers his head while dragging the limb across a small mountain of leaves.

I scent blood before I see it, and the proof is there—dark and tinged with a hint of navy blue, just like Isabella showed me a hundred years ago.

End it, Beta. We're taking this one alive.

No sooner have the words passed through the mind link, there's a snapping of jaws and then the heavy thump of a body meeting the ground. It happens in seconds, ten at the most, and when the injured rogue flicks his attention their way, I lunge.

Our bodies collide and he yowls, crying out as I place my weight on his injured leg while my jaws snap around the scruff of his neck. I break the skin, just a bit, and then I tighten my hold. I'm cutting off his air supply, and he thrashes beneath me, swiping claws against my side, cutting through the corded muscles in my chest, but the struggle doesn't last long.

Each attempt becomes weaker. The force is that of a pup, and soon there's no movement.

He's passed out and I let go, letting him fall back with eyes closed while Cain moves behind me. The heavy dragging pulls my attention, and I raise a brow when he piles all three dead bodies atop each other in a pyre.

We're not burning them. He doesn't verbally respond but tilts his head to the side in question. Waits for my command. *We're taking them with us.*

With us?

Yes.

Because a wolf is waiting at the borders who owes me more than whatever message King Larue sent.

Alpha
XADIEL

reaking through the trees after grabbing a pair of trousers from a nearby storage trunk, one of many throughout this forest, I return to my skin and find my guards standing over the other two rogues. They are kneeling—eerily quiet—while one is on a leash, and the one holding its chain is his companion.

These are the rogues spotted in Anchorage, Alpha.

I know.

The one on the leash is the same wolf seen wandering behind the supermarket there. He was caught through their security feed digging through the garbage and then trekking through a campsite, getting lost within the wilderness. The police and town think they're homeless and hungry, but I know better.

However, at the moment, I'm focusing on the visible differences between the health of the two. It's more than just the scent coming off them. More than the different stages of mutation between every rabid shifter that's trespassed on my lands today.

One is clean and wearing name-brand clothing with a Rolex on his wrist, while rags barely cover the other. One is at ease, while a rash seems to be growing on the other's neck and it runs up to his cheek, leaking as the blisters are open.

"Alpha," the guards all greet in unison, placing a hand over their hearts.

I nod while dragging a body in each hand with Cain doing the same just a few steps behind me. Three dead beasts and one unconscious man; the trail of blood and the deep grooves in the earth tell the story of their demise. Some of their fur has also peeled off, snagging on fallen branches and the bottom of tree trunks during their journey.

The one still breathing isn't looking any better, especially since he shifted minutes after I knocked him out—he had nothing to protect his human skin from the harsh terrain.

"Step back." At the command, the patrol follows, and then we're dumping the carcasses at the trespassers' feet. "Talk."

Neither speaks, but they do watch, flicking their eyes from the dead wolves to me before stopping momentarily at the already healing scratches. Surprise flashes through the eyes of the sentient one, as if he doesn't understand why I'm not hurt, and I file that information away for now.

I have somewhere else to be soon.

A low growl leaves my jowl. Warning. "Talk before I rip your heads off."

No sooner has the last word left my lips than I realize there's a small Bluetooth device in his ear. It's partially hidden beneath his chin-length hair, but the subtle black device flashed twice before returning to its all-black dormant stage. And I'm not the only one that noticed.

Without having to say a word, Cain steps forward, grips the

man's face, and turns it, exposing the wireless earbud. ***Someone's on the line.***

Not a question, but I give Cain a nod and he removes the device. The arsehole tries to protest and opens his mouth to scream, but I unsheathe my claws and bring one to my lips. They're large and dripping in my blood, having torn through the nail beds, and the sight unnerves him.

Everything about me does. Both of them.

Sour, their natural odor deepens with a decaying note I associate with Larue's men, but it's the zombie-like one that finally reacts. His lips begin to curl at the corner, foam dripping down his chin. His chest heaves and his body thrashes, fighting to shift, but something is stopping it. It starts and then stops. Refuses to fully release his animal.

And I'm trying to find the ward. Because I recognize the trail of magic. There's a certain essence to each woven tendril.

But I find nothing. Nothing outside of the collar and the unhealthy color of his eyes. The emaciated body and lack of natural responses.

These wolves are not your typical rogues:

Not like the ones who want to live on their own in the human cities. That kind is peaceful, a wolf that embraces being alone while ignoring the natural need to be with a pack, unlike the other end of the spectrum. The other type of rogue—the more common—has betrayed or hurt their pack members and have been exiled as a result.

They are selfish and violent.

Untrustworthy, but somehow, I don't get that from this collared man.

What have they bloody done to him?

Smash it, Beta. Check his pockets for anything else.

Cain follows through and with two fingers crushes the electronic device before tossing it toward the large warehouse. He digs into the man's pockets and jacket next, finding two mobiles, another earpiece, and a small satchel with stones and a powdery mixture inside.

"Wait. Hand those over."

"Yes, Alpha."

"Beta." Once they're in my hands, I retract the claws of one hand and look through each, noticing right away that one of the phones is still on. There's an ongoing call from an unknown number, and I step closer to the owner of the mobile, squatting down to his level and meeting his eyes that up close, are very familiar. "This visit is going to cost you."

"You have no idea what you've just done."

"Actually, I do." Removing the batteries to power everything off, I toss them at one of the guards awaiting orders, and then turn the small leather pouch in my hand. My finger swipes across the smooth surface, thinking, and finding a crest at the bottom. It's not big, but rather a thumb-sized shield of a sacred tree with a sword at the center of its trunk. *Royal Fae.* "You stupid, stupid man."

"He's coming."

"And I'll be ready."

"His message—"

"Take him to the dungeons and make sure he's comfortable. Our guests will be here for a while." I cut him off, still fingering the emblem. They grab him quickly, a hand over his mouth to block any retort, but it's not fast enough. One sharp tug on the chain within his grip, and he releases the sick wolf beside him.

At once, he begins to shift and the sight breaks my heart. It's inhumane.

More so when his pained whimper slips and those murky eyes meet mine. He's there. For a second, the man hidden beneath what's been done to him meets my gaze, and there's a plea for mercy.

Even as his rabid actions rob him of speech. As he breaks and bleeds as his body morphs into a disfigured animal with little to no body mass.

I swallow hard. This poor wolf.

Forgetting the others, I kneel before this lost soul. He snaps at my face, but doesn't bite—there's fight within him, although it's small. Recognizes me for what and who I am.

I'm not afraid, though. And I show him this as I take a grip of his jaw and place my forehead against his. "I'm sorry."

Two words and the wolf releases a sad noise, something I've never heard come from my brethren before. His suffering is unacceptable—what they've done to him—I'm going to kill every fucking fae or creature involved.

It is a vow.

"May you rest with the goddess." Murky orbs close for a second. His body becomes lax, but then his eyes open and that peek of the wolf within is gone. Now, I'm left with an animal without control and with the intent to hurt anyone within his grasp. Yet he never gets a chance as I snap his neck and then lower him to the ground with gentleness.

This makes me look at the other rogues we killed tonight in a new light.

Out of the four, this one had been the worst, but still, their alterations were plain to see. As if they were the different stages of an experiment on display. This was the message. The threat of what will be.

"Rest with the goddess," the others with me say after a second. They feel this as deeply as I do.

No werewolf wants to hurt a fellow brother.

"This wolf gets a proper burial, Beta."

"Yes, Alpha." *What are they doing to these poor wolves?*

I don't know, Cain. But I will fucking find out. "But this arsehole…" cutting my eyes in the direction of the rubbish "…he gets a proper welcome from the Evergreen pack. He's to have a cell on the lower level, with his still-breathing accomplice as a roommate." Nodding, Cain casts a glance at the dead bodies from our earlier fight. His question is clear. "They'll all stay in the same cell. Dead or alive. Let them spend some quality time together before I visit."

No one says a word, and I stand back, watching my beta walk toward who I'm positive is a lowly messenger—one who reminds me an awful lot of an elder fae I dealt with after meeting Isabella—and knock him out with a solid punch to his temple. His body slumps in the guard's hold and then is tossed over the same man's shoulder. One by one, they pick up a rogue before disappearing, leaving me to stand guard over the border until they return.

"I'm going to kill you, Larue. You and every fucking descendant that's still breathing."

***

SHE'S ALL YOURS, Alpha.

As requested, the spa's empty when I arrive a few hours later. It's late in the evening and I've cleaned myself up, any sign of the earlier disruption now gone and the small wounds as a result are all healed.

Not a trace left behind, although I know better than to hide anything from a seer.

And I'll tell her—take her to the prisoners myself—*but* not now. Not today.

The next few hours are about us. To celebrate the day my life truly began.

At the back exit, I find the owner waiting for me, propping the door with a hand while keeping an ear out in case my mate needs anything. She's also shifting from foot to foot while wearing a cheeky grin, and the sight almost pulls a chuckle from me.

Almost, because a deep-rooted hunger overtakes my senses— burns in my veins—the closer to my female I get. Just a few feet. So close. My wolf thrashes inside my chest with his need, the desire to taste his mate once again, and anything that delays that is a bloody sin.

An eternity with Isabella would never be enough for either of my skins.

Nothing will ever satiate this ferocious need.

Ember and I don't exchange words as I take hold of the door, but she does give me a small bow as we pass each other. I'm keeping the noise level down. Can't ruin the first surprise of the night.

I do send a quick *thank you* through the link, though.

She's been more than accommodating to my requests.

Inhaling roughly, I pick up the subtle notes of jasmine in the air. It's light and teasing, a flirtatious calling that I acknowledge with a low rumble in my throat while stepping inside.

I no longer pay the owner any attention as she leaves, rushing toward her car and then exiting the salon's private parking lot while I turn the lock. Being on the lower level of the mall has its perks, makes it easier to haul products in and out without carrying large quantities of boxes or taking an elevator to one of the higher floors, and right now, it gives me the added benefit of having my luna close.

Completely unaware. Mine to take.

Then I hear her.

Little Moon releases this soft and tender sigh, a content and relaxed sound that almost pulls a purr from deep within my chest. I bite the sound back, no matter how much I want to hum our mating song and add to her happy state.

"It'll be worth it." The whispered words leave a second before there's a rustle of fabric; she's either getting undressed or covering herself with a sheet, but more importantly, she's delighted. It comes through the bond, this little flutter that vibrates within me and leads me to her door where the soft notes of classical music are playing.

Then there's the scent of cedar and mint coming from within; a special blend candle I commissioned for use here and at home that melds with her natural floral notes. The combination is lovely. Heady and decadent with a touch of sex that causes my cock to jerk within my trousers.

I'm throbbing, the beads of pre-come rolling from tip to base and then down my heavy balls. The closer I get, the harsher my heart thumps; I grip myself hard. Squeeze the turgid length the way her tight cunt chokes me and then count to ten.

Then twenty.

I count until the need to mount her eases enough for me to open the door and step inside the candle-lit room. Steps from the doorway, my queen lies on the massage table facing down and squirming, thighs shifting beneath a soft sheet strewn across her round arse. There's also the spike in her heart rate and goosebumps on her skin; I can make out every single shiver that wracks her beautiful body.

Motherfuck, I'd kill anyone who saw her like this. Man or woman. No exception.

Isa's jasmine scent with light notes of musk slam into me then with the force of a battering ram; her arousal is prominent.

That causes me to stop and narrow my eyes. Not because I'm jealous or think she's waiting for someone else. I know it's the candle, an exact replica of her male's pheromones, but how the bloody fuck does—

"I'm ready, my king."

"You sneaky little thing." Toeing off my shoes and socks, I leave them a little past the entrance before pulling off my vest. It ends up beside my trainers on the bamboo flooring, both forgotten as I undo the row of buttons on my denim trousers. I'm not getting naked, but my cock is painfully hard.

The air greets my girth and I hiss, something that catches my female's attention, but before she can turn her head, I have my hand on the back of her neck. Just pin her down while I look over the tray beside us.

Warm massage oil sits inside a copper set that hosts a lit tea candle inside. Light slips from the star cut-outs throughout, and I dip a finger inside to test the temperature. Hot, but pleasant, and I bring that same digit over her spine and run it from the base of her neck to small of her back, before tapping the crack of her arse.

Those goosebumps return and are more pronounced now. Little Moon hums in satisfaction.

Nothing in this world is more precious to me than this woman. My female.

Isabella

For a while now I've been unsettled, fluctuating between excitement and need and a bit of trepidation—it's messing with my head. Because I saw the fight earlier play out, and it was his victory and intelligence, the way he handles each situation with poise and a good heart, that keeps me calm.

Yet I can't deny that I worried for a minute.

Not because he could get hurt, but because I felt his pain.

The atrocity committed against those wolves cuts him deep, and his ire matches my own. The throb in my chest mimics his, and the sorrow after ending the life of the last one still swims through my veins. Yet this is only the beginning, and while I need to talk to those prisoners and dig deeper into what's being done to these shifters, my male needs this. Me.

I felt it in his exhale before he ever stepped a foot inside the room.

From the moment the she-wolves left, rushing out while pretending they were late to a training session—one I knew nothing about—to being brought in here and asked to strip, I've been waiting for him. Because the pampering is one thing, hair and nails are fine, but to be offered a deep-tissue massage booked by my alpha male...*I knew.*

Xadiel's not one to share or let others touch me outside of an appropriate greeting, and even then, there's a small touch of jealousy in his grumble. The way he stares the other person down, daring them to linger.

I'm his. His female.

Untouchable and sacred. A truth he's never stopped proving every day of our lives.

Slipping my eyes to the tray for a second, just one to calm my breathing down as excitement threatens to make me whimper, I pay attention to the little details set up. There are some towels and a few other tools: two wooden rollers, a scalp massager, and hot stones warming on the counter to the left, but these are unnecessary. Knowing him, there will be nothing between my skin and his. Those strong hands will take care of me and I hum at the thought, thighs clenching beneath the high thread count sheet.

"Are you okay?" I ask. Have to. His emotions are always so vivid, like the color of northern lights on a clear night sky.

"I am at peace, love." Xadiel's aura is clear and honest, the shade a light blue while a hint of red and orange dances at the edges. The two are powerful—sexual passion and dominance—and my male is both. "But more importantly, I'm here with you. Let me enjoy you, Little Moon."

"Please."

"Cheeky." There's a grin in his tone that makes my lips twitch, but that's forgotten a second later when a slow drip of heated oil warms from the center of my back to the curve of each asscheek still covered by the sheet. It rolls and spreads, soaking through the material and causing another round of goosebumps to dance across my skin, and more so when callused fingertips follow each drop. "I can scent your arousal."

Playing and taunting, Xadiel adds pressure while traveling a little lower each time, then back again. From just beneath my skull, working loose every knot until I am languid and shaking—horny yet relaxed.

The contradicting emotions play with my body. Thrumming. Winding me up until I start to rise on all fours. From just below the dimple on my back, I remain covered but that doesn't hide the scent of my arousal nor the way I move and arch, trying to get his hands where I desire them most.

But instead of giving me what I want, Xadiel forces me back down with the push of two fingers on the small of my back. Right at the two dimples there.

"Don't move." Gravelly. So much undisguised need in those two words that I can't help but answer with a whimper.

And he likes the sound. That answering purr sets my skin ablaze, more so when those fingers work lower and dip beneath the sheet. At first, it's a skim, just a soft back and forth while pushing the fabric down. Bit by bit. Bunching it at the curve before that purr becomes a low grunt and it's ripped completely off.

Cool air greets my skin. I'm bare and so wet, preening as the heat of his gaze travels over me from my head to my toes. A path those hands follow without words, digging in deeper over each cheek before the sting of his hand settles across each globe.

"Xadiel," I cry out, the one word a plea he ignores. He smacks me again, three times in rapid succession on each side before moving lower, spreading his fingers and encompassing the back of my thigh. Teasing me.

"Why are you naked, Little Moon?" There's amusement in his tone, a natural cockiness that does nothing to abate my arousal. Instead, it's kerosene. Everything he does is. Dousing and stoking and then lighting a match before watching me explode. "Hmmm?"

"You know the answer to that." A whine: I'm unable to gather myself.

"Do I?" After another rough pass, Xadiel strokes from the back of my knee up to where my ass and leg meet. There he runs his thumbs back and forth across the crease, causing my cheeks to jiggle for him.

"Yes." Goosebumps spread and my nipples become impossibly tighter, beading and sensitive, while every minute shift causes a lick of pleasurable fire across each. "Are you upset?"

"Never." *Christ,* he spreads my legs open a little, and at once, the cool air greets my slick skin, causing me to suck in a sharp breath. "Just gives me another reason to punish you."

"Punish me?"

"Damn right." That's all he says. Nothing else, but it's not needed when he finally cups me, grip tight. My male's touch is possessive, just like the emotions coming through our bond.

I'm his. There's no other option, and my heart fills with joy at his need for me.

Not just the sexual, but every aspect.

The good. The bad. Every laugh and tear, Xadiel wants it all.

The heat of his palm feels like heaven, but it's the tight circles—how he adds pressure slowly—building me up until I clench at nothing, that frustrates me. Arousal turns to hunger on its way to a clear, needful rage when he stops.

Then he's running those same torturous fingers from my clit to my entrance before dipping the tip of a thick digit inside. Automatically, I clench. Walls trying to pull him in deeper, but I receive a salacious chuckle instead, and then a light pat from his other hand over the curve of my asscheek.

"My king, please—"

"Will you be my good girl and let me pamper you? Ignore your vision and just feel me?" he asks, cutting me off. He also brings his face down to mine, exhaling roughly against my jaw. "Will you be patient? Let me take care of you?"

"Yes."

"Little liar." Not mad. More of that mirth filters through the bond and his tone, but I'm not given much time to defend myself. Instead, I'm rendered pliant in his hands as he retakes the massage while purring for me. That vibrating rumble calls to me, a decadent song that's just for me, and it feels so good. "Sweetest fucking scent. My heaven."

Long strokes are accompanied by circular motions over my sides, skimming across the side of my breast and down to my hip. First the right side, then the left. Xadiel works through every knot and tightness, leaving me a literal puddle before adding short slapping movements across my upper back until reaching my butt once again.

They go from soft to hard, striking each cheek with enough force that it stings. Yet that pain quickly morphs, the heat and feel of him only elevating my need for his cock. His knot.

I want the delicious burn of being stretched past my limits.

I want to feel him lose himself—own me—before filling me with his come.

"Alpha, please," I moan out, trembling after a particularly sharp swat. Never want him to stop. "More."

"I want to demand you present and fuck you like the dirty girl you are, Little Moon."

"Yes." Lifting my bottom off the table, I meet the next slap halfway. "Fuck me."

"Gods, I love you." Suddenly, I feel his other hand slip between my legs. Xadiel strokes me, soft and slow. Teasing. "My perfect mate."

Those words fill my heart with so much happiness. His feelings for me are always open and free.

"And I love you." Spreading a bit more to give him better access, I begin to lift onto my knees, yet I'm stopped once again. He's determined to keep me as he wants me and the hand smacking lands another sharp swat. This one truly stings; the pain, however, quickly turns into a volcanic rush of pleasure as it settles on my clit, which he pinches. "Fuck me."

I'm so close. My orgasm licks at my senses, but before I fall under, Xadiel pulls away. "Not yet."

"Don't stop." The words leave me on a whimper.

"Not. Yet," he rasps. The massage table I'm on is built to withstand the weight of a shifter. Male or female, and I have a feeling this one was designed with the alpha in mind. By him. And that theory is tested when he climbs up and lays over me, covering me from feet to head while keeping most of his weight off. He's grabbing onto handles I didn't notice were there before. "Not until tonight. I plan to spoil and then eat and finish the night with you writhing on my cock under the moon. Your beast wants to play, love. Will you let me?"

"Please."

"Then be a good girl for me and take a small nap before the women come back. You still have two appointments left before I come back to pick you up. Can you do that for me?"

"How about a taste to hold me over as a compromise."

"That I can do."

A bad idea for me as he brings a hand to my hair and fists my red locks, pulling until my head is arched back and he's meeting my eyes from above. It stings, but then it doesn't matter when Xadiel kisses me.

He pours every ounce of love and his desire for me into the kiss, overtaking my senses. It's all tongue and teeth and filthy, messy and beautiful, but before I can attempt to bite him—tempt him to deepen it—he's off the table and heading for the door.

I'm left breathless while watching him walk away.

Trembling while he opens the door and steps out, but before walking down the hall, he turns, and the look in Xadiel's eyes smolders. Holds me prisoner. "Be ready at seven, Little Moon. I'm hungry."

Alpha
XADIEL

Motherfuck, she's gorgeous.

Sweet and sinful with a decadent touch of perversion that complements my need to mark her. With my seed. With my bite.

I have no shame when it comes to my mate.

Isa's walking toward me with a cheeky smile that always awakens in my presence—a naughtiness that's solely for me—and I'm more than honored to indulge her. Because this female is more than just my mate.

She's my other half. Created by the gods themselves to walk this path by my side.

Wearing a white, long-sleeved dress with a high split over the right leg, she reminds me of our past and beginning. Of a time when she stood before me in a dress much like this one; a temptress coming to demand the attention of her male, but this one is made of a silkier fabric and a nearly sheer overlay strategically placed in open cut areas that highlight her every feature.

Like the thickness of her waist and the flat of her stomach where there are openings on each side, while the deep V at the front ends just above her navel, enhances the perkiness of her tits.

She's also wearing nothing underneath.

I can make out every single sinuous curve through the thin fabric. The tight pebbling of her nipples and the bare flesh of her mound— the thin line that adorns that sweet skin where she's completely devoid of hair everywhere else.

I slide my tongue across a canine and prick my tongue on the sharpness of my fang. They want to drop and my teeth itch to bite her, but I'll play her game for now.

We have all night to mark her.

Isa's lips curl a bit at the corners while pretending to watch the sky above us. It's a beautiful night, colder than earlier this afternoon and the inky night sky is full of stars, yet it's the half moon that shines the brightest.

It calls to me. Gives me a fiery lick of power that causes the beast inside me to stretch and thrash, wanting to be let out, but not *yet.*

Tonight, is about the woman before me with a fresh face and gorgeous blue eyes with cherry red lips. Her needs come first, and right now, the first is to warm her up.

Werewolves run hot by nature. Our bodies are designed to thrive in temperatures as low as -40 degrees, but my little witch isn't. Not without the aid of her magic, yet she doesn't say a word.

The hood of her dress is down, allowing her curled, fiery red locks to bounce around her face and back. Isabella's hair has always been long, styled in layers or at times with a straight blunt cut, but it's always beautiful. Yet today she blew me away with the addition of these messy curls.

Her natural waves are enhanced and the extra tight ringlet at the bottom of her ends makes my fingers twitch. I want to wrap my digit in a spiral and tug.

She knows this too. The gleam in her eyes and the way she bites her lips tell me as much.

Moon Goddess, you have truly blessed me.

"Come." One word, and Little Moon takes my hand without hesitation. She lets me pull her against my bare chest in the deserted back lot of the mall—shivers as I wrap my arms around her back and press our fronts together. Chest to stomach, but then I lift her a bit and bring our faces closer together. Revel in the hum of satisfaction she emits as my natural warmth seeps into her jasmine-scented skin. More so when fur sprouts across my arms and upper torso; she turns her face and nuzzles into the long hairs before kissing the area just above my heart that beats solely for her.

"Are you kidnapping me tonight, my king?" she asks, the words a little muffled in my pelt, and even that I find adorable. "Or is it a game of *chase* that you want?"

Chase.

Run.

Hunt.

My cock throbs and thickens further behind the zipper of my trousers, stretching the fabric to a near-ripping point. Clenching my teeth, I narrow my eyes and meet those azure eyes twinkling up at me now. They silently dare me. Bloody taunting me.

"Bad girl," I growl low, biting back a grin when she squeaks a second later as the deep vibration travels through her. Forces another deep shiver from her. "Are you wanting to start our evening with my come dripping down your legs? Or is it that you miss the taste of your male on your tongue?"

"Yes." Breathy. A bit of a whine, too, and the sweet musk of her arousal heightens.

Raising a brow, I tighten my hold around her back. Purr for her a tiny bit to return the teasing favor. "To which one?"

"Both."

"So greedy." I tsk, lowering one of my hands to her arse and squeezing the plump flesh. "But I love you this way, more so when I deny you."

"Deny me?" Annoyance filters through the bond but I ignore it; we have somewhere to be. Without another word, I shift her and place my hand underneath her bum while keeping her close to my chest. Our position now mimics that of human traditions where a man carries his new bride over the threshold after saying *I do*. "This is mean, Xadiel. Cruel."

"Not at all." Releasing her back for a second, I chuckle when she clings to me. Little Moon wraps her arms around my neck before biting my jaw, pulling a rumble from my chest. My beast likes her little Wiccan teeth. Adores her attempt to mark us in any way she chooses. "Put this on."

Isa looks at the dark green mask with the words *MINE* stitched in gold lettering with a raised brow. "What's this?"

The tethers connecting our souls tug with excitement, even as she tries to look annoyed.

"Cover your eyes." Not a request. A demand.

"Why?" So sassy. So fucking beautiful with that naughty, cheeky grin.

"Because I have a surprise for you, my female. Let your mate spoil you."

STEPPING through the tree lines with Isabella secured in my arms, I slow down my pace. I'd run from the mall to the middle of the forest, an easy feat for a wolf, and enter a place no pack member is allowed inside of. We're surrounded by thick trees and silence, a private stretch of untouched land not far from our home, and not a sound can be heard except for the occasional chirp of a nocturnal animal.

Not that they get close. Instead, they remain outside the perimeter, adding to nature's symphonic melody while the sky above us dances with light. As the gods show their approval—the moon and the stars lighting the pathway—and I step onto the first oversized paver. The walkway for Isa to use is wide and smooth so as to not hurt her bare feet; she still prefers to be barefoot whenever the weather permits, and I'm all too happy to oblige her.

Even though I'd rather carry her everywhere we go.

Even when the beast in me rumbles at the mere thought of her being anywhere but in my arms.

Moreover, Mother Nature calls to her as the Moon Goddess cares for her children.

There's a kinship there. A deep-rooted respect, and over the years I've come to understand a lot about my mate. Not just her big heart and the ability to love and give with no care for what it costs her—I see how truly special she is.

Yes, a seer is one of a kind, but there's more than meets the eye when it comes to her abilities. Fierce, loyal, and deadly when provoked.

Coveted.

He will never have her. Over my cold, dead body.

"Are we there yet?"

My eyes flick down to her face, and there's a pout on her lips. One I quickly duck down to nip. "We are."

"Well…"

Her giddiness tugs at my chest, and I chuckle. "Well, what?"

"Are you going to put me down and let me see?"

"No."

"No?"

"Aye."

"Seriously?" The pucker of her lips becomes more pronounced. "You're being mean again, my king. No knot. No come. And now, no surprise."

"Have I ever told you how much I love it when you get bratty on me?" It's the truth. Ninety percent of the time she's responsible and helpful and takes care of others. She worries and watches the future, trying to pick up anything that will help her people—me—but when she's like this... "Motherfucking perfection is what you are."

Neither the mask nor my heightened sight allows the touch of pink that sweeps across the apple of her cheeks to remain hidden. Even as darkness surrounds us and the sole source of light is coming from the sky above—our destination a few feet away—I make out every detail of that luscious blush. How it deepens. The way it spreads down to her chest the more I stare at her.

"I'm going to shock you."

My shrug makes her huff. "Do it."

"You'd like it...gods help me!" Little Moon yelps, grappling to find purchase on my shirt—anything—when I drop my hold for a second, but then catch her, keeping her upright. She's plastered to my chest and facing forward, chest heaving. "Before the night is through, I will get you back, my love. It's a vow."

"So mote it be?" I'm not being disrespectful, just confident I'll enjoy anything she'd do. Shock me. Bite me. Ride me. I'll take every punishment with a smile. "My little witch is fierce."

"You..." the rest of Isa's response dies on her tongue after I pull the mask off. A surprised gasp follows. She's awestruck, and I feel a hundred motherfucking feet tall.

Nothing makes me happier than seeing this look of wonder on her face.

The way her bottom lip trembles at the sight of the glass ceiling dome with nine-foot-high ceilings and twinkling lights inside. There's also a wood-burning stove warming the space, a fully functioning bathroom, and a king-size bed with thick quilts and all the plush pillows my mate enjoys.

Soft fabrics and plush bedding have never failed to make her happy in our marriage.

"Would you like to go inside, sweetheart?"

"This is beautiful. Xadiel. I can't believe you—"

"I'd do anything to see you smile."

"As I would for you."

My chest swells and then thumps when she turns in my arms and then gives a cute little hop to kiss my chin. She's too short to reach my lips, and I smirk at the small huff that escapes her before trying again. And I let her—a few tries—my cock thickening each time her tits bounce and her mouth presses against my skin.

On the last one, though, I grip her hips and lift until our mouths are hovering. They don't for long, but in those few seconds in between, Isabella wraps those luscious legs around my waist. At once, her thighs clench and a needy mewl slips through her parted lips. She grinds that tight little cunt over my lower abdomen.

"I love you." Little Moon moans into the kiss, swiping her tongue across my lips. Top one and then the bottom one, and I find the action to be sweet. So soft and tender that I'm shocked by blunt teeth digging into the flesh.

It pleasantly stings and I grunt, tasting her arousal in the air, mixing with my blood and the concoction is heady. Fucking brilliant. And just as delicious is the resounding smack I land on her bum. Both cheeks.

It echoes around us. Loud and provocative, and the way her body responds is art.

My female whines for me while arching, lifting her arse a little in invitation. There are goosebumps across her skin, and her heart rate accelerates.

I feel the tight bead of each nipple against my chest, rubbing across my pecs as she shifts and gives in to the pleasurable bite of the spank. *Fucking perfection.*

Rubbing the stinging flesh, I return to her lips and kiss her back. Dirty and quick, I take over her mouth while moving us across the pathway and toward the igloo's front door. The structure's sunken to accommodate the bed and allow a bit more privacy with curtains enclosing the first level of glass. From there, it's all open and free and I want her to parade for me in nothing but her gods-given bare flesh.

Pulling back, I admire the bee-stung lips pouting at me. "Close your eyes for me, Little Moon."

"Why?"

"Because I said so."

Isabella

It's impossible to be upset when his eyes crinkle at the corner and the chuckle he's suppressing becomes a deep rumble in his chest. Does that mean I'll let him get away with that answer? No.

He's aware of this, and the response I get after sending an intense electrical pulse through him is a thing of beauty. It strikes like a whip, the intensity higher than what I'd use on a normal creature, but my alpha wolf is well over seven feet of solid strength. The corded muscles beneath his furry chest ripple, and my open palm takes in every sharp shift: how he bristles right after and those golden eyes become swirled with black.

A growl slips through his lips, and the sound is pure brilliance. Dangerously addictive.

So I do it again while looking up at him from beneath my lashes, my bottom lip caught between my teeth. *Did that hurt, my king?* I'm going to pay for that. Of that, there is no doubt, a fact he confirms when all I get through our link is another warning growl. "Wolf got your tongue?"

"Brat." Gravelly. Edgy. Xadiel exhales roughly and I lick my lips, an act he follows before shaking his head. He's not upset and lives for our playful exchanges as much as I do, but there's another need riding him hard at my direct taunt.

The need to control. To make me submit to my alpha.

It's why a second later I'm thrown over his shoulder while his hand takes a possessive hold of my thigh, fingers curling around my flesh while the tips of his now emerged claws dig into my skin. They don't break through, but the warning is there.

Not that he'd ever hurt me.

On the contrary; I live for the sting. It's why I push him.

Heat spreads across my skin the second we set through the door. Warm and cozy, it's a sensation accompanied by this sense of complete devotion and love. There's also his scent throughout—as if he'd touched or rubbed against every single item within—and the result is lighting my body from within.

I've never felt this before. Not like this.

Something within me reacts, it stretches and pushes, but before I can begin to decipher anything, I'm lowered and turned so I can see the thoughtfulness that went into this space. The warmth coming from the wood-burning stove helps keep the frigid cold out, but with it, there are twinkling lights and a few lit candles, the same as the ones from the spa.

The colors within resemble our home here and back in England. We're both represented, and I can't help but snuggle back into him as I take in every inch of the space. The rugs and bedding are white with creams while the royal green of our crest is placed strategically.

From a set of throw pillows and a velvety lined chair in the corner opposite the bathroom, and even from where we stand still in the entry, I can see it's spacious with modern touches.

"Our private oasis. Our nest." The words slip out before I can stop them, but we both tense. It's instinctual to react—we've both wanted children for so long, and this room would be perfect for the day I go into heat. Being mated to the alpha wolf and carrying his essence in my veins has changed my biological traits, things that are different for a witch but because of our relationship, are now possible.

Female witches conceive on full moons much like other species, but we don't experience heats or frenzied states. Ours is more of a celebration and offerings to the gods and goddesses to bless our union and provide healthy offspring. Some might give their blood—a combined mixture of the fated couple—and feed the earth in a plea that her womb be fertile and healthy to receive their precious gift.

For a werewolf, though, it's a more instinctual ritual.

It overwhelms and controls; the feral hunger forces the female to seek out her male while giving in to her most baser needs. To mate. To fuck. Nothing matters more than satiating the pulsating, near demonic hunger—to take his knot and protect his seed. To be locked together for days on end as a new life begins inside of you.

And I want that. More than anything in this world.

"One day soon, Little Moon. The time is coming." At his words, I look back at Xadiel from over my shoulder and find his golden orbs are now pitch black while his nostrils flare. There's also the bulging of his fur-less muscles and a vibration—this heavy thrum that shakes his torso while traveling through my limbs—wrapping itself around me as if it were a large snake, and the embrace is so lovely.

Without words, it tells me all I need to know. *We're okay. I love you.*

"He'll be such a fierce warrior and king, my male. A revered leader."

His emotions filter through our bond, and his pride makes me smile. So much love already for his unborn pup, yet for a miniscule moment, I can't help but feel guilt. That he's had to wait. That my sacrifice took this from him, but then I'm whirled around to face him and taken aback by the ire in his gaze.

It's directed at me. My uncontrolled emotions.

"Don't." It's a barely contained snarl a second before I'm lifted and brought deeper into our suite. Xadiel doesn't stop until we're at the foot of the bed and I'm sitting atop a plush mattress, the bedding soft and luxurious. With me at the edge, he steps between my parted legs and kneels so our gazes lock. In his I see a bit of reproach, something that makes my heart clench. He's never— "You did the right thing, Isabella. It's because of *you* and those *sacrifices*, that our future is bright. That we'll have the opportunity to raise him and all of our pups…I want ten of the bloody rascals, by the way."

"Ten?" My pussy clenches hard at this. I've never thought past our one blessing—the heartache wouldn't allow me—but this fills my soul with joy. I want a huge family with my male.

A house full.

A crazy schedule and after-school activities and chaotic dinners full of laughter—the screeching of children talking over each other as they tell us about their day. To some that might be too much, but for me, it's my most selfish dream. To live in peace and surrounded by love.

"Your smile and the scent of your arousal tells me you agree."

"I do."

Cupping my face with both hands, my alpha places his lips against mine. The small peck is sweet, but before I can try to deepen it, he pulls back. Now his eyes hold mirth. Cockiness. "Good."

"You're horrible today." This leaves me on a huff, but then it's forgotten when I catch sight of a small bistro set with two tables against the wall to the right. It's made of steel, sturdy to accommodate his weight, and an exact replica of the one inside the family library in England. That, and the delicious treats set atop with a kettle warming. "But I just might forgive you."

"Is that so, love?"

"Yes." I'm answering, but I'm taking in yet another surprise. There are assorted cakes, finger sandwiches, and a wild berry cobbler. Everything I love, but there's also a plate of tuna tartar with a thin layer of sliced avocados and mixed micro greens on top. A few toasted pieces of bread accompany it to one side while English cucumbers take up the opposite edge. "Absolutely, it's a yes."

"And why is that?"

"Because I'm starving." At that, my alpha king throws his head back and laughs, the loud guffaw reverberating through the room. It bounces off the glass while I watch in awe, taking him in, the room, and then every small detail while thanking the deities above. "After all, you did go to a lot of trouble—"

Placing a finger over my lips, Xadiel stands and then bends to pick me up. "This is my pleasure." He walks us over to the table and sits me in one chair while taking the other and placing it beside me. He's so close our knees touch, and every time he inhales, the movement shifts me a bit. "Besides, the hard part was keeping it a secret."

My brows furrow at that. "How did I not see this?"

"I had help." Cocky. Smirking.

"You did?" Only a high-ranking witch would have that kind of power. *But who? There's no trace of a witch being here.* I also don't know how to feel about this. Thrown off by it is one thing, but then what else have I missed? Am I failing them, or worse—

"Stop that, Isabella Evergreen." It's not often I'm full named and my eyes snap to his, narrowed, while a small shiver crests over me. *That tone is going to get me in trouble. Makes me want to present first and ask questions later.* "I can see the wheels turning. Eat this and I'll explain." That's when I notice he's brought a piece of the cobbler to my mouth. Just holds the forkful with a raised brow, and I reply with one of my own while taking the bite. Not going to lie, the dessert is delicious. I want more, but I refuse the next offering until he speaks. Ignore the need to clench my thighs and the wetness coating my flesh. "So hardheaded, my little witch."

"Who?" Need to know first. It's unsettling me.

"Gabriella." The tension drops at once at my sister's name. Her, I trust. Of course, he notices the change in me and my favorite grin crosses his face. He's proud of pulling this off and slowly pushes another bite between my lips; I accept it. I'm fed more of the berry treat and then from a mini chocolate cake. "We spoke about this—my surprise—the last time she was here with Theo, and I mentioned how keeping you unaware was an impossibility. She laughed and told me there was a way and taught me the simple spell. Took a few tries, but I got it, and I also blessed this space for us."

I'm done.

Nothing he could've said would've been sweeter. Meant more.

From a wolf who hated what I am, to now blessing our space.

A glass of wine is offered next; the chilled bottle came from an ice-filled bucket close to where his chair was before. There's also a manila folder beside that, and I ignore it too. How I missed them, I have no clue, but then again, right now I'm filled with so many emotions, and they're all happy.

At ease and free. They're thrumming between us—tugging at the bond—and I find myself becoming jittery. I let him bring the glass to my lips and I sip. Let him feed and care for me.

And only once I'm full does Xadiel eat. He doesn't speak, but the heat in his eyes keeps me on edge—a predator watching his prey. Stalking my every move. My male doesn't have the tea or wine. Instead, he stands and walks over to a small refrigerator inside of what I now realize is one of two small closets. The fridge is just big enough for snacks and drinks, the latter of which he grabs.

Golden orbs with black swirls meet mine as he takes a few deep pulls of the water; I'm tempted to lick his Adam's apple. But then again, everything he does is sexy.

Protective.

Thoughtful.

His ability to learn and conduct a spell to surprise his mate with this beautiful glass dome in the middle of the forest, filling the space with warmth and love. When he tightens his grip on the bottle and the muscles in his arms flex, I'm standing from my chair.

Keeping my eyes on him, I mentally count to four and place a hand over a button that secures the hood to this dress. Undoing the right one, then the left, I let the fabric fall to the floor while shaking my hair out a bit. As I count from five to eight and edge away slowly, I lick my lips and then wink.

"What are you doing, Little Moon?" Xadiel doesn't move, but tilts his head to the side the way I've seen his wolf do a million times. It's instinctual. Attune to me.

"*Calefacies.*" Heat: I'm protected from the cold.

"Answer me, love."

A small smirk forms on my lips while I take two steps back and toward the door. He doesn't follow, just leans forward a bit and inhales deeply. A growl builds and this one is predatory, the signal of a hunter acknowledging its prey.

It carries throughout the room, and while I accept the edge of threat, I don't heed it.

"Nine."

"Isabella." His tone is dangerous. Thrilling.

"Ten." The number hasn't fully left my lips when I turn and take off, slamming the door open and taking off toward the tree line. I don't feel the cold nor the light dusting of snow that's begun to fall. If anything, I'm on fire. Excitement courses throughout my small frame, pulsing with each beat of my heart and it only grows the further I get from my male.

And it's when I reach the first cluster of trees that he howls.

Gods, the sound travels through me from head to toe, settling on my clit as I lean on the nearest trunk. My nails dig into the bark, grappling to steady myself as a rush of wetness drips from my core. It makes a mess of my upper thighs and I'm sure a few drops have marked the ground, leaving a trail of perfume for this wolf to follow.

"Move, Isa. Run," I command myself, but then he snarls and it shocks me. The sound travels around me, nearly corralling me, and it feels as if he'd licked me from my clenching hole to my bundle of nerves before suckling the sensitive flesh. At once my back arches and chest thrusts out, a whine leaving my parted lips.

One he responds to. He's close, but not in a hurry and I can just make out his shadow.

"Come to me, Female." It comes out garbled and a bit distorted through his fangs; he's half shifted and prowling along the tree line. "Please your male."

"No." A whispered response, but I know he heard. His amused chuff makes my heart pitter-patter. His head also snaps in my direction while he licks a sharp canine, taking in the slow way I remove my dress and then hang it on a low branch, exposing my body for him. Only ever him. "Come find me, my king."

As I say this, I'm already rushing away, dodging smaller plants and a raised stump while losing myself to the rush of adrenaline currently coursing through me. It's part exhilaration and desire meeting a touch of fear, but the latter isn't a negative. It's an automatic reaction, and knowing that I'm safe while being chased is freeing. Allows me to let go and enjoy, and when a sharp claw rakes softly across the back of my thigh, I squeal and push myself harder.

My eyes dart around and find nothing.

My senses tell me he's close, his scent strong, but one quick look behind comes up empty.

The alpha wolf is toying with me, but I can play games too.

Not far up ahead, there's a small brook. The width isn't horrible and I'm confident I can jump over it, but before I do…

An annoyed grunt fills the silence and gives me his location. He's to my right and now wet. The fur on his body is plastered to his muscles, and I bite back a laugh. His expression is disgruntled—determined to make me pay.

To my advantage, being able to control the water is a dirty trick I'm not ashamed to use.

Did I know where he was? No.

Did I send water in various directions? Yes.

His body lowers to the ground, pitch-black eyes watching from this position. Xadiel's going to pounce at any moment, the goose-bumps on my arm a clear warning, and I make a quick jump over the brook. My feet land just on the edge. The back of my heel is wet, but I balance myself just in time to see him stop on the opposite side.

A chuckle leaves him. I know it's now or never.

Extending a hand toward the water, I let the power within the substance flow through me and sing. Each drop converges and meets, uniting as a solid yet malleable unit under my command to do with as I please, yet a second after I'm determined to strike again…

I'm pinned beneath him while he bears the brunt of another cold bath.

I shiver, but it's not from the cold as he watches me through black eyes while biting his bottom lip. The sharp fang has pierced his flesh, but he's unbothered. Instead, he rakes his eyes down my flesh from my hair to the wetness between my thighs and hums in satisfaction.

"I win."

"Did you?" Breathy. A little whine.

Xadiel doesn't answer. Instead, I'm flipped onto my hands and knees and forced to spread them wide by one of his. His clawed hands grip my hips—not cutting but gentle—and yank me back until the head of his cock slips into my hole. Just the engorged tip.

Automatically I clench, wanting more, but receive a few short jabs instead. "Xadiel, what—"

"Silence, Queen Evergreen. Not a bloody sound." Five times he does this, toying and flexing before sliding up between my labia and kissing my clit with his bulbous tip. It feels so good. My responding moan tells him so, but all I receive is a sharp spank to the ass with one hand, and the piercing of my hip with the other. "Take it. Take me."

"I'm yours, my…*oh my fuck!*"

In one brutal thrust, Xadiel's buried to the hilt while his body's bent over mine and the hand not on my hip digs into the earth. This isn't gentle or sweet. This is a claiming, and I feel it in every throb and pulse—each snap of his hips that drives me lower to the ground until I'm laying down over the cool grass. It's a complete contrast to the furnace above me, and the contradicting sensations only heighten what I feel.

Loved. Owned.

Lips at my ear, he exhales roughly while driving in deeper. "You have always been mine. Nothing will ever change that."

"Yes."

"My precious Little Moon."

He's thickening, the base expanding while his knot smacks against my labia with each sharp piston, and I can't do anything but reach back and grip his hair. Anchor myself—hold him to me while the pleasure mounts, my body shaking beneath his.

But then his hand circles my throat, and I clench so hard it nearly hurts. But it's the best kind of pain, tightening and releasing while he continues to ride me hard. Not a second of pause; he's all I feel and understand.

It excites me. I enjoy being dominated by my alpha wolf.

The world around me dissolves into warm colors as nature rejoices at or union. "Xadiel, I'm close."

"Good girl. Come for your male," he rasps, pride coming through the bond. Xadiel pushes a little deeper now while bringing the hand at my hip down to my thigh and lifting; it spreads me wide. Makes it easier for him to work the fully expanded knot at the base inside me while the hand at my throat tightens. "I want you dripping down my balls before I lock myself inside of you. Like that, sweetheart. *Motherfuck,* the heat of your cunt is heaven."

Heat. For a split second that word makes me pause, but then I'm lost to my orgasm.

"Oh goddess," I scream, my fingers in his hair tugging so hard I'm sure I've broken a few strands. Not that he cares. If anything, his answering purr is one of contentment. "Xadiel, I'm—"

I'm being pinned, controlled, and now his teeth are embedded deep in my shoulder. It hurts at first, a second or two at most, but then I'm plummeting head first into nirvana. Lose myself to the feelings coursing through me while my mate never stops loving me—if anything, he envelops me in a pelt of warmth while forcing the last bit of his cock deep within my channel.

His knot slips inside and swells to the point we're locked in before the vibrations begin. There are no words to describe the emotions rushing through me, filling my soul with so much happiness—completeness—when the first and second spurt of come paints my walls.

Each one causes me to shake. To whine and press myself closer, and even when I'm full to the brim, I want more. Of the closeness. Of him.

"I'm yours, Little Moon. I love you." With his body warming me, I'm slowly lulled into a semi-conscious state after a few minutes. Exhaustion is hitting me, and between Xadiel's purr and the vibrations of his cock, I can't stay awake for much longer.

However, just before I succumb to sleep, I hear him…

"Happy anniversary, my female," he says so sweetly. A raspy declaration that I acknowledge with a smile. With a promise of my own.

Happy anniversary, my wolf. Know that I will always love you and no other.

Alpha
XADIEL

I t's been a week since our anniversary and we're inside my office at the pack house. Isabella's in my chair while I lean against the desk and my beta sits across from us. We've kept the prisoners without contact—with people or the outside world—and their feedings have been limited at best.

Bread and water twice a day, and both are shoved inside a small opening at the bottom of the steel door keeping them inside. The two alive aren't chained but separated by a few silver bars strategically placed to hurt if you make the wrong move.

What the deceased corpses look like at this point is the greatest cause for their distress.

They scream. Curse. The male fae demands we remove the decaying mess, but his words fall on deaf ears.

"What time did Gamma Grady say he'd—" Cain doesn't get to finish his question as the computer on my desk pings, prompting

Isabella to accept the video call. It takes her two clicks to send the signal to a large screen to the right of my desk, and the sight of Grady that greets us isn't one of the calm and easy-going man I'm used to.

He's always sensible. Nothing unbalances him, but the worry—whatever he's seen has shaken him to the core.

"My Alpha and Luna," Grady addresses first, a fist over his chest before also acknowledging Beta Cain. "Blessed are these eyes to see you."

"Blessed to see you, Gamma," Isabella responds, her head slightly tilted to the side as she concentrates. Knowing her for as long as I have—being able to pick up the subtle changes in her—I'm positive she's seeing something. Her lashes flutter a bit while a glazed-over blankness takes her over. A few minutes pass and no one speaks, allowing her to concentrate, but I catch the worry in Grady and the unease filling Cain. "Hmmm."

That's it. She doesn't say anything but looks at me. *Proceed. I'll speak at the end.*

Everything okay, love?

It will be. Through the bond she sends me reassurance and love, giving me a sharp tug when I don't continue with the meeting right away. *Go on, love. Be a good boy and I'll fix you a cuppa with some of those little sandwiches you love after.*

The cheeky brat.

A low growl ripples through our private link, admonishing, yet all I receive in return is a sweet giggle—one I have no choice but to ignore and turn my attention back to the screen. "Give us an update, Gamma. What's happened? Are you still in Italy?"

"No, Alpha. I'm on Evergreen soil now." For a second there's a small smile on his face, and I understand why. It's been so long for us—too long—since being home. Not that anyone would complain or challenge the decision, but there will always be a part of me that longs for that forest.

Isa knows this and understands. She too misses her coven from time to time.

And while we're each other's resting place—home—there's a level of responsibility we feel toward those under our reign. Isabella loves my wolves as I feel protective over her Wiccan brethren.

"When did you arrive?"

"Last night, Alpha." His eyes shift to Isa. "You're brother opened the portal and is visiting with the former alpha and luna. He has a gift for them he recently discovered from your mum, Luna."

"From my mom?"

"Yes. It's an evil eye amulet that's been blessed and charged since—"

"Before her death." A wistful smile crosses my mate's lips as she remembers. The bond sings with warmth at it. "I remember that day. Gabriella and I helped her. We each gathered the items needed for the ceremony and gave a small bit of our essence per Mom's request. Said it had to be all three of us."

"King Leo has brought and delivered it. As you can imagine, the previous luna was touched and sad at the same time. Your brother is spending the day with them and reminiscing while the rogue we captured is being questioned in one of the cells by two guards."

"Just one?" I ask, raising a brow, my jaw ticking. "There were ten reported outside of Isabella's coven alone, Gamma, not to mention those outside our lands. What happened to the rest?"

"I'm sorry, Alpha. Two days after we arrived, they crossed onto Moore's land and attempted to take a young witch. We fought and killed those who were unreasonable, no amount of asking them to submit helped, but there was one who acknowledged the command. He was rowdy and seemed to be almost drugged, but the wolf inside forced him to lay down at my feet." Grady looks down in shame. "All are dead except for that prisoner and the one who escaped."

"How the bloody hell did one escape?" It leaves me on an angry growl that shakes the walls, causing both men to bare their necks while those outside this room all whimper. It's a chorus of submission to their leader and while the beast is angry, I rein him in. Focus on the touch of my mate, her fingers intertwining with mine, and its soothing effect. She quiets the rabid animal within that wants to admonish his wolves for this could-be costly mistake.

Those hybrid zombie-like creatures can be dangerous.

A threat to both our hidden existence and humanity as a whole.

Not because we fear the humans or their weapons, but because hysteria is never productive. It can lead to stupid mistakes and angry retribution from different species; I will kill to protect mine, be it my mate or my people.

"We don't have an answer to that, Alpha Xadiel. Your father reported the same issue to us with the rogues spotted here. One second, they were here, and the next—"

"Gone." Isa finishes while rubbing her thumb across my knuckles. *He wasn't a wolf.* "Did you sense any magic? A trail, or did anyone feel off?"

Our gamma nods. "Not that night, but two days later one of our guards found a leather pouch hidden within overgrown grass. Nothing inside, just a dark blue residue that no one has touched, and we need permission to hand it over to King Leo."

"Has he been made aware of it?"

"Yes, Luna." Protocol is protocol, and my brother-in-law understands that. "He's the one that found the fae emblem on the lower corner." Lifting the small sack, he points to the crest identical to the one in my possession. This one is lighter in tone, but the same size. "Do we have your permission to hand it over? King Leo thinks there's a way to identify—"

"Tell him to trace the lineage, but it's fae. Of that, I have no doubt and neither does your king."

"Of course, Luna."

"While you are home, who stayed behind to help the Moores?" At my question, appreciation comes through the bond and I give it a playful tug. I'd never leave her people on their own.

"Two guards stayed behind." Since our meeting began, this is the first time Grady has smiled. "They were more than happy to do so."

"Happy to do so?" I repeat and Isa giggles, already knowing.

"Yes, my king. They found their mates."

"Not what I expected, but I'm pleased, nonetheless. We will figure out living arrangements after all this is dealt with. Keep them where they are." At my instructions, Grady nods while shifting his gaze for a moment toward Isabella. As does Cain. They're thinking the same thing I am.

Finding your soulmate is always a joyous moment. Truly makes me happy for those wolves, but I won't deny there's a small pang of regret that flows through me. It will always be there.

In my pain, I'd blindly trusted my aunt and former beta. Took their words and the carefully planned deceit—I forfeited the greatest gift this man could ever receive; her. And I've never been more ashamed of myself than I was the day Little Moon found my mother alive.

Her promise to walk away and forget me still causes my wolf to thrash inside my torso at the

memory. The whole pack still bears the consequences of that betrayal even if we try our best to hide it, yet our luna always knows.

My mate is the blessing we don't deserve but cling to. She soothes our aches with nothing more than a simple smile, trying her best to override a past we can't erase.

The anger. The sadness. The guilt.

That's our burden to carry.

Stop it or I will shock you.

I'd prefer it if you bit me, little witch.

My words have their desired effect, and she blushes. "Please find out what you can from the prisoner and report back, Gamma. Don't expect much. He's pretty far gone, but focus on the location he was taken. I have a feeling that's where we'll get the most information from him."

"Anywhere in particular, geographically, or?"

"The Mediterranean basin. France, to be exact."

THE STENCH IS near overwhelming the second you step inside the lowest level of our prison a few hours later. During our meeting, Cain remained quiet and has been pensive—more than usual—and I'll speak to him after. He's been concerned since our encounter with those creatures a week ago, tightening up the protection details around our perimeters while taking the overnight shift every single night.

It's cut him as deep as it hurt me. No shifter wants to see his kind end up like that.

I'm fine, Xadiel. Angry, but under control.

Giving him a barely perceptible nod, I let him lead the way down the first flight of stairs while Isabella gives my hand one quick squeeze. She's in the middle, pulling me behind her while the few prisoners housed here whimper as we pass. It's rare for my pack to have issues, disruptive behavior between its members, but I do help contain problem wolves for other packs under my ruling.

This structure is a few levels deep and most are underground, an excavated network of tunnels beneath the earth that no one would realize is there outside the members of this pack. Each floor has three diverted sections and the deeper you go, the more dangerous the prisoner.

These two are the lowest of the scum and near rabid when we approach the hallway housing their cell. More so when Cain and I stand side by side and watch them while Little Moon moves behind me. Not out of fear, but because she doesn't want to alert them of her presence just yet.

Although, they sense something is off. Both shift nervous glances around, but a single growl from me has them stilling and exposing the changes a week in isolation created.

The wolf is skinnier and the boxers given are almost falling off, adding to his haggard appearance. Unhealed wounds and bruises—an unset broken leg and fresh burns. The latter markings, though, were left behind by the silver bars. It's clear he tried to get around them multiple times and reach the fae male, but failed. There's also the mucus-like film over his eyes now, similar to the rogue we killed last week, and the loss of normal responses built in to all shifters.

Because werewolves yield to dominance—the hierarchy and power of an alpha—and no one is higher than me.

His beast senses me and for a minute or two bares its neck, but then rationality disappears, and it thrashes. Snarls and bares a recently chipped fang while puffing out its non-existent chest; he's trying to shift but can't. The difference between the arrogant rogue I met during the altercation and this one is quite obvious—sad. He can't control the most basic need any shifter is gifted: being one with his other skin.

Not fully. His transformation starts and stops multiple times before he falls to his knees from exertion, the injured leg unable to keep him steady, and he glares at us until catching sight of Little Moon.

Then he shrinks back on a whimper, and she takes her place beside me. So much fear.

It overwhelms the space and drowns out the scent of rotted, swarming-with-flies flesh not far from him. Two bodies per side of the cell, but this new odor is quite potent. An odd combination, but the notes are there, and I'm not understanding how a werewolf can stink like spoiled eggs. How it can overpower literal corpses mere feet from him.

"*Cedrus*," she says while scrunching up her adorable nose, and the foul stench disappears. Not a trace left, and I bite back a smirk at the scent she chose. Cedar. Me.

"Thank you, Luna." Cain smiles, his body a bit more relaxed. *Wanker.* "I've never had an odor affect me so…" he gives a small shudder while Isa suppresses a giggle "…goddess bless you and your gifts."

"This mediocre witch is unworthy of being a carrier." A smaller voice speaks up from across the cell, the same calm and cocky fae. His expression is haughty and challenging while Little Moon simply raises a perfectly arched brow. "My sister will fix that, though. She's coming for you, *my queen*."

"I'm going to rip your bloody tongue out," I hiss from between clenched teeth, moving a step closer to the bars. Every muscle in my body expands and my fangs drop, but a hand on my arm stops me from moving forward. She also reaches around me and removes the keys from my back pocket; these prisoners aren't given electricity and everything is run the same way we did a hundred years ago.

They get a hole in the ground, no running water outside of a quick hose down once every few weeks, and the sole source of light comes from lit torches that are maintained sporadically.

If they spend time in pure darkness, I do not give a single fuck.

This is a prison, not a spa.

Relax, my king. I want him to talk.

I can only be so patient.

Understood and appreciated.

"I'd be very careful, you right cunt. Don't disrespect our luna." Cain's anger and power spreads throughout the hall, his effect less than mine but sharp and strong. Both men are smart enough not to respond, but not Isabella. She has no fear. Knows that her rank is higher than mine.

If there's anyone in complete control of how this ends, it's her.

No one is above my little witch.

"You look very familiar." Her blue eyes are on the fae bastard, narrowed yet knowing. "Reminds me of someone from our past. Do you know who, Xadiel?"

"I'm beginning to see it." And I do. I'll never forget that piece of shit.

"Same obnoxiousness. Same defiance."

He doesn't respond, but a sudden red flush overtakes his face and upper body. His mouth drops open, but there's no scream. It's as though he's being strangled, and I smile in satisfaction.

Isabella tilts her head while her fingers expand and then turn in a circle, calling something over. That pull grows—the shift in magic is felt by all—and so does the dark gleam in her eyes. Because while my female is sweet and full of so much love, she can also be vindictive—a killer when needed.

"Merde," he grits out, hand pounding on his chest while an aura tinged with dark blue grows larger around him. And the more pronounced it becomes, the weaker he is, to the point he slumps back against the solid stone wall behind him. "Please stop."

"What's your name?"

"I will...*fils de pute!*"

"That's not very nice. Let's try this again." Isabella once told me that while her power of sight isn't as strong as Gabriella's gift to take and give life, I have to disagree. There are many ways to kill a person, but my mate is blessed with seeing the future and protecting those she loves, while also bending the blood within an enemy's veins. Like now, she calls to his life's essence with the sweetest voice. Just three words: ***veni ad me.***

Now his cries rend the air, filling every cavern of this tunnel and the ones above it with his pain-filled screams. And no matter how much he pleads and begs, it's not until he whispers a broken *Gaston* that my mate stops.

"That's better." Her hold on him eases, but doesn't relinquish in its totality. "Now...why are you here? What's Larue doing to my wolves?"

"I will never betray my king." Gaston spits on the ground by his feet. His lips are dry and cracked, the appearance as if they're cooked. "His power is supreme."

Isa throws her head back and laughs, the sound so melodious to her alpha. "Is that what he's told you?"

"It's what I know..." he trails off and is smart to do so. He'd wanted to insult her but cannot handle the level of pain she will inflict or my instinct to rip out his throat. Instead, he swallows hard and closes his eyes. "King Larue is coming for what is his."

"And I will kill him." A matter-of-fact promise from my witch. One I will take care of personally with honor. "While you, Monsieur Gaston, are nothing more than a distraction in the grand scheme of things. Did you really believe he'd send someone of importance here with this lot of malfunctioned experiments meant to be hybrids? That I wouldn't be able to tell you force mutated this poor animal's blood with that of an ancient fae, realigning their DNA to your convenience? This was pathetic at best and you know it."

"Shut. Up."

"And what about your sister? She couldn't even find a simple book hidden inside a child's bedroom, disappointing your king."

"She's going to kill you and take her rightful place."

Ignoring his remark, my female dusted her hands off on her slim-fit, denim trousers. The action is that of boredom. Gives his threat unimportance. "Just like Bartolo, too. Was he your failure of a father or grandfather? Such an amazing family you have there."

The woman she speaks of I only saw once, and my attention had been on Isa back then. Bartolo, however, I took great pleasure in torturing that elder fae—hunting him down and ultimately, being the cause of his death. Just like I'd known there was something familiar about this tool, that elite air of rubbish they all seem to rub around in; I'd dealt with it before.

That same stale stench of death follows this one, too. His mortality is reaching its end.

At her insult, he stands and charges toward the bars keeping him locked inside. Makes it as far as a few inches from the solid silver door before Isabella strikes again. This time, though, she calls to his blood with a level of ire—malice—I've never seen before in her.

Gaston drops to his knees and punches his chest several times as if that would alleviate his pain, but Little Moon doubles down. There is no stopping her and I don't interfere either until a tiny bit of blood dots her left nostril. It reminds me of the last time she pushed herself this hard, and I place my hand on her nape.

I just touch her. Massage the area with my warm palm and gradually she lets go, leaning into my touch while trying to regain her composure. No one says anything, but the tatters of the wolf still alive are shivering in a corner while covering his face with his front paw. It's a natural reaction for a werewolf when afraid and in the presence of an alpha wolf or female.

His eyes are also clearer. Still a nasty shade of green, but less infected-like.

Are you seeing that? Cain's mind link has me nodding, but I don't take my eyes off the shifter. *That's the second time he's responded to dominance or danger since we walked in. Do you think…?*

I don't know, but get him out of this cell and into one by himself. We need to monitor his behavior away from this arsehole.

Yes, Alpha.

"Come on, Little Moon. Let's get you to rest for a bit."

"Not before I say one more thing." Her eyes dart between the two males, one with pity and the other with disdain. "Your king wants the stones, but he will never have them. That's a vow made by this powerful witch with her blood." The moment those words leave her, a cut appears over her right wrist and rivulets of red trail down to the floor, becoming smoke upon contact. No other trace is left. Completely vanished. "I am the daughter of the fallen Wiccan King Paolo Moore, the Luna Supreme of all werewolves, and a vindictive seer. My blessing is your downfall. My thirst for vengeance will bathe this world with royal fae blood."

Isabella

**A HUNDRED YEARS AGO:
AFTER DEATH...**

Thanatos, please hear my prayer.

It's been a week of total darkness.

Of self-reproach. Of sorrow.

Like the world is at a standstill and not even the gods can breathe without choking on the crumbling pain of losing a beloved child. Because in a way, that's what my sister and I are. Chosen and raised with expectations placed over our heads and a life controlled by a path we never had a voice in, and right now, all I'm left with is my faith and a vow to do what must be done.

To maintain my composure while those I care about crumble around me.

To protect our people and help restore peace, even if it is temporary.

Thanatos, please hear my prayer.

Because everyone who knows Gabriella—who loves my sister—is fighting the feeling of hurt, loss, and the rabid rage that filters through our thoughts during moments of weakness. And while I understand them, no one outside of her mate can begin to comprehend what I'm experiencing as her sister. There's a special bond between siblings, but as a twin, I lived her death as she did.

The piercing of the blade and the shock that followed.

The worries for her mate and then regret at leaving him behind.

Gabby's pain is mine, one I plan to avenge after securing her rebirth, but right now, I have no choice but to be at the next stage of the process: acceptance.

I've had a long time to prepare, thanks to our father's warnings, and settle my thoughts. Learned long ago to discern the consequences of reacting impulsively—the detriment that follows blind ire —which is currently forcing those I love to lash out.

At the world with their mourning song and vows of retribution.

At me with empty stares and broken condolences.

And while they don't outright say it; I carry the blame. As a witch, I can sense emotions and auras, the vibrations each person emits, and most around me feel as though I've failed them. For not seeing. By not warning anyone, but that's the heart's reaction after losing so much.

My people have been hunted and killed, they lost their beloved king and queen, and now this. Despair is their gateway to unleash the hurt while I struggle to maintain the peace we so desperately need. Not just for every Wiccan coven, but for vampires and wolves just as much.

Thanatos, please hear my prayer.

Everyone wants to spill blood—demands revenge—but to do so will negate what the Moore coven has sacrificed. They don't see it, but we are guaranteeing their survival even if hate consumes them at the moment.

Only Xadiel and Leo see what this is doing to me. One tries to help me through the pain, while the other mourns her with me, but they themselves have unspoken questions.

Leo's young and lost. He's hurt by the betrayal of our uncle, still reeling from the death of our parents—Dad's final words—while my mate tries to be supportive.

Yet what no one understands is how heavy my burdens truly are. How this gift comes with a hefty curse, the responsibility to protect yet not interfere while vowing to follow the gods' will.

Even when it eviscerates a part of my soul. Even when it hurts those I love.

This ache in my chest won't abate, tightening with each intake of air, stinging as it fills me with nothing but the acrid reminder that I'm alive and my twin—best friend—is not.

But she will be one day. Can't give up.

That's what I cling to. The words in father's grimoire are precise, a sacred prayer to the god of death in our time of need. And more than once, I've spoken them out loud, but I've yet to receive a response.

For over a hundred and sixty-eight hours, magic itself has stopped.

"Just breathe, Isa. Don't ignore the pain, but breathe through it." Xadiel's warm arms encircle my waist while bending enough to place a gentle kiss atop my head. He's been with me since I felt her soul detach from her body, as Meera did what she could to stabilize her disoriented tethers, keeping one to prevent her from fully entering the underworld. I needed a piece of Gabby to linger, and after Theo buried himself with her at the end of their vampiric ceremony, I finished the official binding with my blood and a tendril of my magic as a sacrifice.

Her essence will never fully perish. I'll do everything to bring her back.

"Any word on where Elise and her siblings fled to?"

"None, but all guards are on the lookout." One of his hands moves my hair aside, placing the long red tendrils over the opposite shoulder. His nose replaces where the locks had been, just breathing me in while his voice remains low. "We'll find her, Little Moon. Her entire family will pay for their betrayal."

"I know." It might not be for some time, but Elise Veltross will have a date with me. The time and place are already set in stone. "But continue pushing them toward North America. That's where her destiny lies."

"Okay. Isa, I…" Exhaling roughly, he trails off, hesitating to ask or make any comments on what's happened. He's been supportive, a pillar to me and Leo, but I owe him this. Even if this exposes just how much I've kept to myself.

"Go on. Ask me." Steeling myself, I become rigid in his arms, but I'm gifted a *shhh* sound from him while his arm around my midsection tightens and his other hand comes to my face, cupping my jaw. The longer he holds me, the more pliant I become, and it's not long before every ounce of fight leaves me.

I'm too exhausted and my shoulders can't continue to hold up this weight.

"Is this about the stones Larue spoke about?"

"Yes."

"Did you know this would happen?"

And there it is. The one question I dread, but can't deny.

Stepping out of his embrace, I keep my back to him while walking toward the base of an old hollow oak on the Moore property. This tree was our special hiding place for so many years. Where we spent hours talking and sharing energies, working on small spells, and sometimes just taking an afternoon nap. There were sleepovers. Gossip sessions. Where Leo hid while I rushed to find Gabriella the night our parents were murdered.

It's also a distraction at the moment. I don't want to see the disappointment on Xadiel's face after the truth comes out.

"Our parents knew they were going to die, King Xadiel," I say, voice low and breaking a bit at the end. "For months, my father tried to see a way out of the inevitable, but every path he'd take would lead to the fall of our kingdom and the death of his children…all except for me."

"Isa—"

"Let me get this all out, and if in the end, you hate me, I'll accept that." His growl is one of displeasure, but to be honest, I hate myself enough already, and adding another name to the list just makes sense. "On the day of our birth, the God of Death and the Goddess of the Earth blessed our lives. Princess twins given more power than our parents and with very specific gifts; I see the future, and she can give or take a life. I'm the warning, and she's the solution. However, many coveted these powers, and we've spent most of our lives turning down potential suitors who swore we were mates."

"Give me their names and I'll kill them all."

"That's probably one of the sweetest things you've said to me since we met," I tease, still looking ahead, my watery eyes focused on the carving we begged our dad to help us with. We were maybe fourteen at the time, and with his help were able to pyrograph each initial with a spell that taught us control. "You have such a way with words."

"I try."

"Never stop." Taking in a deep breath, I exhale slowly.

"I vow it." He's close enough that his warmth settles against my back, but my male doesn't touch me. "Now, go on. Let me help you shoulder this burden."

A knot forms in my throat at that and my lips tremble, but I bite back my emotions. Now isn't the time to break down. Not until I can guarantee my sister's return. "One of those possible mates was Larue's son, Ruben. The same idiot that Theo returned with a warning to the fae kingdom is the same immature prick that dared to threaten my father for my hand. They want me, not Gabriella."

"Why?" An angry rumble.

"Because you can't control that which can kill you, but you can bend the future with enough warning."

"But doesn't what bends eventually straighten?"

"Exactly." Looking at him from over my shoulder, I give him a sad smile. "Most people don't understand that, Xadiel. Life has many twists and turns—deviations out of our control, but the destination is always the same." Behind him, Leo waves us over, but I shake my head and he understands, disappearing back into the house. This is an overdue conversation. "And to come back and win this inevitable war, because one is coming that will involve all creatures, I had to let her die and with it, take the stone inside her chest. Between her and Theo, they hold two keys—"

"The stone and what else?"

"Theodore has the Stygian blade and Gabriella carries the stone blessed by Thanatos himself; both are meant to be gifts—a way to gain favor from Aries. Or better yet, trick him."

"How so, Little Moon?"

"Larue believes that to become powerful you must defeat a god, and that will only bring catastrophic destruction for many." He doesn't say anything, and I take that as my cue to carry on. "Just like my father accepted his fate without my sister's interference, though he could've lived a little longer with it, he saw just like I have that the ending would've been the same. The only difference is that if she died before meeting her mate, there was no coming back for her."

"And you, Isabella? What is your ending?"

"You and Theo would've also died in that war."

"That's not what I asked, Isabella. What happens to you and your stone?"

"This one..." raising two fingers, I tap the center of my forehead to show him the placement "...is safe for the time being. But more importantly, when all is said and done, I will be safe and by your side, if you'll have me."

"It's where you belong for the rest of our days." My werewolf reaches a hand out toward me and I meet it halfway, intertwining our fingers. As they lock, I let him feel my energy the way I've done with my siblings so many times in the past, opening my emotions to him. "That's beautiful, sweetheart. Every part of your gentle soul was born to meld with my animal spirit. By blood and pact."

"We are one."

"We truly are." One tug and I'm pulled against him and wrapped up in his warm embrace. His lips lower to mine and meet them in a soft kiss, just a soft peck before his eyes close. "Together, sweetheart. Let's pray together."

"Thank you."

"Never thank me for loving you. Just lead, and I will always follow."

Nodding, I close my eyes and repeat the same words written in my father's book. "Thanatos, please hear my prayer—"

I'm here, my child. Open your eyes for me.

Alpha
XADIEL

I am the daughter of the fallen Wiccan King Paolo Moore, the Luna Supreme of all werewolves, and a vindictive seer. My blessing is your downfall. My thirst for vengeance will bathe this world with royal fae blood.

I can't get Isabella's words or the sight of her blood vow out of my head. Not because I don't trust my female, but because I worry about her emotional state. For far too long, she's carried this heavy burden—the responsibility of steering her siblings down the correct path while caring for them the way a parent would—even if it broke her while doing so.

And while I shoulder what I can, there's still so much Little Moon keeps to herself.

To protect those she loves. To ensure the future of more than just her coven.

"But they don't see it." No one does. Her family doesn't realize just how much she's done, not truly. They trust her gift; most will say Gabriella's death was the higher price, but I don't.

Those that stay behind always suffer the most.

My female's been mourning since before we met, dealing with the consequences of a responsibility placed upon her shoulders while the world continued to spin. Then and now, she's done the best she could by her siblings, by our people, but what I saw in her eyes in that cell—I'm angry.

Beneath the ire, there was hurt. Our bond sang between us, but not with joy; she was drowning. Some of it is self-loathing, undeserved anger toward what she sometimes feels is a curse, and I understand because with power comes responsibility. As a leader, you don't get to hide when problems arise. Instead, you're looked to for answers.

We protect. We solve. We let our emotions show in the quiet of the night when we're alone.

My wolf thrashes within me, snarling at the vivid memory of her pain. His claws rake my insides while I fight to swallow back my natural response. Anything that hurts my female is unacceptable—a declaration of war.

"Xadiel?" I look up at my female's voice; she's standing in the doorway to my home office with two cups of coffee in her hand. These are her favorite mugs; a his-and-hers set given to us last Christmas by our godchildren. They'd written *Alpha* and *Luna* by hand in permanent ink and decorated each with symbols of our status: a wolf in love with a witch. "Feel like having a cuppa with me?"

"Always, love." Placing my pen down, I push aside a contract for housing I'd been finalizing before standing. It's for a recently mated she-wolf transferring from a pack in Oregon, the niece of the alpha in charge there, after meeting her mate. He's a warrior and next in line for an elite position in the royal pack—one of our older members is retiring next year—and she agreed to the move. All parties involved are happy. "How do you want yours?"

"Sit. I'm preparing it."

"So bossy."

"No. More like worried." I frown at that, not liking the quick flash of sadness in her eyes while demanding I comply. And I do, but raise a brow for her to elaborate. "Don't give me that look, Alpha. Why are you upset? I felt it through the bond and—"

I'm in front of her before she's able to finish, my hands cupping her cheeks. "I love you, Isabella."

"You're such a sweet talker." There's a quick quirk of her lips, but she bites back the grin, embedding her teeth into the plump flesh of her bottom one instead. At the sight, a low growl rumbles past my teeth and she shakes her head, unable to hide the smile this time. She also smacks my chest with more strength than ever before, but I don't think Isa's aware of it. "But I've always known that."

"Have you, now." *Could she be…*

"I do." Cheeky. Mischief in her blue eyes, yet it's the *I do* I'm choosing to focus on.

"So much brattiness for a queen, Isabella." Immediately there's the feel of her powers saying *hello,* curling around me, and it's a sensation I welcome. I'm also not surprised by the warning shock I feel a second later nor the chuckle that follows. "Is this how you'll behave while planning our ceremony? Will you become one of those lunazillas, love?"

"First, I'm *your* brat." Another rumble of approval leaves me, more so when it's accompanied by a nip to my chin. "And second, what the hell is a lunazilla? Where did you get this word from?"

"Heard it on the television once." Her amusement causes me to drop a hand from her face and poke her ribs, earning an adorable squeal. I do it more than once, too, knowing exactly where to touch to get the loudest giggle. "It's something humans say about their brides, but with you being my luna supreme, I—"

Now she doesn't hold back, gasping for breath in between laughs. "Luna. Zilla." Little Moon's body is shaking, the sounds coming from her mouth now sound more like a yip, and I stop breathing for a moment. *This is a sign. She's changing.* "Goddess, you're adorable."

I don't say anything, though. Instead, I dig my fingers into her hips and pull her close, lowering my face down until I can skim her parted lips with mine. "Werewolves aren't adorable."

"Yours is…" she's looking up at me from beneath long lashes, expression coy "…just for me." And motherfuck if my wolf doesn't approve, responding with a purr—her sound—making my mate happy. It flows between us, the bond tugging playfully inside my chest. "And now that it's cleared up…"

"Speak, love."

"What upset you a few minutes ago? You were sad and angry, Xadiel…I don't like it."

"Nothing for you to stress over."

"Don't lie." Slipping from my hold, Isa turns toward the coffee station a few steps from us and after placing our mugs down, she opens the top left drawer. The pods are there, organized by flavor and brand, but it's the dark blend with notes of mocha that she picks up. One for her. One for me.

And I watch her without responding. We have our rituals and I follow her lead, letting Isabella make a cup—our individual preferences—before handing me one, grabbing hers, and then tugging me by my unoccupied hand back to my desk. This surprises me. I thought we'd head outside to our patio, but instead, I'm pushed back onto my chair so she can settle atop my lap afterward.

My female doesn't talk, but she does take a sip of her hot cuppa and then hums. Nudges me to do the same, and is only satisfied when half my coffee is gone; she always makes it right. Dark and just a thin layer of sweet cream foam on top. "Thank you, Isa."

"My pleasure…" I'm gifted a quick peck on my cheek "…now tell me."

"I promise nothing's wrong, Little Moon."

"Explain, Alpha. What can I do to help?"

"Be happy." It's the truth. That's all I've ever wanted for her, and right now, my mate needs me to keep a cool head. But more importantly, I'll be here to catch her if she stumbles.

Isabella's pain at the path she's had to walk alone at times, be it while I denied our bond or after her sister passed, has left a mark. One I plan to erase by loving her completely until the Moon Goddess calls us home. "To take care of yourself first and let someone else worry about the future. Let me shoulder what weighs you down. Let me be the one who protects and sacrifices—"

"You do so every day, Xadiel." Six words couldn't affect me more than these. It's in my nature to serve her—to love, honor, and put her pleasure above mine—but I also worry that when the time comes, Little Moon will endanger herself for the sake of others. "I'm blessed to call you mine."

Gripping her chin, I bring our faces closer. Lips hovering. "And you are my world. Remember that."

"I know." Her eyes glaze over for a few seconds, but when I blink, it's gone. Whatever she saw had her smiling. Blushing too. "You'll show me soon enough."

My brows furrow. "Haven't I yet?"

"Not like that," she says, tone a bit coquettish while her lithe thighs clench and my cock throbs. My trousers feel tight as the scent of her arousal also blooms in the air, sweeter, but before I can demand she tells me, my office line rings. This line is for pack business only and my first reaction is to mind-link Cain about the fae prisoner, but Isa picks up the phone and hands it over while shaking her head. ***This is a pack in need.***

"Xadiel Evergreen speaking."

"My King, this is the Alpha Craig of the Moon Valley pack in Oregon. I'm so sorry to call you like this, but—"

"Is this about the transfer? I have your niece's paperwork ready to be signed."

"No, my king. We have a problem."

"Please speak freely. What happened?" As I say this, I take in

Little Moon's body language. There's more than just a knowing expression, it's resignation. *What do you see, love?* "Is it rogues?"

"I don't know."

"What do you mean, you don't know?"

"I truly don't know, but all of our crops have been decimated." His stress comes through the line, and so does the confusion. There's anger and self-reproach, but heavier is the sense of worry. Of not knowing how to take care of those relying on him for their safety and survival. Moreover, it's the same sense of responsibility I have for every wolf and packs around the world. "My king, everything is burned and the soil ruined, but more than that financial loss is the decaying scent that lingers throughout the pack. Like death surrounds us, and the patrol guards—I—couldn't find anyone on my lands, but the stench left behind is unlike anything we've encountered in the past."

They need help, Xadiel.

Is this what you saw?

I can't bloody help but be concerned. The trespassers here, what little we've learned about the infected wolves, and now this…

Larue is coming, and it's the woman in my lap he's trying to draw out.

Yes. It's the same kind of rogues the male fae brought here.

Nodding at her, I run a hand down my face. "I'll send Beta Cain to investigate. He'll take a few trackers with him and we will scour the land."

"Thank you, Alpha. We are so thankful for your help."

"I'll also need a financial report on the losses incurred, Craig. Every last cent will be honored by the royal pack, including what's needed to till the soil and replant the crops."

"Alpha Xadiel, I'm so thankful for your help," Craig says, much calmer than when he first rang. His wolf also responds with a sharp bark, a quick sound that I understand as him being grateful. "Blessed be my king. Blessed be our royal crown."

Isabella

Later that night, I'm sitting beneath a grouping of western hemlocks that have grown intertwined. It's a few minutes past midnight; the night is cold and the ground is covered by a light layer of snow. Small gusts of wind circle around me, breaking around large trunks before reuniting in sparse, open spaces while creating a low whistling sound that carries throughout.

And yet, I feel at ease and warm within the darkness these trunks create while the full moon illuminates the rest of the surrounding forest. The three large trees sit alone and undisturbed—their deep, thick roots create a quaint little opening at the center big enough to fit a blanket and candles while hiding me from the outside world.

Not that I'm avoiding anyone, but right now, as I close my eyes and inhale nature's fresh scent, I feel centered.

My fingers dig into the earth as the thundering of paws passes close to my tree. The pack is acknowledging their luna. I sense their joy, while my favorite wolf howls up at the star-filled sky. Xadiel's not far, even as every werewolf shifts to celebrate the Moon Goddess and her blessings, he's in tune with my every breath.

If I make any sudden movements, there's a questioning tug in the bond.

If I ignore him, I receive a mental bark as a warning.

"Gods, I love him." Another loud and dominant growl rings through the forest, signaling my pack is traveling east of me. His call resonates deep within my chest, and the small note of annoyance in the tone pulls a wide smile from me. *Have fun, my king. I'll be waiting for you.*

Your place is on my back, Little Moon. Never again.

Since the day of our mating, this is the first time I don't participate in a pack run. He's a bit grumpy, and the response from his end comes out garbled. His wolf is fully present, merging with his naturally deep tone to voice their displeasure, something I find cute.

I love him all rumbly and demanding—needing me.

I'll make it up to you, Alpha.

You will.

Two words, and they send a pleasant shiver down my spine. Cause my nipples to pebble and my core to throb, and it's heightened when I pick up on the sound of heavy paws pounding the forest floor. It's a gait I recognize. The pattern and strength behind each step warm my heart—starting low yet coming up fast—the vibrations rush through my limbs as I dig my fingertips deep into the earth while a whimper slips through my lips.

All around me, life sways and breathes.

Each exhale strengthens my connection to these lands.

But it's when my favorite wolf rubs his snout against my leg a second later that I find my strength and open my eyes.

Xadiel's action is sweet; he's leaving his scent on my skin while simultaneously soothing my now-racing heart. But then again, he knows he's both the cause and effect. Fully shifted, he's glorious at well over seven feet tall, and his midnight black fur shines under the moonlight. Over the years, he's become more handsome, more distinguished, and the little bit of white around his snout makes me want to nuzzle his jaw.

In his human form, there are no grey hairs, but this touch occurred after our bite, and he knows I love it.

Will you be okay? His cold, wet nose skims up my thigh and midsection before pressing against my neck. I don't miss the way his chest expands with every heavy inhale, nostrils flared against my skin. ***Fuck, you smell delicious, Little Moon.***

"Yes." Breathy. A small tremble, but I find the strength to pull back and create a bit of space. Enough to control myself; our wolves need this run. "I'll tell you all about my adventure later." His response to that? A roll of those gorgeous, golden-with-black-swirl eyes. "Behave, Alpha. Wouldn't want to be accused of being adorable."

So cheeky.

"You love it." That earns me a quick nip to my mating bite, the pleasurable pulse settling on my clit, and I shift away once more. If I let this beast continue to tempt me, I will be on all fours within the next sixty seconds. "Now go, my love. Lead our pack."

Xadiel nods once before his snout comes near my cheek, licking the flushed skin from apple to chin. A wolfish kiss.

He leaves right after, reuniting with the others mere seconds later, and their harmonious howls warm my heart. Their animals need this. To run and hunt and feed, but this time I won't be there and soon enough they'll understand why.

I have a visitor coming. One I need answers from.

Relaxing my breathing, I find my center while the earth lulls me with its ancient song. The soothing waves run from my fingertip to my chest, a low cadence full of peace that I accept with a grateful heart. I've grown to love these moments of silence over the years—they've reminded me of a past life that at times feels foreign yet so embedded within my DNA.

This was Gabriella's favorite pastime in our youth. To sit and breathe in the land while life swayed for her—I miss her.

We're twins. Connected in ways no one will ever fully understand, and when we lost her, this gave me a way to honor Gabby. To feel close.

The soil between my fingers changes then, no longer loose and grainy, but more of an inky gel that shifts like the crashing waves upon the shore. It rises like the tide, submerging my hands until reaching my elbow, and then…nothing. Everything stops. No noises. Not so much as the sound of my breathing can be heard, but I do feel him.

I don't need to look up to know that a powerful being is mere feet from me.

"Hello, sweet child," a voice says then, and my eyes snap toward a tall figure leaning against an opposite tree, his figure easily seen through the opening. He's wearing a black robe, the heavy fabric hiding his frame while the hood covers most of his face, yet the markings that travel from his chin down to his neck stand out as if glowing. It's an intricate and bold design. The vine of thorns looks as if it's real—his shackles and crown—tying him to his position as God of Death.

But right now, as he stands beneath the canopy of the forest, they appear to be lit on fire. The flames are an eerily clear blue, sharp and ominous, and they greet me as if we're long-lost friends. And in a sense, we are. He's tied to Gabriella, the reason she can control and give life, and more importantly, now he's her father-in-law.

Life has a way of coming full circle. And this god broke the rules of the underworld and defied his brethren to give his son the woman who owns his heart. Thanatos has my respect, always will, and one day soon, Gabby and I will each repay him the favor.

Because true love never truly dies. It lingers and waits—gets angry and is ignored—but never abandons.

Each thorn in his tattoo is a tendril brimming with magic. Strong.

Powerful. Moreover, I can't stop the grin that spreads across my face. "Blessed be, God Thanatos."

"Blessed be, Luna Supreme." Pushing off the tree, he enters the space I've created for myself inside the western hemlocks and at once, the flames of my white candles begin to dance. They're brighter—rise higher, while the natural warmth he emits almost overwhelms the space. Yet, I'm used to it. Xadiel is a furnace and so warm, and while I attempt to recreate the exact temperature through spells, Thanatos does so without trying. His magic knows. His grin dares me to say something. "How have you been, my child?"

"Awaiting your arrival." I'm honest, and he'd never accept anything else. We both knew this day would come. Thanatos warned me, and I'd be an idiot to forget.

"I know." He lowers himself to sit across from me, head tilted to the side as we hear a distant howl. In the distance, we hear the deep howl of a wolf, and he chuckles. "Your mate knows I'm here. Not happy about it, but he's respectful nonetheless."

"He worries for me. No disrespect is meant."

"Again, I know." Thanatos looks like he wants to say something else, but shakes his head instead and closes his eyes. In the times we've met in the past, he's done this. Quiet and contemplative, but always aware. Thinking. "Xadiel is a good alpha and wolf. An honest man."

"Understanding, too."

"That, he is."

My male has given and loved me without pause. Without reproach or anger.

"But that's not why you're here." As the last syllable slips past my lips, I get a crackle in my mind. The open connection between his consciousness and mine.

Are you okay, or do I need to return?

Mentally, I giggle. *Thanatos sends his regards, my king. Please enjoy your run.*

I'll remain close.

"Judging by the smile on your face, I'd say he's contacted you."

"Yes," I respond. Thanatos's eyes remain closed, yet I don't question how he knows. Instead, I relax my breathing. Let myself fall back into the trance-like state I'd been in before his arrival. Except this time, I feel more. My senses appear sharper. The world around me becomes a series of electrical currents attached to colors while the candles I'd lit are extinguished. Not by me. Not by him. But I don't question this as I focus on the newness surrounding me: some of the strands are luminescent while others are so dark you can't discern them from our surroundings. Shrouded in black by the lack of light, this cropping of trees is thick—intertwined— obstructing the light of the full moon and stars from reaching us.

If you step outside, though, and walk a few feet forward, it's a different world. Lulls me with its brilliance while the silence cocoons me. It's not uncomfortable. On the contrary, I find that his presence alone speaks louder than any warning could.

Things will be changing soon. Pain is unavoidable.

"The time is coming soon, Isabella," Thanatos says a few minutes later, opening his all-black eyes to meet mine. He doesn't elaborate, and I don't need him to. I've seen Gabriella's arrival and know what it signals—the inevitable clock has been ticking since the moment she took her first breath as a vampire after being turned by her mate. "Our deal is now complete, and everything that was done to protect those you love is now out of my hands. I can no longer stop the natural order of life; many will die, and the path is as it should be."

Exhaling roughly, I place a hand over my flat abdomen. "Everything?"

"Yes, Isabella." His lips quirk, and it throws me back. In the times we've met, Thanatos hasn't been one for smiles or idle chitchat. With him everything is direct and without pause, something I appreciate. "That which was taken has been returned." I should be happy about this. Elated. Yet, I can't disguise the sudden bout of dread that fills my chest. *How long before Larue...?* "The road will be difficult, but much in the mortal realm is. You know what must be done."

"How much time do I have?" With Xadiel. My family.

"King Larue," Thanatos says his name with disgust, "is preparing to strike now that Gabriella's back and so is her stone. I did my part in protecting the onyx gem inside her chest by safe-keeping it in the underworld, but her rebirth couldn't stop its return to this realm. It belongs to her, Isabella, as Gaia's belongs to you. Moreover, he needs you both: one alive and the other dead, to strike against the same gods he worships and then curses. In his cocki-ness, he underestimates you, dear one. Show him. Accept who you are."

For some reason, his words remind me of Larue's warning before Gabby's death.

My patience is waning, young one. You will come to me of your own volition and comply—behave like the good girl you were raised to be—or be forced to watch them all die. His tone is mocking. He's self-assured. *One by one, I will kill them while you watch. Your sister. Her husband. Your mate. Each one will die because of your selfish-ness before my son takes you as his bride. By choice or by force, you will become our whore. The clock is ticking, Isabella. Choose wisely.*

"Will my sacrifice save them?"

"The love of a queen will make them rise."

"Thanatos, I—"

"Say hello to Gabriella for me." I'm given another small smile before I blink and he's gone. As are the colorful pulses and this heightened plane of existence I'd been experiencing. Yet as I turn my face to look toward the tree he'd first been standing against, I find a knowing golden pair of eyes.

Xadiel's wolf is just outside the entrance of my nook. His gaze is intense and understanding—he doesn't say anything or shift back to his human skin. Instead, he carefully moves around the limited space, shifting me forward just enough that he can curl his large body around mine, soothing my soul. Keeping me warm and surrounded by his love, I accept it, sending all my devotion through our bond while my mind is a chaotic mess.

Rapid snippets of our life together flow through my mind…

Our beginning and the hurt; these wolves were lost within a grieving that robbed them of kindness and rationality, but that ended quickly and without complaint. My male has spent a hundred years trying to repay me for something that isn't his fault nor mine, not realizing that there's nothing purer than his honest heart. He's given me a place to lay my head and calm my fears, a place to share my pain as I have his—and the pack's trust.

And being his mate and their queen, I've felt it all.

Know that this is where I'm meant to be and that the alpha king is my home.

One I will kill to protect.

Because I've lied to those I love the most.

I'm the keeper of all secrets, and when the time comes, I don't know if they'll ever forgive me. But what must be done, I'll do out of love and loyalty. To my family. To my mate.

To the little one I dream of every night.

Isabella

"I'm not that easy to pin, my luna." Xadiel taunts me, feet a few inches apart and stance lax, while I take in his every move. His cockiness is cute but I don't tell him that, choosing instead to keep my cool after failing to land a jab to his ribs. He's trying to distract me—break my concentration—by flexing those shirtless abdominal muscles and pecs at me. A tease. A delicious prize for later, but right now I ignore him and focus on my breathing. On the vibrations of the earth and the sway of magic that's just outside my reach, yet it thunders like my personal cheerleader. "But please give it an honest try. I do enjoy that spandex-covered body squirming all over mine."

It's been two weeks since Thanatos visited and Gamma Grady left England to come home, stopping in Oregon on his way back. He'd taken the trip for our beta, keeping him home while his twins celebrated a milestone: their first hunt. And while the adorable twosome took down some rabbits in their human skin with nothing more than small, sharp fangs—they don't shift until hitting puberty —our pride has been tainted by sadness.

It's been a stressful time, one full of monitoring the rising sightings of these modified rogues, and the lack of answers we've encountered—a few happy matings, too—but the focus remains on protecting every wolf, no matter if they are pack or not. No one deserves what's been done to these shifters, and even though the one in captivity responded to my power, there hasn't been much progress to remove what's been done to him.

Instead, he just lies still. Doesn't eat unless we force him.

We've also gotten film of the destruction left by the attack in Oregon, and while heartbreaking, I'm proud of the way Xadiel's handled everything. Financially and emotionally, as their king, he's given them the backing to rebuild.

"That's what you think," I say, stretching my neck from side to side. We're currently behind our home, on a private stretch of cleared land that we use for training: both my magic and hand-to-hand combat, the latter of which my mate sees to personally. Because he didn't lie all those years ago when he promised to be by my side for every potion, incantation, and punch I throw.

My alpha king is patient and kind and takes my safety as a priority, especially when it comes to my fighting skills. Because while I'll never be a shifter; I've been given traits that quietly simmer beneath the surface of my skin since our mating that need to be nurtured. They're latent and prickling against my magic, fighting to break free, but for now, they remain subdued by both circumstance and sacrifice.

That which was taken has been returned.

The God of Death's words, while thrilling, worry me. Xadiel, too.

He never asked what we discussed, but I shared what I could without jeopardizing his safety. My male knows Larue will strike, that he's after my sister and me for different reasons, just not how close we are to the end—what I must do to ensure our pup's future.

You know what must be done.

And I do. I need to awaken a part of me that hasn't risen since I stopped the female fae from killing Leo and taking the grimoire my father left behind—the instructions inside were too valuable then and now. It's why I've hidden it inside the hemlock trees that Thanatos found me in. My siblings will know how to find it when the time comes.

"It's a fact." His smirk is deadly. The dark ink on his skin under the sun is a distraction, and the way his eyes crinkle at the corner with mirth tells me he's more than aware of this.

Game. On. "And you say I'm the bratty one?"

"Then teach me a lesson, sweetheart."

Concentrating, I focus on a heavy rock near the tree line. It's just big enough to surprise him, but it barely trembles. That day my ire and hatred caused the world around me to bend in a way that evades me now; I controlled the shard of glass, and the desire to kill that female was my sole focus.

I need to regain control over that gift. It will come in handy when the time comes.

Because Larue and his army of power-hungry fae aren't done; he was held back—the price for his failures has been steep and my responsibility to fulfill.

"Watch your back, old man." At that, he clicks his teeth at me, a playful warning I do not heed. And I show him as much by blowing a kiss and sending a wink his way. "I'll try to take it easy on you, though. It'll be a gentle, steady ride this time."

Arms crossed over his bare chest, he licks a sharp canine. "How I love you, Little Moon. Even if you're unable to take me down without magic."

"Is that so?"

"Yes."

"I'm going to enjoy this." Opening my right hand, I reactivate the perimeter spell around us to dull my powers. Not eliminated, but they become dormant while within this contained space once it's up, and as I test the strength, it yanks back hard, causing me to smirk. "You ready?"

Xadiel's golden eyes narrow, and the black swirl of his wolf appears, showing me he's here. Yet it's not necessary; I feel him everywhere and always.

But this works to my advantage as he keeps switching his attention from my face to my hands without acknowledging my taunt. He's trying to find any subtle shift, and because I'm feeling playful, I start bouncing on the tips of my toes—stretching my neck from side to side while pretending I'm limbering up.

Instead, I'm following one of the earliest pieces of advice Xadiel ever gave me: never show your hand until it's too late.

"Will you be making the first move today, or...?" he asks, pushing me to make a quick and unprepared attack, but I flash my lashes instead. My quick survey of the land also throws him off but gifts me more than just a moment of hesitation on his part. Xadiel's not one to take it easy on me, something I appreciate, and I want to make him proud. In this space, I'm without my premonition or enchantments.

Equals. Because brute strength doesn't get you far, something my male preaches to his army. *Braun will fail if you're not thinking critically—never underestimate an enemy.*

"Maybe."

"So sassy today," he tsks, although the purr in his chest is louder. He's trying to distract me with the sound. "Is that your strategy? How you'll make me sweat?"

No, but I'll be more than happy to lick your wounds after.

Xadiel tries to reply, but I close the mind link and refocus. I'm looking for a point of weakness myself—that golden opportunity that doesn't come often— because this alpha is a fierce warrior. Strong and fast and can read his opponents with clear precision, but I'm different.

I have my moments. They're not often, and I've never truly pinned him in the century we've been mates unless you count mounting his glorious length, yet today, I'm feeling lucky. Almost *cocky*. There's this elevated thrill that causes my core to throb and wetness to ruin the gusset of my lace panties. And that rumble in his chest grows as his nostrils flare. Louder. Headier.

Not yet. Tonight.

"I can scent your need, female. So pretty."

"It's the excitement that comes from knowing I'm seconds away from mounting my king. I can almost feel you beneath me, Xadiel..." this leaves me on a whimper and his responding, pleased growl doesn't cool my desire, only stokes it "...spreading my thighs obscenely wide—"

"You're going to pay for this." Doesn't move. Still waiting.

"Promise?" Circling left, I find a cluster of bruises that weren't there this morning before he left to train with the elite and our beta. The three are no larger than a half-dollar coin and on the right side of his left knee; I fight back a grin. I might not be able to pin him, but at the very least, dropping the sexy giant to his knees comes with some benefits. "But I'm going to enjoy proving you wrong, Xadiel."

"Is that so?"

"Yes."

"How?" Two steps back and he shifts forward, matching my stride now. "By avoiding me?"

"No, but I am interested in a bet..." Trailing off, I tap my bottom lip to draw his attention there. Which works and when he licks his own, I give him my back. Before my next intake of breath, he's hovering close. Not touching, but his exhalation warms the top of my head. His body completely towers over mine, blocking out any bit of sunlight from touching me. *Perfect.*

"A bet? With me?" That sinful voice is deeper, the barely controlled hunger clear.

I nod. "Unless you're scared."

"Of you? Always, my witch." How much has changed since we met; a word that once came with animosity is now reverent. Sweet. "You're cunning and fierce; I would never doubt you."

"Smart man." Leaning back, I press myself against his front for a second. Just long enough that his hands find purchase on my hips, pinning me in place. Right where I want to be. "Which makes this even sweeter."

Before he can respond, I kick back against the hurt knee with all my strength and we teeter, stumbling while his grip remains unyielding. Another advantage and I launch a second blow, focusing on the same leg before stomping his foot.

His grip loosens as a muffled curse escapes him, the sound garbled and dark as his wolf comes forward. Yet it's enough for me to turn and meet his heated gaze—nearly black eyes with just a rim of gold on the outside remaining—narrowing while his half-shift makes me smile. My powerful male stands naked and proud now with fur sprouted across his arms, legs, and chest—while the rest of him bulges—fights to control the full turn into a wolf.

Goddess, he's glorious. Mine.

I take three steps back and he snaps his teeth at me.

I take a fighting stance, legs shoulder width apart with one foot slightly in front of the other.

I raise my fists, thumbs tightly over the first and second knuckles of my pointer and middle finger.

In response, Xadiel snarls. A warning to my direct challenge.

My focus on his knee was never about bringing him down with a hit but forcing a mistake, and I further taunt him when I bare my Wiccan teeth in response. Pushing his alpha instincts, the same ones that will never allow me to be harmed, to react.

Xadiel's hard in his half-shift, the knot at the base throbbing while a string of pre-come clings to the slit on the bulbous head. It slowly drips down to the grass and my mouth waters; I lick my lips.

"Come to me, Isabella." His tone is gravelly. Hungry. Ravenous.

Moreover, I'm shaking my head before he finished with the command. "No."

"Last chance, Little Moon. Come." Again, I ignore his demand. It's a stalemate and his chest expands, taking in my excited scent and clear defiance. Xadiel's seven-foot frame shivers and his head tilts back, every muscle in his body bulging and tight—ready to attack—while a deep growl reverberates through the field and our pack.

And our people answer him, their low howl a song of submission where his mate has denied him.

I shift my feet a little wider apart, center myself, and his head snaps back—eyes the color of onyx now stare at me. His wolf is in full control. The black-tipped claws of his feet dig into the grass and dirt below, leaving huge gouges behind in their wake. Then, there's the curl of his lips back over his teeth, snapping at me twice while I remain as I am.

I'm not afraid.

I'm amused—his jaw ticks, and for a few beats we just stare. There's a countdown in my head, the numbers ten through three ticking between each of my heartbeats before he lunges. One leap; he's aiming to tackle me and pin me beneath his strong body. Prove how strong and virile a mate he is, the pleasure only he can provide.

Because this man isn't angry. Oh no. He's hard and wanting—needing to claim his defiant female. I've tugged the wolf's tail, and he will bite me.

And I'll let you, my love. You can destroy me after.

Gods, it takes everything in me not to shiver. To give in.

Xadiel's fingertips graze my waist for just a second, but I pivot. In slow motion we pass each other, him tumbling forward before re-finding his grip in the dirt, but it's too late. Recognition flashes across his eyes a second too late as I use a trick he taught me during one of our earliest sparring sessions.

Any weakness is worth exploiting, especially when I'm so much smaller.

Thank you, my king.

I flip over him and land on his back. Again, he stumbles but remains upright, until I kick the back of his bruised knee. Twice on the same leg, I know it must hurt, and his garbled curses confirm as much while making my heart clench. Hurting him hurts me, but disappointing him would be worse.

With both hands on his shoulders, I jump slightly and bear all my weight on the weak point. My tower of a mate fights it and almost pulls me over his body, but I refuse to budge. Screaming through gritting teeth, I spring myself up and then come down hard a final time.

Xadiel drops to one knee, growling low. "That was a dirty move, Isabella."

Leaning down, I exhale against his neck. "I know."

"You're going to pay for that." Chest vibrating, his clawed right hand is tapping against the ground. "By my hand and my cock."

"I'm aware." Kissing the skin there, I make him shiver while one of his hands quickly grips the back of my thigh. Holding tight, his claws slightly digging into my skin while the other comes to my neck. No pressure. No pull. "But all is fair in love and war, right?"

"Good girl."

I'm anxious and breathing hard. I know he'll retaliate. "And I won." ***I need you again.***

All I get is a grunt in response before swiftly being flipped over and caught midair, like a ragdoll, and held above his mouth by my thighs. I'm suspended while his onyx eyes smolder, the right one giving me a wink while he runs his nose down the seam of my yoga pants.

I'm wet. Have been since we started.

Not a day goes by without the feel of him stretching me—the slight burn his size creates is a worshipped one—and I'll never stop thanking the gods for his stubbornness at a moment when I was done. He followed and claimed me, gave me his knot for the first time under the rain, and has stuck by my side ever since.

Our connection is powerful. This all-consuming tether that sings and pulls—only finds peace when we're together and no measure of time will satiate. Because I always want more.

Of him. Of our life together.

But more importantly, I'll do whatever I must to protect it.

The rough swipe of his tongue across my spandex-covered core makes me squirm. I'm fighting his hold on me but the brute only smirks, the subtle movement a feather-like kiss to my soaked labia. It's a complete contrast to his earlier touch, the grip on my legs, yet just as powerful.

Moreover, Xadiel knows this. How easily I surrender to him.

Without conscious thought, a whine escapes the back of my throat. It's a plea to my male, that *I desire him,* and he responds with a purr. Each vibration pulses right over where I need him most, pulling a deep and wanton moan from me.

"Please, Your Majesty. I deserve a reward."

"Hmmm." That's all. No move to take me, but then my lids close in frustration.

"Xadiel, I—" One quick breath, a jerk, and my eyes snap open. He's lying flat on his back with my pussy near his face while the tearing of fabric follows a second later. It stings, but then the cool air over my tender, wet flesh feels good. Soothes the shock to my system.

His dark eyes watch me from beneath long lashes, and I moan.

I'm clenching and trembling. I'm leaving a mess across his chest and chin.

Please, baby.

My male shivers beneath me, grip tightening in response to the mind link before pressing a tender kiss to my clit. "Now you've won, Isabella. Pinned your king."

Alpha
XADIEL

Her whine at my words is my undoing.

I'm not gentle nor do I take my time; I eat her like the starved beast I am. My tongue slides through her dripping folds, dragging from her entrance to clit as a growl rips from deep within my chest at her taste. Isa's always been sweet, but right now, there's something else and it's an addictive decadence I want to gorge myself on.

Cock hard and painful, I rake a sharp fang across her flesh before turning her to face my throbbing length. She's so tiny compared to my seven-foot frame. A literal doll I can manipulate and position to my liking, and right now, I want her just like this.

Squirming and whimpering, at my mercy as I suck her clit between my lips and flick it rapidly with the tip of my tongue. Wetness drips from her clenching hole and onto my chin, soaking my short beard, and nothing makes me prouder than to carry her scent with me.

Being marked by her is a privilege. The world will always know that I am hers, but I'm also a possessive son of a bitch, wanting to snap the neck of anyone who's gifted a small taste of this sweetness that's mine. Only mine.

It's a contradicting stance. I know this, but no one ever said love was rational.

This possessive need is archaic and controlling, but I am an animal ruled by instinct and our bond. And I follow both. Unwavering and faithful while always putting my female's desires before my own.

"Xadiel, please," she cries out when I slide two fingers over her rosebud and down to her entrance, circling her tiny flexing hole. Isa clenches at nothing, wanting me to finger fuck her, but I nip her clit instead. There's a tiny tear in her dermis because of it and a few drops of blood seeping through, her life's essence mixing with her juices as they slide across my tongue. This is bloody nirvana. My weakness, and I purr against her sopping flesh, causing another rush of her arousal to drip down my fingers. "Oh, *Gods*. Oh, *fuck*."

"Such a perfect little pussy my mate has. So pretty and pink." On the next swipe of my thick tongue across her bundle of nerves, I bury two fingers inside her cunt. Deep and fast, loving the way she undulates above me while my cock bobs a few inches from her face. Her warm puffs of breath caress the taut skin. "That's it, baby girl. Squeeze my fingers…ride them."

And she does. Like my perfect slutty doll.

Her lush ass bounces above my face with each gyration, taking my fingers to the hilt and then dragging them out slowly while I suckle her clit. Laving the tiny bundle with bites and pressure, sealing the cuts with my spit, while my tongue doesn't leave a single trace behind. While her slickness—the headiness of her arousal—causes pre-come to drip from my cock.

I feel each bead. How it pools at the tip and then rolls down the underside to my knot and then swollen balls. Balls she's currently caressing with delicate fingers, running them from the expanded base of my dick down to the perineum before cupping my sack and giving it a firm squeeze.

"I want to taste you, Xadiel. Feed me, my king."

Motherfuck, she's my literal wet dream come to life. The Moon Goddess couldn't have designed a better match for me—this woman was created to fulfill every aspect of my life, but it's her sexual appetite—one that matches my own—that causes my beast to snap.

It's all her fault.

Couldn't contain him.

Before her next intake of breath, I sit up while keeping her in place: upside down and with my cock now at her lips. Her thighs are splayed open and body shivering and her wet slit is parted while the fingers that'd been buried deep now rub her swollen cunt with tight circles.

"Open your mouth, Little Moon. I'm going to fuck that pretty little throat of yours." Before I'm done speaking, she's already taking the engorged head between her lips. I hiss, muscles contracting while never pausing my possessive hold on her cunt. Her clit is swollen and I feel each pulse—watch in rapture as her arousal drips from her entrance and down my fingertips before dripping down to my palm. "Gods, baby. Like that."

Isabella suckles the head, flicking the slit at the tip while letting out a pleasure-filled hum that I match with a loud groan, adding pressure to my hold on her before slapping her labia twice with enough bite to make her scream. And the moment those lips part, I buck into her mouth and nearly come when she gags on my girth.

Not that it stops her. If anything, she's hungrier for me.

Bobbing her head in time with each pump of my hips, vibrating in my hold as I take turns between spanking and licking every drop of her slick. She's canting her hips in search of more, whining for me to make her come, but I hold back.

For a few minutes, I let her whimper around my cock. Just watch as her saliva drips down my length and knot, while her tongue adds pressure to the underside. It's the sexiest kind of torture. Feels so fucking good, and I'm an evil arsehole for pulling her off—just high enough that she can't do anything but plead. Unintelligible sounds leave her. Isabella fights my hold but I attack without mercy.

Nipping. Licking. Suckling her sensitive flesh without pause.

"Xadiel, I'm—"

"Do not hold back from me, Female. Give your king his reward," I purr against her, raking a sharp tooth over the swollen bud before burying my tongue deep into her cunt. Her keening sounds are loud, reverberating throughout the forest, and my beast deepens his call. The sounds merge and create a sensual soundtrack, as sweet as the scent of her desires, but it's the way she grips me with a hand—her hold desperate—that I enjoy the most. "Good girl."

"Male, I hunger for you." She's close and frustrated—arching and squirming—trying to reach my cock, and I reward her with a rough snap of my hips. My dick slides across her tongue to her throat from the tip to my knot without pause. I take what she so willingly offers and eat her pussy with punishing strokes, fucking into her hole with short jabs as I take her mouth. Moreover, between the plumpness of her lips and the way she swallows, I'm close. Expanding to the point of pain and throbbing, but it's the way she wraps a small, delicate hand around my knot, squeezing tight, that pulls the first rope of come from me.

It's fast and sudden. Slamming into me with enough force that I lose myself and bite hard right above her clit and catch a little bit of the hood. Little Moon's orgasm is near violent as I draw blood, her entire body pulsing while I fill her tiny mouth with my spend, some dribbling out the sides while I drink from her.

I'm not a vampire but understand the draw. Just for her. And more so when it's mixed with her slick; a heady combination that I devour while sealing the wound—soothing the sting—and she licks me clean. Once she's done, Isabella nuzzles me and then relaxes in my hold and I lay back on the grass, bringing her with me. She's easy to flip around and maneuver, placing her over my body so that we're face to face.

"Hi." Grin salacious. Blue eyes are so bright.

"Hello, love." Lifting a hand to her face, I sweep the still wet pads of my digits to her cheeks and sweep them back and forth. Motherfuck, she's beautiful and tender. All mine. "You good?"

"More than," she croons, stretching a bit. "Feeling relaxed and full of pride."

"Pride?"

"Of course, Xadiel." Her expression is sassy and amused. Preening. "After all, I did pin the werewolf king and got a nice orgasm as a reward."

"You cheeky little minx."

"Doesn't change the fact I pinned you. Fair and square."

"Not at all." My claws unsheathe, and I walk two fingers from my unoccupied hand up her spine. "But that means I can demand a rematch."

"Technically…there are rules you're not following." Goosebumps rise across her skin while a small gyration over my abdomen follows. "You need to file for this, wait for my acceptance, and then set a date."

"I make the rules."

"Says who?"

"Your slick cunt grinding on me." Removing my hands from her body, I bite back a grin. "Now run, little witch. I'm going to earn my title back."

<hr>

WE SPENT most of the afternoon out in the woods, playing a naked game of hide and fuck until my female tapped out and pouted for me to carry her back home. It was then I carried her home, smug and puffing my chest out while she burrowed her face in my neck. Moreover, we remained this way while entering our bedroom, during our shower, and even now as she slips on a simple off-white long-sleeved crop top and matching joggers. On her feet she has a pair of ankle-length socks while her red locks are pulled into a high pony-tail. No makeup. Fresh and bare and so fucking beautiful.

"Ready for supper, Little Moon? You haven't eaten since lunch and you have to be starving."

"Shut it," she huffs, giving me the evil eye, but the twitch of her lips negates any annoyance. "By the way, is your knee okay? Those bruises looked painful."

"They're fine. Cain was being a right cunt after I kicked him into a tree." *Alpha, you have visitors. They're heading your way.* Faith sends the message, and it's the perfect timing. A few days ago, I received a call and news that will make Isabella happy. Something she wants but never asks for, thinking she's being selfish.

This woman doesn't have a single self-serving bone in her body.

Thank you, Faith. Let them in, please.

Of course, Alpha. Luna will be so excited.

"…you're not listening to me, Xadiel. Something happen?" Isabella waves a hand in front of my face, jumping a bit to reach my line of sight. "Were more rogues spotted?"

"Calm down, love." Smiling, I bend down just low enough to seal her lips with mine. The kiss is gentle and soft, just a tender sweep across her plump mouth until she whimpers for me. *Such a lovely sound.* "It was just Cain alerting me to the proposed transfer of funds for the Oregon pack. He received and accounted for all the losses, and then needed my approval to up the total by ten percent to cover any inconsequentials."

"Tell me Grady isn't helping him? That man needs rest and time with his mate." My luna purses her lips, brows knitted. "Give them both tonight and tomorrow off. We can handle whatever is left tomorrow…will you need to travel and oversee the progress soon, too?"

"Breathe, and yes on all accounts." I'd already given everyone the night off to relax, as the next few days will be busy. Faith, Cain's mate, greeting our guests was the last active duty of the day. "Everything can wait."

"Good." Satisfied with herself, Isa turns toward her vanity and picks up a bottle of perfume and spritzes a few drops across each wrist and the hollow of her throat. The floral notes match her natural scent with an added touch of citrus that pleases my wolf and me. "I love it when you listen."

"Yes, dear."

"Now who's being cheeky?" Giving me a wink, she crooks a finger for me to follow her out the room, and I do for more than one reason. There's a presence in the air the second we step onto the stairs, a familiar and familial call that causes Isa to pause and her hand to press against her chest.

She doesn't say anything to me.

Doesn't so much as pause as she rushes down the steps and heads directly to where our visitors await. They're sitting on our couches, all proper and regal, while sipping from a cup that I know isn't briming with tea. Instead, there's a tinge of red on their lips, ones they spread into a wide grin at the sight of my female.

Especially her twin. "Took you long enough to realize I'm here, Isabella. Is my brother-in-law keeping you distracted?"

Isabella

"I'm going to kick your arse." Why this comes out in a British accent, I have no clue, but it does as the surprise hits me full force. It needs work. I don't sound like my werewolves at all, and I can sense Xadiel's amusement through the bond. I ignore it as I stare at my sister a few feet from me, smirking and carrying herself with a lightness that pulls a grin from me no matter how much I want to fight it. "Why didn't you tell me you were coming?"

"It's called a surprise…*surprise*!" At her squeal, Theo chuckles beside her while giving me a nod. His attention soon shifts to Xadiel and the two exchange looks, but no one says anything and I won't ruin this moment by asking my mate what that was about.

Instead, I focus on my sister. Alive and vibrating in her seat—what she's waiting for, I have no clue, and a second later I take matters into my own hands. I take the steps between us, rushing to where she sits and then we're hugging. Placing our foreheads against the other's while intertwining our fingers—giving the other access to our souls.

We feed off each other, feel the good and bad and even those moments of uncertainty, but I'm happy to see that her tethers are joyous. Even as a hybrid now, a witch changed into a vampire, her tethers remain the same, like a warm hug after such a long separation.

I don't begrudge her the time away after her rebirth. I understand the need to be with her mate and enjoy the life—the time lost—but I've missed her. Leo, too.

Our familial connection. The ties twins share.

It's the memories of our youth and the time in our coven. It's learning spells and playing in the forest.

Our parents. Our people.

"By blood and pact…"

"We are one," I answer her, unable to stop the tear that slips from my right eye. Hers are also glassy, but unlike me, her vampiric change doesn't allow them to fall. They just shine.

"Always, Isa. Remember that." After a few minutes, she pulls back and steps past me with a grin, greeting Xadiel with nothing but warmth. They embrace, and I can't help but endure a small pang of hurt. Not because they're close, but because I don't truly think I'll ever have good relationship with Gabby's mate.

When she died, he blamed me. Not so much with words, but actions, and while I understand that grief is an uncontrollable emotion—an intensive explosion of pain that chokes you—I felt his ire. His hate.

Justified within his sorrow, Theodore wished it was me instead.

Do I blame him for a natural reaction after losing the woman he loves? No.

Do I still think he holds a certain level of animosity toward me? Yes.

Even after she was gone, I approached him multiple times, helped him where I could—dealt with Elise—nothing was ever truly solved between us. It's something I've learned to live with and ignore, smiling at my sister and mate as they laugh at something.

Luckily, my stomach rumbles then and I blush. "Sorry."

Immediately, Xadiel looks over and smirks. "Nonsense, Little Moon. Time to eat, love."

"It can wait a bit. They just—"

"Come on, Isa." Gabriella cuts me off, patting Xadiel's arm and then coming back to me. Her slim, yet slightly colder hand grips mine and tugs me toward the dining area. "Let's go feed."

<hr>

I'M HAPPY, yet off balance.

The four of us are sitting in the dining room and chatting, them more than me, as I bask in the sounds around me. While my sister and her mate drink from a golden chalice, the contents inside deep red and a little thick, my husband cuts into his steak. Two of them sip, and the other chews, while I can't stop the visions and memories from clashing into each other.

I'm here. With them.

Yet will this moment last?

In my mind, we're kids again and kicking up a fuss over having to clean the altar, wanting to go out instead of taking care of what we cluttered. I hear Mom's patient voice explaining the importance of showing respect and taking care of the sacred space where we pray and reflect. Then, just as fast, I'm watching the first time Gabriella saved a being—the family cat—and how it freaked her out after. I listen to Dad comfort her and explain, sitting us both down to explain how special we are.

Something I still struggle with. This has felt more and more like a curse each day.

It's an emotion that makes me feel guilty. This path led me to Xadiel, and while I'd never forsake him—the weight on my shoulders sometimes breaks my back—I can't help but ask myself *what if we were normal?*

Just a simple witch. A stable life.

I blink, and the answer hits me straight in the chest.

Destruction and chaos without any stopping the torture our people would succumb to. Humanity would crumble and war would ravish lands, leaving behind nothing but ashes in its wake. Xadiel and Theo would fight, kill many of the rising enemies, but each is betrayed.

Right-hand men, trusted generals—would become their executioners.

My father would be forced to watch his wife and daughters become slaves. Leo would die.

"Isabella?" My mate's voice brings me out of the horrific images and then there's a clang, and the sharp sound of metal crashing onto a plate refocuses my attention. Three sets of eyes are looking at me, but the one's I meet are Xadiel's. "What did you see, love?"

"Something that will never be." It's croaky, my throat tight as the sight of so many dead corpses, the faces all staring at me, tries to take me under the vision again. "I asked a question, and the answer hit me hard. Nothing to worry about."

"What do you mean, you asked?" I'm surprised Theo's the one speaking. More so because his expression is soft, not the usual clenching jaw or hard eyes. "Who did you ask?"

"The universe." My male reaches over, in his hand a glass with water that he brings to my lips, urging me to take a sip. Which I do, needing the moment to collect myself. And only when my throat is able to swallow past the lump, when I feel centered, do I answer. I'm also feeling a little guilty to admit this. "I couldn't help but ask where our lives would be if we'd never been given gifts—"

"I've asked that many times, but never got a response." Gabby cuts me off, but more surprising is her admission. "Not because of who I am with, but more so because of those I miss."

"Wouldn't have mattered, Gabby." At my response, Xadiel's

becomes tense beside me. His worry is palpable, and I reach out for his hand still holding the glass. Without pause, I remove the water and place it down so I can intertwine our fingers. *I could never regret you, love. Never you.* "Our unions were blessed and created to withstand what's to come. Without each other we would've failed, and the outcome would be catastrophic."

"How bad?" Xadiel asks, his gravelly tone deeper than normal.

Swallowing hard, I turn my face toward his. "A life of servitude or death."

"And now?"

"Destiny changed that, Xadiel." He's so handsome. The best part of me. "Because of you, I have something to fight for. A life. A future family." Pulling my hand from his, I cup his chin with the same and smile. This one is honest and truly felt; I will do what must be done to protect what we have. "The path to happiness is paved with tears, but the destination is blessed. What I saw was a direct answer to my question, not our reality. What could've been can't be if I have you."

"Always." A promise to his female.

The other two remain quiet and when I look over, my sister's expression tells me she has questions, while her mate seems appeased by my answer, giving me a nod. No one says anything else, maybe because I was forthcoming in my answer, but it's because it doesn't affect our future.

What could've or should've are irrelevant in this scenario.

My emotions are just that—mine. Nothing more than a personal reflection.

"You've barely touched your food." Theodore's statement makes me frown for a second; this is the most he's spoken to me in years, but before I can answer, a new presence is felt. Powerful and also familial. Gabby must sense him, too, as a grin spreads across her face.

It's coming closer. Rushing toward the house, and the flood of warmth that fills my soul has me pushing my chair back and standing, heading toward the door while my sister follows closely.

That's how I love to see you. Happy and carefree.

Did you do this? How do you keep surprising me, Xadiel?

A loud, rumbly laugh filters from the dining room. Its owner tugs at our bond playfully. *An apprentice never shares the learned secrets of the trade. Just know that it's magic.*

It's my turn to snort. *I'll remember that the day I give you my bite.*

Your bite? The pulse through our bond is full of desire. Want.

A seer never shares her naughty visions…

Female, I will—

He doesn't get to finish as I break the connection when a smiling face stops before us. His smile is wide and his posture regal, yet he will always be our little brother. "You going to just stand there, Gabby?"

"Gods, Leo. I can't believe you're all grown up." Her words aren't meant to make us sad, but the truth is she's missed so much. This is also the first time she's seen him since coming back, having been away with her mate, yet as they embrace, hugging tight and speaking low, I let go of my doubts.

Of the *what ifs*. Of a little of the guilt I carry daily.

A large, thick arm wraps around my midsection and pulls me against a solid chest. His woodsy and mint scent wraps around me as his lips press against my ear. "This is because of you, Little Moon. Never forget that."

Nodding, I keep my attention on Theodore joining my siblings. How they share a quick hug and then keep talking, Leo answering every question Gabriella has. There's also a squeal when he hands her a gift, an identical box to the one he brought me not long ago with a message from our aunt.

It's Aunt Silla. She needs to speak with you.

I make a mental note to ask him about it tomorrow. For tonight, I'm going to relax and not give anything else away as my brother looks over and waves us over. This reunion is a hundred years in the making, all three Moore children together after enduring so much, and I need this as much as they do.

"Are you okay?"

Tilting my head up, I nod at my alpha with a grin. "You've made me so happy, my male. Thank you."

"That's all that matters to me."

"Enough whispering, you two, get over here."

"His Majesty spoke, Xadiel," I say loud enough so everyone hears and while Gabby laughs, our brother groans. "We mustn't make him wait."

"So mean, my luna," he chides, a hint of claw breaking through and playfully digging into my side.

"Did you know I will bite, too?"

Alpha Evergreen shivers, and my smile widens. "Baby, that's the second time—"

I don't get to answer or evade him, and that makes it sweeter. My brother and sister pull me away and walk us back into the dining room, each holding one of my hands tight. Just like with Gabriella earlier, I share my energy with Leo and it's a bittersweet remembrance of our coven in Italy.

<hr>

"...Dad was so pissed at me," my brother grumbles, while the rest of us laugh. He's taking it in good stride, being made the subject of most of our stories, but this he's a little grouchy over. "I took the blame, but it was Gabriella who knocked the glass hands over. The damned things hit the ground and shattered into a million pieces."

"I warned you both to quit messing around in his office. Didn't I?"

"Yes, but you weren't specific as to the why." Leo points out, and I shrug. "A little heads up would've been nice."

"So warning you beforehand and during weren't enough?" I

laugh, remembering his roll of the eyes pre-disaster and the sulking after he got sent to the stables to clean out Onyx and Pearl's stalls. "He got a full week of free labor out of you that time."

"How often did this happen?" Xadiel asks before taking a sip from his gin. We're all gathered outside and around an outdoor fireplace, relaxing after a nice meal as flurries crash to the ground. I'm full, lethargic, and becoming sleepier by the second under the protection of our roofed deck—more so because my mate has me in his lap and snuggled against his chest. "Who was the troublemaker of the three?"

"I was the good child." At my yawned reply, the other two snort. "What?"

"You were never caught because you saw the outcome, sister. That's called *cheating*."

"And *you* paid me in sweets to help you avoid getting caught, Gabby."

"She what?" Leo scowls at us, knocking back his own drink. It's weird seeing him like this—an adult now—and not the little kid we did everything to protect back then. Now, we're all older and wiser. We'll live long and happy lives as our bodies age slowly. *So mote it be.*

Outside of humans, our species isn't hindered by time. We can be killed, yes, but it's not easy and natural causes or diseases isn't something we worry about.

"Not my fault you didn't think to bribe me."

"Seriously? A few pastries would've saved me?"

"Yes." No shame, but I do yawn again. Longer this time, a heavier than normal exhaustion settling deep.

"And that's my cue to take this one to bed." He kisses the top of my head. "Ready?"

"Yeah." My male stands with me in his arms, ignoring the teasing grin on my sister's face, but then I remember something and begin to squirm. Want him to put me down. "We need to show them their rooms and get—"

"Already done, Luna Evergreen." Seeing the confusion on my face, Xadiel nuzzles my jaw and then bids everyone goodbye. I do the same, having him lean me over my siblings to give each a kiss on the cheek and then a small smile for Theodore, before returning my attention to the man carrying me up the stairs and into our room bridal style, not pausing until he's placed me in the middle of our bed. He's never been concerned with showing affection in front of others—his family or mine or our people—and I love it. Never ceases to send a pleasure-filled thrill through me, but having him alone is my favorite time of the day. In our room. With his focus on me. "I've known for quite some time they were coming and had Faith prepare the rooms on this floor for them. Both suites are ready; I was hoping Leo would show up after I sent him the picture of you two hugging."

"You did?"

"I did. There's nothing I wouldn't do to see you like this."

"Like what?"

"At peace. Truly content." After taking off my socks, he removed my pants and panties in one tug. My top is next, seconds before my bra, and only once I'm bare does his chest rumble for me in that purr that sets my blood ablaze. "Now take a nap. I'll be back in a few hours."

"Where are you going?" Even as I ask this, fatigue takes a deeper hold of me. More than anything, I think it's the roller-coaster ride of emotions I've been on lately. The coming to terms with choices and truths and the inevitable departure I must take. Then, another thought hits me and I try to sit up, but he just places his large, warm palm on my flat stomach to hold me in place. "Seriously?"

"Yes. Rest."

A huff escapes me, but that too turns into a yawn. "Is everything okay, Xadiel?"

"While they're here, I want you to relax and enjoy yourself, my queen. You more than earned the time off."

"That doesn't answer my question."

"Luna, all is as it should be." Climbing up the bed, he hovers above my thighs before lowering his head and kissing my knees. One leg, then the other, getting higher with each one until he's licking from clit to belly button, causing goosebumps to rise and a shiver to crest, my pussy slick. Moreover, he doesn't stop—nipping my abdomen and then laving each beaded nipple—licking and sucking my flesh until our mouths meet in a heated kiss. It's over before I'm satisfied. I'll never have enough of him. "Your people are safe, and all this king is doing is returning two phone calls: one to the Oregon pack, and the other to my parents. I promise."

"Yeah?" Breathless. Aching for more, but I understand pack business. Sometimes having to wait is worth it when the reward is sweeter. Dirtier. "Tell them I said *hi* and *I love them*."

"Aye." Another kiss, much softer. "Now be a good girl for me and rest, Little Moon. Your male is coming back as soon as he can to fuck that pretty little cunt and swallow your cries."

Isabella

I'm walking through the house late at night, heading toward the kitchen area. It's empty, which makes no sense since my siblings are here and Xadiel should be in his office, and yet, I know I'm alone. It's an eerie feeling, this almost out-of-body experience where my surroundings are familiar, yet strange all at once. The walls and decor are the same, but the scents are off.

There's no cedar with a hint of mint lingering in the air.

There's no rippling bond always pulling me in my mate's direction.

"What the hell?" I say out loud at the sudden faint sound of a child's giggle, my words echoing while my flip-flops slap against the flooring. Something else that makes me pause; I'm not one to wear shoes indoors. Hardly ever. I'm a socks or bare feet kind of witch, and that's when I take in the rest of me. Wearing yesterday's clothes, the same comfortable set Xadiel ripped from my body, but now with a red blot at the center of my chest.

It's not large and looks like blood. but when I pull the ribbed top away from my body, there's no lesion there. Not a damn thing outside of the normal.

Another child's laugh, and I turn around in a full circle. No one is here, but that sound is familiar to me. It fills me with a warmth that quickly becomes dread.

Walking further toward the kitchen, I pass our formal dining and find flowers on the table. Again, not out of the norm, but I don't recall ever buying a wolf arrangement of forget-me-nots. Their blue hue is pretty, and I know I've seen this flower before somewhere of importance, but the where evades me.

Why is this important, though? That's the better question. What am I missing?

"Xadiel," I call out, hoping he pops out somewhere and this will all lead to another surprise. I'm pleased by them, to be honest. It's fresh and new, this not knowing everything, but the lack of bond— him—is starting to unsettle me.

Yet the moment I give our connection a tug, I find emptiness. No love. Not a trace of its presence ever being there.

"What the—"

"You've already said this, young one. Are you seeing or hearing things?" This new entity slams into my awareness with the weight of a sledgehammer; I bring a hand to my forehead and try to massage the ache. My head hurts. I feel pressure—*him.* "Are you done playing games?"

"Show yourself."

"For a royal, your etiquette leaves a lot to be desired, Princess."

"It's Luna, to you." The more this man talks, the more I recognize his voice. His patronizing tone. That aura of superiority. "Although, it's better if you don't call me anything at all and leave. You're not welcomed here."

"You wound me, Isabella." King Larue steps out of the kitchen's entryway, dressed in a royal blue suit and matching robe over it. On his neck there's a rather long and intricate gold chain, woven like a rope with a large pendant hanging just below his sternum. It's large, an oval with a tree inside, it's wide branches delicately etched to show the most minute detail while a diamond encrusted sword sits inside the trunk. *Fae crest.* "I thought we had an understanding all this time. I've been patient and too lenient—let you play house with that mutt when your place is at my feet."

"I'll never serve you."

"You will." Closer, he moves until I'm within arm's reach. But the closer he gets, the more I realize his physical presence isn't completely solid. There's a highlighted tinge to it—subtle, yet it gives him away. "Or I'll kill him. Him, and that vampire-loving cunt you call a sister and her puppet. Heed my warning, Isabella. Don't make me hurt you."

"You touch them, and I'll end your entire bloodline. That's my vow, King Larue." There's a sudden crash, the sound of glass shattering upon impact loud, but I don't so much as flinch. "My patience for threats has its limits."

"It's comical, really. A mere witch threatening—"

"I'm not a mere anything, and you know this. You're misogyny has no place in my home."

"I'm going to beat that smart mouth out of you."

"We'll see."

"Sooner than you think. My first gift will come with a note." He reaches for my face, but his body here isn't solid. Instead, it goes through me and all I feel is a light shift in the air. So subtle that had I not been seeing him, I wouldn't pick up on it. "It's already started, young one. I will destroy everything you love, one by one, until you crawl to me and beg for mercy. And I'll be compassionate enough to forgive you."

"Get out of my head." As I say this, I pick up on someone else getting close. They're just outside this level of sub-consciousness I'm currently in. "Leave, and don't come back."

"Is that a threat?" His smirk is full of condescending mirth, yet he fades a little more. Light seeps through. "Because it's quite amusing, mon cheri."

"It's a promise. Nothing good will come from your obsession."

"Why is that?" he asks. Curious. A little more subdued.

"Because Gods are not children to be fooled. You will never kill Aries or Hades or Thanatos." It's my turn to smirk. "They're watching you."

"This you've seen?"

"Leave." From deep in my gut, I feel a shift in me. The air around me. It's as if all this time the home I was inside of had been muffled—muted—and colors now burst to life around me. This cosmic shift pulsates and grounds me, while that magic within me, the one I use to protect Leo all those years ago, bursts free. One second, Larue is calmly watching me, and the next—

"Isabella?" another voice suddenly calls out, pulling from that…*what the hell was that?* Blinking, I realize I'm dressed and in the entryway to my kitchen, yes, but no longer in whatever trap Larue had set up. Instead, I'm now looking into Theodore's concerned, yet questioning gaze. "Are you okay? I've been calling your name for a few minutes."

Frowning, I bring a hand to my right temple and rub the skin there. I can feel the start of a migraine forming. "I'm fine."

Not really. Anything but and I want my mate. *Where is Xadiel?*

"You're as shit a liar as Gabriella is." Shifting my eyes around the space, I try to find the subtle differences I took notice of while in that trance and come up empty. Yet as his words register, I pause and snap my attention to him. They narrow, too. "Ask your sister. I'm not one to sugarcoat. You both can't hide anything; your expressions are too open."

"Only with those I trust."

"And you trust me?" The mere thought surprises him. I'd be laughing if what happened, this entire night, wasn't so bizarre already. *Does Larue know about my future child?* "We don't have the most—"

"I'm sorry. It's been a long night and I'd rather not have this conversation right now." My words come off cold, but being told what I already know isn't my idea of fun after everything that's happened. He doesn't see me as someone he can *trust*. He *blames* me for her death still. "I'm just going to ring Xadiel and head back to bed. Good night."

Turning, I make it four steps before I hear him exhale roughly. "I don't hate you, Isa."

"Come again?"

"Can we please talk? I just need a few minutes of your time."

"Okay." What else can I say? Pointing toward the kitchen, I wait for him to proceed and then follow. In the breakfast nook, there's a large built-in booth with bench seating my mate built; it's nestled into large bay windows overlooking our back deck area. "Go ahead and take a seat. I'm going to grab something to drink…would you like anything?"

"I'm fine."

As he goes to sit, I head straight for the fridge and grab a can of pop. It's cold, but I want it freezing with the good kind of ice for this conversation. Luckily, one of the few things I insisted on in this kitchen was a specialty ice maker. These little nuggets are easy to chew, and to me taste better, too.

Once I have my items, I return and take the bench across from him and facing the kitchen entryway. We don't talk at first while I open and pour my drink, nor as I take the few first sips, but the silence is too much for me.

So is his gaze. Not hostile, but more contemplative.

"What's on your mind, Theodore?"

"I owe you an apology, Isabella." For the second time tonight,

I'm caught off guard. Don't quite know how to respond either and remain quiet. "When everything happened, I wasn't fair to you. At that moment, the pain was too deep to think logically or see past it. I'd just lost her and—"

"You felt I should've warned her." Not a question. A statement.

"Yes." His expression and response are honest; I can respect that.

"That's fair, but answer me this much…can you evade fate?"

"I believe in making my own destiny. Will defy death himself, and have."

"Yet she was still taken from you," I say this, and then take another sip of my drink. And while I know my words anger him, I'm a little raw and shaken at the moment. The words bubble out of me before I can stop them, too. "But that's the bad end of the oracle stick, Theo. Everyone wants answers and help and the easy road—I got stuck with the task of carrying fate on my shoulders and doing everything I must to protect those I love. You think I wanted her to be taken from us? That I haven't cried myself to sleep as the guilt eats at me?"

"Just help me understand. Why not warn us?"

"Her death was written to happen before she met you."

"What are you talking about? What does that mean?"

"Do you remember what my father said to you when he begged you to protect her?"

"Paolo said it had to be me. That I'd understand once we met."

"And why is that? Why did a royal wizard—someone with his strength—allow himself to be killed?"

"Isabella, I—"

"She would've died had he not intervened and sacrificed himself. My parents died to protect their children because my father saw what I did." Anger slams into me, and I know I'm shaking. It feels as if the entire room is. "We saw Larue's rise and the betrayal of our own people. We saw her rushing to save him and being wounded in the crossfire, a blow that couldn't be healed in time to save her. For weeks, we tried to find a loophole. Anything to save her, because gods be damned, what's the point of being a powerful seer without helping those you love."

"And you saw me?"

"I saw you." Theo's eyes shift behind me, and I know it's Xadiel. His scent hits me first and then his hands, big and strong, warm my shoulders while giving me support. He's towering over me, calming the volatile tremors I've been fighting back since my interaction with Larue. I'm feeling raw—exposed and unsettled by that giggle. "You were our only hope, Theodore. Between your ties to Thanatos and her carrying his stone, I knew we could negotiate and bring her back if she were ever put in danger. Every time I saw her walking a path, your protection shielded her—I saw her death, but the rebirth was worth it. You demanded what no mortal could from your father while I sacrificed my children until she was given back to us."

"You did what? Why the fuck would you—"

"Because she's my sister." A tear escapes and then another, but I don't hide my pain. Being strong sometimes is exhausting. "This was the only route I found to secure her long and happy life with you. It had to be or not at all, and that's a shitty decision to have to make, but I did and I don't regret it. The safety of our people and my family is all that's ever truly mattered to me."

I'm tired, Xadiel. So tired.

I've got you, beautiful. Always lean on me.

"I'm sorry, Isa. Truly sorry for my blindness."

Standing, I give him a small smile while Xadiel's quick to scoop me up in his arms. "I know you are, and there's no need for apologies between family. Everyone has a role to play, and sometimes sacrifices have to be made. Just trust me that in the end, all will be as it should. I'd never truly endanger those I love."

"Come on, Little Moon. Time for bed—and to stay there." My male's voice is a bit terse and I get it. He doesn't like me being upset, but I'm thankful he controlled himself. This conversation is long overdue, even if at the wrong moment. My body is shutting down on me. My mind wants a break. "We'll see you tomorrow, Theo."

"Good night."

With a nod, Xadiel heads for the entryway, but I tap his shoulder and he pauses. It's just enough time for me to look back at my brother-in-law. "Make sure that blade isn't in this realm anymore. Send it back, Theodore. It has to go back."

Isabella

"You've been silent, Isa," Gabriella says to my right while placing three clear quartz on the ground. Each sits in front of one of us; three children here celebrating our parents while our mates are somewhere in the territory. *More than likely our jail.* They've given us this time to reconnect without the mating bond tugging at our attention, and I appreciate it.

We haven't had a ceremony for our parents since their death. Leo and I refused to do so without Gabby, knowing our parents understood that the grief was too much for our hearts to contain. And while I know my brother remained strong all these years for me, this has weighed on him, too.

He was a teenager when they passed. Needed them the most out of three of us.

Wiccans celebrate life in every form. You shed one skin to presume another, even if that new life isn't of this realm. Sometimes our loved ones take on a guardian shield, an intermediate between this life and the next to guide us through each phase of our evolution as sentient creatures.

Our parents didn't want to start over in another flesh.

They remained in chosen limbo to parent us from beyond the grave.

Inhaling deep, I take in the fragrant scent of lavender and patchouli I've missed so much as I find my center and let go of my encounter with Larue. *He will never hurt my child. I will kill him first.* Around us, we've laid our mother's favorite flowers while Dad's complementary scent mixes, giving us the comfort we've missed since being children. The incense burns inside a golden bowl while the trees sway, the breeze sweeping all around but not dispersing the scent. It's a contained circle, our powers rising to greet each other while melding and fortifying the space.

The trees also sway for us on this beautiful day as we reconnect, allowing the sun to break through the treetops and illuminate our altar. We've combined our memories and given them an offering of all their favorite things: Dad's favorite human songs are playing the background while Mom's snacks sit atop a pretty cake stand I pilfered from the kitchen. I bought this white-with-a-flower-patterned display with her in mind, remembering an old one she had but was unable to keep full thanks to her family.

All her children love sweets. It's a weakness.

"Would you believe me if I said it's been a crazy few months? That I'm worried?"

"Without a doubt. What have you seen, Sister?" Leo squeezes my hand as the next song kicks on, and it's the one they danced to at their last wedding. Because every decade or so, the renewal of their vows was a big affair. From traditional to not, my father indulged my mother in whatever her heart desired, and that time, she wanted one that reminded her of a song she heard on the radio.

A ballad about eternity with your soulmate. About never letting go.

"It's what I know."

At that moment, the sky opens and a torrential downpour encompasses the area, yet it doesn't reach us. Our area is warm and dry, our circle protected, and I give thanks to Gaia for the protection.

She's all around me. Covering me in her shelter on the days I don't know how to put a foot in front of the other.

"He's coming, isn't he?" At her question, I flick my eyes in Gabriella's direction. She's angry, and her normally green irises are blood red—the part of her that's a vampire shows her fangs—while the hand not holding mine digs into the ground. The new mixing with the old; she indulges every living creature while letting her demon greet us. "Larue hasn't given up?"

"Yes, and it will be brutal." I will not lie about this. They must prepare for when I'm not here. "Everything is as father foretold."

"Then we fight." Leo's baritone is deeper now, almost identical to our father's. And if I were to close my eyes, I swear he'd be the one talking. "They laid their lives down so we could live—to protect what they cared about most. There's no other choice."

"No. There isn't." Opening myself, I show them a little of what has been building inside of me. *Let go, Isa. It's time to let it all go.* In my head, it's Mom's voice I hear while it feels as though the world has stopped moving. Power, an unexplained electrical force, lashes through us and I welcome it. *This is yours. Take it, and don't be afraid.* The three crystals rise from their places and hover above our heads, catching the light from the sun while the rain washes away the dirt. I exhale and each piece snaps, creating a halo of quartz icicles. "It's time to pay with kindness for what they've stolen. I want my peace back, and only standing atop his corpse will I get it."

"So mote it be," they replied in unison while the stone shards drop, creating an unyielding barrier as the storm around us deepens. Our hands release and my siblings stretch their hands out, testing out the same intense pulse I feel go through mine. It feels as if something has been released, an energy we've been teased with all our lives, and it's a pleasant sensation.

Almost freeing, as in sync, we begin to sway from side to side. Taking in the song playing, reliving the memories attached—the scent that will forever remind us of our parents.

"Te amo." Leo and Gabby repeat the sentiment a few seconds before I hear my wolf in the distance, his howl one of worry as he runs closer. Both mates are rushing in our direction, yet I know our bonds are calm. My sister and I are angry, yet settled, and as they burst through the thick vegetation across from where we sit, they stop out of respect. Each eyes us in slow procession, but neither speak. Each take inventory of what we're doing and then lower themselves against the closest tree to watch over us.

And under their watchful eye, the circle of protection expands, and they too are safe from the storm. It's how we continue with our ceremony, siblings holding hands and speaking low. We had so much to say. It became a bit of a confessional with the dead, but it was needed. Cathartic.

My shoulders are less burdened. I can breathe a little clearer, and when the time comes to chant a sacred prayer for those who have passed, Theo and Xadiel join us.

It was almost a perfect gathering.

Leo will find his mate soon. She'll complete us.

LATER THAT EVENING as the rain yielded and the earth became dark, the men asked Leo to join them in Xadiel's office. I'm sure they're discussing our prisoners and the rogue issue; it's not uncommon for kings to seek council from those they consider allies, but I think it has more to do with Gabriella and me.

They're giving us this time alone to catch up and bond, to revive our twin connection that was severed years ago.

However, I'm still thinking about his goodbye and trying to control the flush that's trying to bloom. My lips still tingle where he kissed me, bending me back until my red hair swept across the forest floor, and I blushed for the king. Until I let out a low whine after his gentle pat on the ass, not caring who was watching.

That male knows I thrive under his affection, just as he enjoys my sassiness. The way I challenge him from time to time, while on other occasions, I'm needy—clingy.

I'm a lucky witch.

The thudding of paws draws me out of my thoughts as two males and a she-wolf bid me a quick *Luna* in greeting, not pausing as they sweep past the perimeter. They're guarding this section of the forest, their trail about a hundred yards from our fire, and my sister is amused by the little wave I send them back.

She doesn't say anything at first. Instead, she looks into the high, dancing flames with a smirk on her face after mimicking my hand gesture.

"Spit it out, Sister."

"It's nothing. Just nice to see you so smitten." Gabriella shrugs and picks up a thermos Theo prepared for her; it's full of blood and tints her lips in a pretty cherry color after a few sips. "Xadiel makes you happy."

"He does."

"Has a sexy British accent..." my sister trails off while placing her drink down, and simultaneously, I'm thrown into a memory of the last time she said the same thing.

"And lastly, you'll kick his huge arse when he forgets those two things."

I snort at the last one. "Really? Arse?"

"He's British." Gabby shrugs. "It's fitting."

"True." For a beat we're quiet, but I'm the first to break the silence. "The accent is sexy. Especially in that deep baritone of his."

"Don't tell Theo, but I agree. Although, Italians do give them a run for their money."

"You're thinking about the last time I said that, aren't you?"

"Maybe." For a beat we're quiet, but then we're laughing just like we did the last time—barely breathing and choking, but leaning on each other before we both lay back flat on the ground and look up at the star-filled Alaskan sky. This is something we did in our teens: gossiped and ate sweets we pilfered from the kitchen and then fell asleep outside while watching the sky turn from inky to sky blue. "I've missed you, Sister."

"And I, you." Her fingers intertwine with mine, that same familial hum greeting and melding, filling a void I'd been missing. "I remember, you know. My memories are all there from my time in the underworld. At the time, my being understood that you were important to me, as were Leo and Theodore, but something about your visits always tugged at me the hardest."

"My visits were never meant to upset you, Gabriella."

"But they did." That hurts, and I can't stop the emotion from marking my expression. She sees that and shakes her head, begging me with her eyes not to look away. To let her explain. "It wasn't a bad thing, Sister. In death, you made me feel alive."

"I don't understand." It's low, the hoot of an owl almost drowning the sound out.

"You came and talked to me for hours on end. You did my hair, helped me decorate the space my father-in-law gifted me, and kept me up to date on how our brother was doing—brought him with you on his birthday so I never missed out on any milestones." A sad smile overtakes her face, and I don't like it. All I've ever done is fight for my siblings' happiness and bright future. "Isa, you included me in your lives even when I didn't understand the why, and I'll forever be thankful for that."

I'm shaking my head before she's done speaking. "Stop. Never thank me for that."

"Someone's got to do it." This time it's a hiss. Sharp and angry. "You gave up children and a peaceful life beside your mate to care for your family. People don't see the offerings you've made and the emptiness inside of you, but those are things I *feel* as your twin. Like a living, breathing, entity—your longing breaks my heart."

"I could never let you go." It's my truth.

"And now it's time for you to be a little selfish, don't you think?"

"Haven't I been selfish enough? I lived while you—"

"I was safe," she says, another hissing sound coming through at the end. "You know, I heard you talk with Thanatos many times over the years, never truly understanding what you meant when you said: *life goes on but those left behind live in the real purgatory*, but I do now. More and more I realize that you've been left behind to carry all the blame and responsibility, and I can't allow that anymore."

"Gabriella, I'm fine. I promise."

"I'm not going to let this go, *Isabella*." Her arched brow and haughty purse of the lips reminds me of Mom, and my lips twitch. "Listen—we don't know how all of this will end or how long the inevitable war will last, but I want to walk into battle with my heart at ease. Please, for me, be selfish and do something purely for you."

"I want my luna ceremony." The words are out before I can stop them.

"You never had one?" She's appalled, nearly spitting the question out.

"More like a temporary one…"

"What the heck does that even mean? Why didn't you—"

"Because all I ever wanted was my family to be there with me."

"Done." The softest looks overtake her features, and those red eyes become green. There's a giddy air surrounding her, too. Almost vibrating. "We need to start planning immediately. Get a dress, decorations, location, and the guest list…"

"Why the trail off?" I ask, not understanding the now puzzled look.

"Do you want everyone from our coven there?"

"Yes. Of course."

"What about Aunt Silla?" I'm not sure, and the sudden coldness coming from her side isn't welcoming, either. "To be honest, no clue yet. Leo says she wants to speak with me, but I'm yet to make a move. No part of me trusts her."

"I'm having the same trouble. Something doesn't feel right."

"Then we'll put her on the maybe list with a huge red question mark and move on."

"Are you going to call her?"

"Should I?" A shooting star draws my attention at that moment, and I close my eyes long enough to make a simple wish. *Bless us with a long and fulfilled life.* As soon as I do, I open them and look over, finding Gabriella doing the same. Another memory comes to mind at that, a happy one of our parents telling us stories about different gods and their powers. How they came to be and how this symbol in the sky meant they were looking down at us, listening to our heart's longing.

"I want to be present when you do."

"Okay. That can definitely be arranged." We fall back into silence, just enjoying the night. It's how our mates find us a few hours later, languid and sharing the occasional giggle with commentary. They don't ask the *why* and we don't tell, but right as Xadiel picks me up, he says something to Theo. They exchange words, completely ignorant of our earlier conversation, and their lilt is sexy. Moreover, I'm not the only one paying attention; I find Gabriella doing the same right before we're both thrown over the shoulders of our men.

It's also why when she whispers the word *accents,* I lose it.

Loud and embarrassing, she follows it with a snort that sends us right back to being twenty summers and discussing this for the first time. Both men don't know how to react. To an outsider we appear drunk, but the bond with Xadiel thrums with pleasure at seeing me so amused.

He's dying to ask me. He even tugs on our connection.

Yet all that does is amp up my laughter, causing Gabriella to do the same while they just shrug. *Good boys.*

Alpha

XADIEL

I'm never settled when we are apart. It's like an itch, a never-ending need to see her and be the cause of her happiness at all hours of the day. And while the wolf and I understand she deserves this time to reconnect with her siblings, I want to be greedy with her. To pick her up and carry her with me everywhere I go, and more so after spending most of the day apart yesterday.

In both forms, I'm protective of her. As consumed and amazed by our bond as she is.

The yearning has never shifted or slowed. Instead, it's grown over the last century, and I worry for what's to come; I hate seeing her distressed.

Last night, I'd been gone for two fucking hours. A hundred and twenty bloody minutes while returning phone calls to Oregon and my parents, the latter of which will be visiting soon, and walked in

161

on our bond near screeching. Something set her off. And while I don't think it was her conversation with Theodore, I'm angry at him for his part.

Try as I might, I can't contain my glare. The way my claws keep breaking through and withdrawing—I want to seek retribution on her behalf, but that will only upset her more. Fighting him will hurt Gabriella, and that will destroy my luna.

She puts everyone before herself.

Leo's picks up on my mood. He knows me—is like a little brother—and gives me a questioning stare that I shrug off. Now isn't the time, yet a low growl slips from my lips as we enter my office.

"Anyone want a drink?" I ask tersely, heading toward the small bar next to the coffee station. Grabbing the gin, I pour myself a few fingers' worth and then turn to look at the other two. One nods, while the other's expression is hard. Yet I'm not intimidated by the vampire king. Never have been. "Here."

"Thanks." Leo takes the glass from me and knocks it back, not savoring a single note of the expensive spirit. This batch is exclusively made for me by an old distiller in the UK, and it comes from the dried leaves of a single mulberry tree. The woodsy with hints of citrus is quite unique as it blooms on your palate, and yet he chugged it back as if it was cheap pint. "And don't look at me like that, X. This rogue problem has me on edge, too. They're not normal."

If anything can shift the tension, it's this. My concern over my people is embedded deep—overrides the words I need to exchange with Theodore for now. I want revenge for those who've been hurt by an arsehole fae and his followers on an ego trip to destroy our world.

Stripping a wolf of his essence, turning them into mindless creatures surviving on pain is inhumane. They've made their captives a zombie army. Mindless and voiceless and surviving through daily torture until nothing is left but a rotted corpse.

"What do you know about these hybrids?" Theo asks.

"How do you know they're hybrids?" I raise a brow. "We just found out—"

"Word has begun to spread, Xadiel. It's one of the reasons we chose to come now, apart from our mates spending time together." He rubs his chin, eyes flashing pure black for a second before returning to their natural color. "A few have been spotted near my castle, but they don't seem to want any interaction with my army. It's almost as if they're afraid to come near the borderline and just stand, literally stand outside it with lifeless eyes."

"You say they don't want to come close?"

"Not at all. My general says they seem petrified to be there."

"Interesting." It reminds me of our captive's response to Isabella. "We had a similar instance here—I have one in my dungeons. Him and the fae wanker that brought him to my lands. Their failed attack is how we discovered these wolves are being given their blood under Larue's command."

"That son of a bitch," Leonardo spits out from between clenched teeth, leaning forward in his seat. "That's—"

"I know." Pouring another drink, this one I take a sip from before going around to the other side of my desk. "Those wolves are dying. Slowly wasting away, and the one I gave a mercy kill to showed himself moments before I broke his neck. They're watching and fighting to break through, but can't."

"And you say the one here reacted to my sister?"

"Yes." Turning on the computer, I bring up the video surveillance of the prison and their rooms to be exact. With a few clicks of the mouse, I adjust so that it's a split screen view and turn the monitor. I point at the wolf, who at the moment is still in his animal's skin and is simply curled up sleeping. "At first, he was afraid and nothing like the werewolf that fought me, but at her anger, his entire being seemed to regress into his prior consciousness. The wolf in his eyes showed understanding and relaxed, even laid down and reacted to authority."

"I have a theory," Theodore starts but stops. His attention is now on the fae and his yelling—we can't hear him, but he's ranting while pointing toward an area out of view. "Can I test it?"

"Don't see the problem in it."

"Good." The vampire rubs his chin, already standing up. "Can you have your beta escort Gabriella and Isabella to the wolf's cell? If I'm right, there's a solution to this."

AFTER SPEAKING WITH CAIN, I left instructions and make my way to the cells with my brothers-in-law. No one spoke as we descended. They took in the space with contemplative expressions until we reached the wolf's cell.

His bars are silver, but on this floor I keep minor offenders: those who need to cool off after being maliciously aggressive during training, or someone who comes looking to be a part of this pack without references. Here we vet them and decide whether to release or remove them from my lands.

There's a bed that he's choosing to ignore, a toilet, and a sink for water. Meals are delivered twice a day, a bit of raw meat to keep his strength up, but he's ignored that too.

It's almost as if he's afraid to move, yet at peace to be.

Yet the moment we enter, he rises into a low attack stance. The power radiating from us makes the pelt at the back of his neck rise and his lips curl over his dirty fangs. His reaction isn't the smartest, daring us to come closer, but at the very least he's not foaming at the mouth or throwing himself at the metal doors to attack.

This shows understanding of power and the basic assessment of an enemy: never attack first that which is stronger. You wait and check for any weaknesses you can possibly explore.

"He's lost a lot of fur," Theo notes, taking in the patches by his flank and face. Some are red and look rash-like. "Has he been seen by a medic?"

"We've tried twice now, but both times he's attacked the staff. And before you ask us to tranquilize him, we don't know if any medication will have an adverse reaction with what's already in his system. We'd hoped it would've been flushed out by now, but he's the same as the day Isa last visited the jail."

No sooner has the last word slipped past my lips than the twins arrive, each at ease and undisturbed by the scene in front of them, but the prisoner reacts differently.

Lowering his head completely atop his paws, he stills and whines. Literally whines as a distressed pup would after being chided.

"Get a little closer," Theo asks, seeing something I don't yet.

Yet as the two come right up against the bars, I see what he does, but there's more to it. One is a seer and the other controls the essence of life, but their gifts have morphed, even if Gabriella isn't truly aware of it.

I saw it with my own eyes the day her sister passed. Her telekinetic abilities are tied to her emotions, and the one that seems to control this trait is ire. Anger over a loved one being abused or hurt. Anger over the manipulations and destruction of her people—home.

It pulses around us now, and all eyes turn to her.

"Isa?" Gabby calls out, flicking her attention between her sibling and the prisoner, but my female is locked in on the poor wolf watching her with trepidation. "Xadiel, what is happening to my sister?"

"The day you died, the stone inside her head was unlocked," I say lowly as the power Isa contains spreads and shields, much like she did during their ceremony for prior Wiccan king and queen. The siblings didn't pick up then that it was her moving and creating the safe space—always protective—and not the parents that they honored.

"How the hell did I not realize this? I was there."

"You were a kid, Leo. She reacted to the pain and blood being drained, the screams of her people, and then you being threatened."

"Like a mother would." This comes from Theodore, and a deeper understanding dawns on him. Not that he's ever been a right arsehole to her—I'd snap his neck without thinking twice if he was ever outright hostile—but there's always been a level of distance between them. And it's because I understand, would absolutely lose my shit if something happened to Isa, that I've let time heal the wounds left behind after his mate's death. "Motherfuck."

"Come." One word, and all eyes turn toward my female. She's not looking at us, though. Her attention is on the male slowly crawling forward on his belly. "I'm not going to hurt you. No one is."

"Sister, what is—"

"Do you trust me, Gabby?"

"Always will."

"Then give me your hand." Without a second of doubt, Gabriella does as asked and then the room becomes pitch black for a second, every lit torch extinguished and then relit, but the flame is bright blue with a tinge of green at the center. Heat surrounds us while the male screams, his wolf snarling, yet remains docile.

"*Veni ad me*," they chant together, and we watch in silence as the prisoner's aura shifts as if his body and spirit were two separate entities before being forced to work in unison. He half shifts at the command, his human features coming and going as fast as we blink, before he sits on his haunches and screams.

Yet they don't stop, and we don't interrupt. Nothing can be heard but their low chant and the werewolf's cries, going from growl to man as his skin splits at the wrist and a blue substance pours out of him. Drop by drop, the fae blood exits his body until nothing is left and he falls in a naked heap on the floor.

"It's not one, but both," Theo hisses. His face contorts, his demon emerging at the sight of his mate gritting her teeth through each chant.

I suspect the same, but don't voice it. My Isa knows how to play with an essence, but not end it. Gabriella can terminate and revive a soul, but not drain this form of sickness without help.

Without her sister. They feed off each other's magic.

"One manipulates while the other moves it. They control it." Both nod at my response, yet from the corners of my eyes, I watch them tense—muscles coiled tight and ready to step in if something were to go wrong. And at the same time, my fangs drop and claws unsheathe while standing to my full height. "This is what Larue is after. The power they wield."

The rogue is breathing and dirty—malnourished and exhausted—but I pick up immediate gratitude. His animal is resting and weak, but manages to rumble weakly in appreciation from his chest.

"Holy shit." Gabriella is the first to react a few minutes after, stumbling a bit. Her mate is quick to rush over, helping support her body while Little Moon continues to look at the blue blood. Doesn't react when I move within arm's reach in case she needs me. "I've never felt something like that before. The rush of power or the emotions attached."

"Are you hurt?" Theo asks her, but she simply shakes her head and lays a kiss on his cheek. "And you, Isabella? You okay?"

His question pleases me. His mate, too.

"I'm—"

She's cut off by the werewolf on the ground, his voice rough and croaky. "Agua."

"Did he just ask for water in Spanish?" Leo asks, but I'm noticing something else. Something more worrisome.

My nostrils flare, and the answer is right there. My mate senses this too as she turns to me with frightened eyes.

"Xadiel, he's not a rogue."

"Agua. Por favor."

Cain, get the pack doctor to the cells. It's urgent.

Yes, Alpha. His hesitancy comes through the line. Worry. *Are you okay? Luna?*

We're fine, but they saved the prisoner. He needs help.

Blessed be. I'm on my way.

In the time I'd mind linked my beta, Little Moon opened the cell door and rushed in, her family in tow. The men lifted the hurt wolf while the women got him water, and it's Theodore I find speaking to him in the wolf's Spaniard tongue.

He's comforting him. One of my brethren.

"What pack are you from?" I ask, knowing he understands as werewolves are fluent in more than one language, as are most species outside of humans. We must be able to communicate with each other no matter what region we reside in.

"My king. I'm sorry." He grimaces as he speaks, the rich accent coming through. He's also trying to bow, a natural reaction I stop with a command to lie back. "They took me while I ran patrols. My pack is pequeño, sits right on the border between France and España."

"Don't exert yourself. Just rest and answer what you can."

"Si, my alpha."

"And your rank?"

"Alpha's son."

"Pack name?"

"Lunar Pack."

"Diego Lunar's heir. Armando Lunar." Not a question, but he still nods, and anger exudes from me. My aura darkens—my beast insulted by their lack of trust in me— and it extends toward my subject. Immediately, he bows his head in shame. "How long were you missing without informing your king? Why the fuck would your father hide this?"

"Alpha," Isa places a dainty hand on my chest, pushing me back from towering over him. The others have also moved aside; it's just my mate controlling me, and I let her, taking a few steps back so the injured man can breathe. "We will deal with this, but he's not who you should be running at. Look at him, my love. He's hurt."

Her words calm me. Her touch keeps my wolf subdued.

"You're right, but I will not stand for this." At that moment, Cain and the doctor rush in, moving to attend the young alpha-to-be.

Him being an heir explains his challenging demeanor out in the forest. His father's decision to keep this from me will be dealt with.

"Cain, call every bloody alpha and have them meet us in Oregon next week. No excuses, and anyone who does not attend will lose their fucking title. I'll fight and strip them myself."

Isabella

Leo's been gone for a few days now, having been called back by Augusto for an elder meeting. They're aware of what's happening—having had their own encounters—and need to prepare for war.

A huge part of me feels guilt over the battle so many will participate in and might not come home from. I think about their families—spouses who will kiss one last time, not knowing their promise to return soon will be unfulfilled.

"Penny for your thoughts." Gabby bumps her shoulder with mine, smile on her face while her hands are holding up two different color schemes. One is a variation of neutrals with a mint green accent, and the other is the colors of the Evergreen crest.

It's white with a rich green and touches of gold, and while I'm partial to light colors, my heart flutters at the colors of the royal pack.

It's what's right.

"Crest."

"Sold." She adds it my ceremony binder, tossing the other in the trash. "We need to settle the list before I leave. Faith and Momma Evergreen can help you with the rest, but I want to help as much as I can."

"You've done a lot."

"I've missed a lot." Letting out a tired sigh, she stretches her neck from side to side. Exhales slowly. "We all have regrets, Sister. This is mine. How much I wasn't here for."

"But you're here now."

"I am." Picking up her pen, she pulls a highlighted sheet in front of her and taps it with the capped end. "We've narrowed this down to royal pack members, alpha couples under the Evergreen aegis, and your closest family and friends. Agreed?"

"Yes." I know where she's going with this.

"And Aunt Silla? Leo left you her number."

"I know you're busy and there are more important things to focus on, but can you call her, Isa?"

"Who?" I ask, sending a quick text to Faith who's currently at the pack hospital with an injured wrist. She fell wrong during a sparring session, and I'm making sure she's okay. "Who am I missing?"

"Aunt Silla."

That makes me pause, and I frown at him. Between pack duties and my ceremony, I haven't had time to breathe. Priority for me is helping those hurt—finding more wolves like Armando and ridding them of the poison, stripping them of their beast. Killing my wolves. "I will, but I can't guarantee the when, little brother. I'm not quite ready yet."

"She's family, Isa. Hurting, too."

Exhaling roughly, I ask, "Does it mean that much to you?"

"Yes."

"Then give her my number." My phone pings then with an incoming message. A quick swipe across the screen shows it's Faith

letting me know she's okay. It's just a sprain. "I'll make time for her after the ceremony, but not before. Okay?"

"Yes, Luna Supreme."

"You've been dying to do that, Your Highness?"

"My promise to make you eat a frog still stands, Sister."

"Go home before I make that your reality." His laughter booms throughout the house before I'm engulfed in a tight hug, lifted off the ground while Xadiel chuckles. No help whatsoever from behind his desk while Gabriella and Theo are out exploring Anchorage. "You're lucky I love you."

"By pact and blood."

"We are one."

"She can be on the invite list, but that's it for now."

"Works for me." Her eyes skims down the list, stopping at another grouping of names. Tero, Meera, and Marcia. "What about the royal vampire court?"

"If they do not attend, I will be personally offended."

"Good. They'll be thrilled." It's been so long since I've seen those three, but Meera does keep in contact with me. Through Messenger or FaceTime, we make it a point to connect once a month. "Now, let's talk about the flower arrangements…"

***

Gabriella and Theodore left yesterday, and I feel off. It's been building in me since I watched them drive off, heading toward the airport with Seattle as their destination. She has an exhibit coming up; a seven deadly sins feature, and I'm the subject of one of those paintings.

We have a standing invitation to go, too. The plan is to spend a week with them there and then travel back two nights before to start the traditional unity ceremony festivities.

Because this is more than just an official Luna ceremony; I want to wed him. Tie myself to Xadiel in every way that a woman could give herself to a man. Because one day soon, he's going to need that reassurance. The knowledge that I belong to him and only him in this life, and every single one we meet.

Is it a bit rushed? Yes.

Do I care about extravagance and showing off our wealth? No.

All I need is to see him at the end of the aisle, handsome and smirking at me after a night of rough, animalistic sex. I want to be claimed and bitten. Sore yet needing more as I pledge myself to him.

To be the best mate. To help protect and care for our people.

I will never let Larue take that from me. I've been patient enough, while Xadiel accepted to go the untraditional route once to appease me, and now I want to please him.

"He's going to love this," I say out loud, giving a full turn inside the glass-domed igloo he gave me for our anniversary. Knowing we'll be leaving next week and he'll be back from Oregon tonight with his parents—they'll be staying until after the ceremony— who've come to help and celebrate with us, this is my only opportunity to set up my surprise.

Weddings, mates, or a simple binding: all species have their own customs.

Werewolves are no different.

The night before, the mated males will hunt in their human skin for their brides. She-wolves will be hidden throughout the property, evading their spouses in an adult game of hide-and-seek until captured, with the prey on her knees once captured. Hunted and then mounted; I'll hide and run and let Xadiel follow me throughout our lands while leading him to our glass-domed paradise in the woods.

This is my gift for him. A night full of making every single one of his fantasies a reality.

I'm giving him the chase he craves and the obedience he demands.

I'll be wearing a near see-through white dress that's the exact replica of the one I wore the day I entered his pack lands back in England. The one he fisted and tugged and that drove him wild as he ate my pussy. The way his eyes turned molten still causes a wave of desire to rush through me.

I clench at nothing. I miss the way he stretches me.

"He'll be back tonight. Just a few more hours." Checking the fridge a final time, I make sure our favorite drinks and snacks are stocked up—that the room is clean and dust free—while the bedding is freshly washed and folded. It'll be ready for use once I get back; all I'll need is to sneak away with the pretense of getting ready, give myself just enough time to get the last-minute prep done, and then dress up for him.

We'll be leaving in a few days and while I could have someone help me with this, I can't stand the thought of anyone's scent inside this space. This is mine and his. No one else should ever step inside.

"I should head back." Turning, I find the same folder from our anniversary lying atop the table; it calls my attention, and while I'm curious, I don't open it. If this is for me, I'll see it soon enough, but I do put it away in the small bedside table on the left side of the bed. His side.

The drawer barely closes when there's a sudden pang in my chest. It's sharp and steals my breath, causing me to sit atop the mattress. I'm clutching the area, rubbing my hand across it, when I'm bombarded by the sudden shouts of wolves asking for my location.

Gamma, what's going on?

Luna, where are you? His voice is frantic, not at all the calm and rational man I know. *Are you safe?*

I'm fine. Setting up my gift for Xadiel. There's a fighting pressure in the mind link, multiple people trying to speak at once. *What the hell is going on, Grady? Why are so many people shouting at once?*

My nerves are shot. That dreaded feeling grows with each tick of silence, but then my reality crashes and the world stops.

It's the beta's twins, Luna. They're missing.

I'm on my way. Start combing every inch of the woods. Do not wait for me. Hesitancy comes through his end. As if there's something he doesn't want to tell me. ***Tell me. Whatever it is, just tell me.***

There's a note for you. It was left attached to the swings they'd been playing on.

———

I'M BACK at the pack house within minutes, having opened a portal that led me to the backyard where Faith was crying—kneeling where the kids liked to play—while Grady assembled a group of elite who stayed behind to protect as the search party. They didn't notice me at first, focused on the task at hand until I kneeled beside my friend.

"Where is the note, Faith?" A hush fell over those here, all except my godchildren's mother who met my eyes and fell apart. I don't have pups of my own, but her devastation is one I understand and feel. Yet I can't fall apart. When Xadiel left, he wanted me to go with him but I couldn't.

It wasn't a vision. It wasn't a lack of wanting to be beside him.

There was a little voice in my head that told me to stay. Same for the emotions, this dread-like sensation since my sister flew back home.

I knew I had to be here. *It's my job to take care of them.*

"Luna, they were just here and now…" Tears fall like torrents down her pretty face, and my heart clenches with guilt. More and more, I've felt as of late that everything is my fault. That had I given in to the demands of that asshole, my loved ones would be here.

What if my father accepted the marriage proposal instead of telling Larue piss off?

What if I turned myself in during our first face-to-face meeting and accepted my fate?

"We're going to find them, sweetheart. I will never allow anything to happen to your pups, or any other under my protection while I'm alive. Do you understand? Do you trust me, Faith?"

"Yes, Luna."

Wiping the tears under her eyes, I give her a small smile. "Give me the note and help me find them." Slowly, she stands and pulls out a crumbled piece of paper from her back pocket. And while she opens it and extends the corners, I turn toward Grady. "Has anyone alerted Xadiel and our beta?"

"I've tried to call a few times, but I think they're already on the plane. Signal seems to be blocked."

"Did you leave a message?"

"Yes, Luna."

"Thank you." When I'm done, Faith is holding out the note and I take it from her stiff fingers. It's not long. Just a few lines written in an ancient font used by the elders of my coven. Not many practice this, but my father made sure his children could read and write using these symbols as a means to communicate in times of danger. The fact they know and used this lights my veins on fire. Anger pours out of me in waves. It's an explosion of hatred and fear that causes the wolves around me to growl in warning.

Not at me, but at whatever has me reacting in such a way.

You know where to find the innocent ones. How they are upon your arrival is entirely up to you. Dead or alive, it makes no difference to me as long as you see.

King Larue

Isabella

"**D**o you know where they are?" Faith asks, her voice as shaky as her entire frame, and my heart breaks for her.

"Not yet, but I know how to find them and that's what's important." When they asked Xadiel and me to become the kids' godparents, we held a small blessing ceremony. One to welcome the pups and share their names with the pack, and two, to tie them to the four of us. "Please stay here and wait for me."

"Luna, please—"

"I'm going to bring them home, Faith. Please trust me." *I need to focus, and you must be strong for me and them. This is where you'll help me the most.*

"Okay." This leaves her on a whimper, but she nods and steps back. Knows I'm not doing this to be mean, but because I need to concentrate, and the urge to console her as the luna is distracting. My first impulse is always to soothe. "I'll be ready for them."

"Thank you."

There's a small, invisible string that attaches each child to the four of us. Most can't see it, blind and unable to discern past what's in front of their faces, while a secret world is just beyond a thin veil. Unless you know what you're looking for. If you've opened yourself and allowed the third eye that all creatures are born with to develop, allowing the mind to see past blocks and glamour—to accept the intricacies in auras and tethers as those with mystical powers do.

So I close my lids and breathe out slowly, searching for that tiny purple string that hides behind Xadiel's all-encompassing love. It's there, though, and after a few short tugs, I get a flicker of a response.

It's faint, as if they're slumbering, and my eyes snap open. I don't give out instructions, but the elite and our gamma follow me nonetheless as I cross the yard and step through the tree line, making my way down the trail here that circles back to my home here. It's a connection from one property to the other, an access very few people are allowed to use, but we catch the children's scent almost automatically.

And the closer to my home we get, the stronger it becomes. As if we've just missed them, but once we reach my backyard, it fades away. Becomes lighter and lighter, a faint whisper and I pause, my head snapping left as the string tightens and tugs. It's telling me they're not here. That I need to continue, and as I turn right, I'm hit with a vision.

All I see is my favorite grouping of trees and a shadow inside. It's tall and ominous, nearly blocking the entrance, but what scares me is the glinting of metal in its hand.

I take off without another word, rushing through the forest without a care in the world other than reaching the kids in time. There's no doubt in my mind Larue will hurt them to get me to comply, and true fear sinks into every inch of me.

Children are sacred. Untouchable.

The pounding of paws follows me. Most of the guards have changed, the snapping of bones an echo in the quiet forest as I run with Grady a few steps behind me. They cover our flanks, ears and snouts twitching every so often as they look out for intruders or catch the scents we're looking for.

The hemlock trees.

Gamma Grady gets into formation with the others, keeping me at the center since they know where I'm heading. We're not that far; this is an area I know well, and it's now tainted. The stench of his faes is unmistakable, but not all from the Larue's kingdom believe in the idiocies of their king.

They don't all smell like dark magic and decaying health, just his devotees.

The area my siblings and I used not long ago to celebrate our parents has been kicked up, the soil and items stomped on, but it doesn't matter as mixed in with all this nastiness is the tether of Emmett and Eve. The string is pointing to the cavern within the trees, my favorite hiding spot on these lands, and I don't hesitate to rush inside.

"Luna, wait!" Grady yells when I push forward, but there's no stopping me. Before anyone can stop me or get in my way, I'm inside the opening and breathing out in pure relief at the sight of the pups asleep and covered by one of the blankets I left last time. They're breathing and seem to be okay, but I still drop to my knees and check them.

Faith, we found them. They're safe and sleeping.

A ripple of emotions hits me, and it's part hers and the other pure relief that's all mine. My eyes tear up, and my body shudders with the sob I'm repressing.

Now isn't the time to break down.

Thank the goddess. Thank you, Luna.

Her response is choked, and I simply respond with: ***They're safe and that's all that matters. We'll be back in a few minutes.***

I love you, Isabella. Werewolves are blessed to have you as our queen.

I don't respond as a renewed sense of guilt hits me in the chest. *They were taken because of me.*

The tears that fall now are beyond my control, but I grit my teeth and open my palms face down, gliding them a few inches above the twins bodies. I'm using an ancient technique you learn as a young witch to locate injuries in case of emergencies. Because before we can cast a spell or create a tonic to treat the effect, you must know the cause, and I'm relieved to find none. Not so much as a scratch or drug in their system, and when I throw my head back to thank the gods, my eyes land on a note stabbed into the tree by a sleek dagger. The handle is black, a pearl-like quality with shine and a single golden line down the middle.

When Grady enters, he doesn't notice it.

Neither do the two warriors that gently lift the children after the gamma steps out, rushing back to the house with them in their arms. Everyone's in a rush, and I stand after a few seconds, dusting myself off while the men remaining wait outside of my space.

They're talking. Discussing how this happened—who was on patrol duty and sending the two elite trackers to scour the area to make sure no intruders remain.

And while Grady turns his back, reaching for his cell phone while telling them there's still no word from their alpha, I snatch the note but leave the dagger.

I'm not touching that thing. Who knows what it could be laced with.

"Ready to head back?"

"Are you okay, Luna?"

Am I? No. Not one bit, but I nod and smile before beginning the trek back home. No one questions the paper in my hand as it looks just like the previous, same dark symbols I've yet to read, and it isn't until dinnertime and the kids have been given the all-clear from the pack doctor that I'm able to open it.

For someone who sees, you've been blind. Manipulation is my gift, a bend of reality, and I've gifted you comfort instead of loss. But you've angered the hand that feeds.

I blocked your gift once. I move in ways you'll never predict, and my close ties know how to block your sun.

Come to me, young one. Come home, or it'll be your mate's head that I deliver next.

My kingdom awaits their next queen.

King Larue

Hands shaking, I fist the thick paper while flashes of my failures play like a movie reel. Things I should've seen but didn't, like today with the twins, are front and center.

Was this his doing?

Am I so cocky in my abilities that I'm putting this pack—my mate—selfishly in jealousy?

I have to leave.

Xadiel's not home yet, which is a blessing and a curse, making the decision easier for me.

Since the moment we met, I knew this day would come. That my heart would break as I read the symbols of a note, telling me my time was up, but this hits harder than a simple threat. Than Thanatos confirming that some will die and the bigger picture is worth the sacrifice.

Problem is, I can't let others get hurt, or otherwise…

Breathe, Isa. Don't fall for this trap.

I know I shouldn't, but emotions are fluctuating from one extreme to the next so rapidly, it's getting harder to stand. Both sides of the coin have merit. I'm panicking—I know this—when the scent of patchouli surrounds me like a warm embrace.

"Dad," I choke out, my chest constricting so hard I gasp. I'm a chaotic mess, warring with rationality and the impulse to give my life to save my mate, but this stops me.

It feels as though his hand is on my shoulder and squeezing. Patient and comforting, but it's the voice in my head that settles me.

Takes me back to the days when our family was together. Sharing meals, talking about the new spells we learned from the oracle, and his advice when frustration settled in after failing at an elemental concept.

Think rationally. Emotions don't solve problems, but rather create them. To win, you have to keep a clear head.

And he's right. It's why I stop and think over my options as the presence causes the golden globe of the earth to spin and shift until I'm staring at North America; Canada, to be exact.

"Is that where he is?" Not that I'm expecting a yes or no, but the silence in a way is confirmation. No action means no change. "Now, to lead Xadiel to me after I turn myself over."

He needs to unite with my family, all three nations working together while the blade in Theo's possession must be returned to his father or gifted to Aries. Fight fire with fire.

If Larue wants to kill a god, then I'll win over the deity's favor first. Canada might be the beginning or end, and after noticing the coordinates at the bottom of the note, I smile.

"Thank you, Dad. I'll take it from here." His essence dissipates while my mind works overtime. I know I need to hurry before my mate returns; Xadiel will never let me sacrifice myself to buy us time. But then it hits me. "There's a faster way to do this than scribing."

Without pause, I write him a letter, seal it with a kiss, and place it on his desk before heading to the dungeons. No one stops or questions me. Most are still reeling from the abduction of the twins, and I take advantage of the fact. Or maybe it's the rage they see in my expression, the volatile emotions of a witch pushed to her limits, and steer clear of their rampaging luna.

Once inside and entering the lowest level, I find the male fae already waiting. As if expecting my arrival, his smirk irks me. It ignites this darkness within me that feeds off my emotions—strong and passionate—and it bends to my will and offers its service.

The smile falls as soon as our eyes meet.

Now he shuffles back as far as the shackles allow him and presses against the opposite wall. "I'm just a messenger. I—"

"Where is he?"

"You have the coordinates...*fuck*!" his screams rend the air followed by the sound of him gagging. *Not enough. More pain.* "Please don't kill me. He's my king and I cannot deny him."

"So you're against his regime? You want him to fall?" The questions are rhetorical as this man is a loyalist, not an anarchist. He's here because he wants to be top of the food chain—a friend of my enemy while reaping the benefits of other's pain. "Answer me."

"Yes."

"Liar." The decomposed bodies of killed rogues are nothing but fragments of toxic flesh and bones. Bones that I'm slowly using as throwing knives. One to the shoulder, and one to his thigh so far. I control them with my mind. They rise and snap in half, all the while he pisses himself like the pathetic minion he is. "Where. Is. He?"

"I don't...merde!" The next two out of three hit him with enough force that they break through his flesh and embed deep into the stone, pinning him in place. That last one, though, I show no mercy —slice his flesh from left to right, leaving behind a huge gash in his abdomen before it also stabs through his torso and into the cold wall. "No more."

"One more?"

"No! I'll tell you."

"Go on. Where's Larue?"

"He's in Quebec. On the gulf."

"Thank you." Turning to leave, I look over at him a final time. Xadiel will need this note, one I attach to the wall with another sharp bone, keeping just out of reach of this imbecile.

The power of the stone is growing.

Each time it's easier to use, and the fear it instills on this prisoner is worth it even with the newly acquired migraine forming at my temples. I didn't have to touch his filth or enter the room, but I left my mark behind.

I will have no mercy.

Come and find me, my king.

A portal opens with my set location—I use a bit of the fae dust Thiago confiscated from this prisoner—and immediately, I'm hit with the scent of the sea. Clean and crisp, yet the essence of those who await me on the other side is pungent. *This is a trap. Brace yourself, Isa.*

But then I think about my male: will he survive the choice I'm taking away from him? Will he forgive me for not allowing him to provide and protect?

Because there is no other way.

I'd never risk him. I love him too much.

Their scents turn my stomach as I step through, but then it doesn't matter—can't rationalize anymore—as blinding pain drops me to my knees before a face I promised to disfigure before killing greets my line of sight.

"Long time no see, my queen." Female: I know that voice. Could never forget it.

"Fuck you."

"I'm truly going to enjoy this." Her fingers snap, and another blow lands, this one to the area where my skull and my neck meet. It all goes black.

Alpha
XADIEL

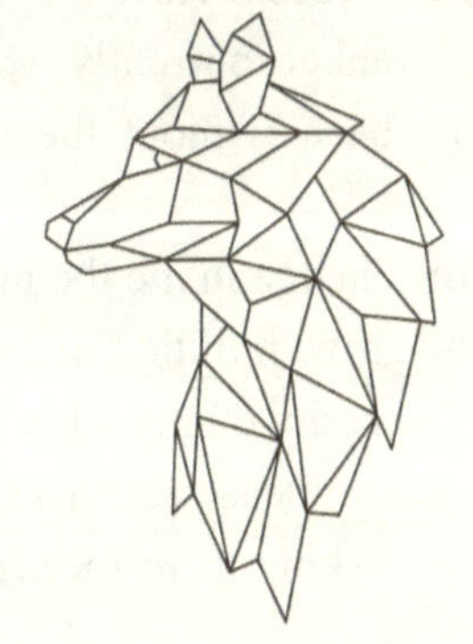

What this pack lacks in members, it does not lack in size. Oregon is beautiful, the land's fertile—and Hillsborough is the perfect location for this farming community of wolves who thrive here, the burning of their crops not included.

In the days since I arrived, we've gone over his plans and budget while visiting the cleaned-out acres already being tilled by machinery I purchased for them. In return, they'll supplement other wolf packs in the region and across the US with organically grown and harvested produce under the Evergreen agreement. In addition, they'll also help their fellow brethren and trap, not kill, any rogues that fit the description and videos of the men I've sent to every pack around the world.

Alpha Craig agrees and has entered a treaty with most of the other heads of packs in attendance, but at the moment, I'm ready to send them all to piss off and de-rank the latter ten. These arseholes think too highly of themselves. Seem to believe they have a voice in the matter, and the beast inside me is pacing—clawing at my insides to be let out and teach them a lesson in respect.

About ninety percent of these men and women understand the urgency to band together and eliminate the menace to not only our kind, but most of all, to my queen. How this is a threat to our families—children—yet the wanker currently speaking is testing the patience of a man who's been without the woman who holds his heart for days.

A few have noticed the change in me the more he talks.

Bare their necks at the growl building in my chest.

"…this is not our fight, and we have only been involved because of your mate, Your Highness. Please reconsider, as she's not a wolf. She will never be one, and asking us to sacrifice ourselves for her is a crime."

"You will respect the crown, Alpha Lester. Understood?" my father snarls then, slamming a hand atop the table in front of us. He's to my left, while Cain is on my right, inside of an auditorium the Oregon pack uses for assemblies. It's a nice building, clean and accommodating, but not the opulence the royal pack usually offers while demanding their attendance. "One more indirect or direct insult, and I will personally take that as a challenge. I might not be the king, but I have no problem with—"

I hold a hand up, and my father quiets. Fuming and glowering at the younger alpha, he complies with my request as does everyone else. For a second, I shift my eyes around the room and most of the women here, the mates of these males and a few female alphas themselves, are glaring with open hostility toward the section in the middle where the ones disagreeing sit.

The air is tinged with anger. Most are showing their aggression over the matter. Whether it's pro-compliance or a high request, I reconsider my stance.

Reconsider. That word does something to me the more I mull it over in my head.

And it's not just my wolf that unleashes a growl that makes every member in attendance bow their head out of instinct. Because we're all animals at the end of the day. Our genetic makeup is intertwined with the wolf inside, creating a symbiotic harmony that can be volatile at times when provoked.

I'm more than angry at this point. I'm the most dangerous predator inside this building.

Standing from my seat, I take the short stairs down and walk toward the center. Unable to contain it, those opposing me let out an embarrassing whimper the closer I get—arching back when I bare my teeth in warning.

"You dare to say my mate isn't worthy?" As the words leave my chest in a garbled snarl, my claws unsheathe and fangs drop, shirt ripping as my muscles expand. My trousers are tailored to not fall during a half-shift; they tear but cover me as per my luna's request.

Werewolves don't have qualms over nudity, but my female is possessive and I adore it.

"My king, she's a witch. Royal or not, her kind is beneath us." This time it's the Spaniard alpha that speaks up. He's part of the problem and also the father of the infected wolf my mate saved. And to hear him imply she's anything but perfect, I don't hold back. "All of this is her fault. We've never quarreled with the fae before, Alpha Xadiel. She's brought nothing but—"

"Silence, Diego. You've done enough, along with the group sitting beside you." It takes everything in me not to rip his vocal cords out, more so when they share nervous glances. I'm fighting to control my urges, remind myself that leading means letting your people speak their minds, even if you discipline them brutally afterward.

I will never forgive or forget this offense.

"My king, what have we—"

"One more word, and you won't live long enough to see your

mate reunite with her son." He's smart enough to heed the direct threat, the color draining from his face. "Did you believe I wouldn't look into this matter, Diego? That they'd use your bloody son, then save him, while your wife cries herself to sleep every night, blaming and cursing the crown because of your selfish deed?"

"Amor, what is he talking about?"

"Answer your wife."

"Sit down, Eloisa. This isn't—"

He's cut off by my hand around his neck, his feet dangling off the ground while I dig a single nail into his cheek and tap his tooth with the pointed tip. "You will answer her. You will explain to everyone here why you worked with the fae king to betray your brethren. Your king." His face turns purple in my hold, within seconds swelling from the pressure, and I drop him like a sack of potatoes before kneeling to his choking level. Make sure his bloodshot eyes meet mine. "This betrayal will cost you dearly, Diego. Now speak."

"King Larue approached me a few years ago after I'd made a bad business decision and we were on the brink of losing it all."

"How? What did you do, Diego?" his mate asks, her expression one of shock and pain. Betrayal. "What could make you sink low enough to help that hijo de puta."

"That son of a bitch, as you call him, bailed us out." the middle-aged alpha spits, narrowing his eyes at her. "We'd be poor, Eloisa. Dirt poor and without our title or pack."

"Why would we lose our pack over—"

"Insurance fraud that called the attention of the Spanish govern-ment. They were looking into our chain of hotels and spas—more than likely to confiscate."

"And?" When he looks my way again, it dawns just how deep I dug. What his punishment will be for his treason. The revolt he started failed because those who were with him are now scrunching their brows and looking around, embarrassed. Second guessing the lies this rubbish of a wolf spread, swearing they'd take their sons and daughters, do the same to the children of all leaders within packs.

To his detriment, though, I received a phone call two days before they arrived from the head of a group of elders in the European wolfen lodge, a group of ex-leaders and scholars that help the crown with the investigation of pack crimes and negligence by its leaders. They're worried. Rightfully so, as news of Diego Lunar's businesses being investigated began circulating in the national media back home —by the government of the country, and because of the ties uncovered with the *National Fae Trust.*

Because why would a wolf who abhors the idea of a queen who's not a wolf do business with anyone outside of his people? The answer to that: because he's an arsehole. An opportunist with greed and expectations of grandeur he'll never reach.

This scum wants the title of king and needed the backing. Moreover, when the original plan to pack his pockets with fraudulent money failed before challenging me, Larue offered his help with the promise of allegiance. The price: a small favor.

Control the crown, control the people.

His greed is his downfall. His willingness to hurt his family is despicable.

"I was going to challenge King Xadiel for the crown. Needed the money to buy support."

Gasps of outrage fill the room, many shaking in their seats at the audacity. The loudest of them all are his wife and son, who just entered. He's still a bit underweight and recuperating from the broken leg I gave him during our fight, but it will repair itself.

As he regains his strength, the rest will fall into place.

"Armando?"

"Hola, Mama." At her son's voice, Eloisa rushes over and hugs him. She's crying, checking for injuries as all mothers would, while the rest continue looking at her failure of a mate. Killing a pack member is never an easy thing to do—destroying the bond between mates—but I'm left with little to no choice. "I'm okay."

"How?" she asks, astonished after what she's seen. Her mate had been cruel enough to show her a video of what they'd done to him;

this was corroborated by their beta, who Cain killed yesterday. Right before his death, he cracked and handed over all their files, pictures, and video proof of the facility—his son doesn't remember much, had been drugged at the time but reacted with a flinch at the sight of a tall and heavily guarded building in Canada.

The only thing I don't have is an address, but I will. Nothing stays hidden for long.

"Queen Isabella and her sister saved me. I'm alive because of our king and luna."

"Lies! That's impossible! King Larue swore—" Diego's face is turned to the right by the force of an open-palmed smack from his mate. She doesn't stop at one, hurling insult after insult, and we don't stop her. This woman was lied to, her pup abused, and all by the man who vowed to love and protect their family. "Enough, Eloisa. We can discuss this after."

"There is no after."

"What the hell are you speaking about, woman."

"I, Eloisa Lunar, reject—"

"Don't you fucking dare! I am your mate!" He attempts to raise a fist at her as an intimidation tactic, and that's a big *no-no*. You never hit a woman. Ever. And that limb he raised to try and hurt her; I snap it as if it were a pretzel. His screams fill the space and the closest to him look down, their shame reaching me.

"Carry on, Eloisa. Keep in mind, though, once it's done, there will be no going back."

While rejection is frowned upon, and I almost fell for a lie once, I cannot judge her desire to be free of him. Her pain is hers to deal with. Her life shouldn't be tied to such a man, mate or not—sometimes those we love are horrible beings.

"King Xadiel, I could never forgive a man who has hurt our child in such a manner." Taking in a deep breath, she shudders as a sob gets caught in her throat, nearly choking her. "You disgust me, Diego. I've forgiven so much—infidelities and verbal abuse—but this…this, never. I reject you, Diego Lunar, as my mate and alpha. I denounce our union, even if that angers the Moon Goddess."

They both stagger. The pain of the bond being ripped from their very soul leaves them weak.

Unable to utter another word and while clutching his chest, I pick Diego up by the neck and dig my claws in. Grin in his face as the flesh gives way and blood begins to drip; his hours are numbered. "I never forgive traitors."

His followers whimper, angry and regretful after being duped by this waste of sperm.

One by one, they fall to their knees, necks bared. Their worry makes my nose wrinkle, and the heavy stink of their fear causing my nostrils to burn.

"Alpha, can I make a request?" At the sound of his voice, I turn my face toward Armando and nod. "Please make it quick. My mother is weak and while the bond is broken, a piece still lingers and it will damage her further."

His hate for the man is palpable. We showed him everything, and while angry and full of resentment, his first thought is his mother. Her pain.

"You are going to be one hell of a leader, Armando. Make me proud."

"Thank you, King Xadiel."

I use very little effort to throw Diego across the room and toward my beta, who doesn't cushion his fall but does take him into custody. "He'll be traveling back home with us. Make the arrangements necessary to leave within the hour. I've been without my mate long enough."

"Yes, my king," Cain answers with a smirk, knowing that I'm more than making a point.

If you are against her, you are my enemy. I take it personally.

"Anyone else have a problem fighting alongside the royal army if called upon?"

"No," everyone answers. Even those still on the floor.

"Do you have a problem with my female being a witch?"

"No."

"Does anyone here wish to challenge me for the title of King of Werewolves? The floor is open." Crickets. Not a single sound. "Good. However, those that opposed still have their penance to deal with. I will not strip you of your titles this time because you were lied to and acted out of fear…unless you pass out on me or my beta. Each of you will have an opponent to face off against next month; I will set the date, and you will be given ten minutes to either make us submit or stay alert long enough to be declared the loser."

"Beta." The chorus is loud and resolute. Cain snorts through our link, and I bite back a grin. He's as bloodthirsty as I am. He's also insulted over their treatment of my luna.

"I never said you had a choice, just that you'd see one of us." The color drains once again from their faces, and I raise a brow, daring them to argue with me. They don't, and after a few minutes, I dismiss everyone while leaving a few last-minute instructions to the Oregon leader.

Then I head home.

I need my mate. Controlling my ire during that meeting took a herculean effort.

I NOTICE the missed calls the moment we land.

A lot of them, and Cain has some, too. There are texts and even emails, almost all from Gamma Grady, and each one depicts a level of urgency that has us running to the pack house from my private airstrip in wolf form. The distance isn't great, and within a few minutes we're changing back and dressed—and find Grady pacing back and forth while my father delivers Diego to a lower-level cell.

His mind is restless. His emotions are full of guilt.

I get pieces and sporadic words through the link he shares with us:

Missing.

Beta twins.

Luna.

Failure.

"What the fuck is going on?" I growl, my lungs expanding as I try to find my mate's scent trail. There are a few, but they're light, and when I give the bond a gentle tug, it's blocked.

Little Moon, where are you? I'm home.

Nothing. Not so much as static.

This is unlike her. We're never apart, and the few times it's happened, welcoming the other home is joyous. Loving.

"Alpha, I'm so sorry. I don't know—"

"Where is my mate? What happened to the twins?"

"Answer him," Cain growls out, reacting as any loving father would, and pins the gamma against the ground, mere steps from the front door. "Where are my children? Our luna?"

"The kids are safe, love." Faith's standing at the doorway now, tears running down her cheeks, her face pallid. "Isabella found them and brought them home, but—"

"Found them? Did they wander off?"

"No." She shakes her head as the feeling of dread builds in my gut. My limbs are beginning to throb while my heart clenches painfully—is Isa hurt? My wolf gnashes and claws fully extend while raking them down my insides.

He has to see her. I need to hold her.

"Where. Is. She?" This is the alpha king speaking. I'm no longer their friend but giving a direct fucking order to tell me where my female is. "Answer me!"

"Faith, love…what happened?" Cain pushes off Grady, still angry, but taps him on the chest in apology. The latter doesn't get offended and understands, squeezing the beta's arm. Our gamma has a son himself, a close-to-elite guard he still worries about—yet what I get from him is guilt. Drowning in it. "Talk, baby."

"We don't know how," she chokes out while Cain pulls her to

him. He tips her face up and whispers *breathe*. While she tries to get ahold of herself, Gamma Grady stands and pulls out his mobile, tapping on our security app icon to pull something up for me. He highlights a few areas in three videos and forwards them, causing my cell to ping. I'm trying to be understanding as she's had such a right scare with the pups, but the longer it takes, the darker my aura gets. Projects toward them.

"Intruders snuck unto our lands in between a shift change at the border, my king. Literal seconds from what we found on the video by station four," Grady says then, saving her from further questioning, and taps his mobile. "I've sent you the moments that matter. Before the children were taken, and then our luna visiting the fae prisoner."

Faith shudders on a sob, and Cain looks at me with an expression that begs me to understand. The problem is, I'm beginning to lose the tenuous hold on my beast—he won't be rational.

He wants answers.

Demands to know where his woman is. Nothing else matters to him at the moment.

"Faith, finish. I'm trying here, but the longer you bloody take, the harsher he will be once out. Where the fuck is Isa?"

Whimpering, she nods. "Two fae males snuck onto our lands and took the children from the playground, Alpha. No harm came to them. On camera, they're seen saying a few words that cause my pups to fall asleep, and then them being placed inside Luna's favorite hemlocks. She found them there covered and unharmed."

"And?"

"Please watch the videos I sent you, my king. They show every-thing," Grady answers, neck bared and looking toward the ground. The twins are safe, but his aura is defeated—so much hurt.

Something isn't adding up. "Explain what?"

"That's the problem, Alpha. She left."

At that, an angry howl rips through my chest. The sound is loud and malicious, scaring everyone within hearing distance as the common areas become desolate—not a single pack member can be seen outside these three, who are now on their knees.

My beast is almost out. I'm giving him the control he wants to search our lands for Little Moon when a hand touches my back. I'm thrown off for a second, ready to snap at whoever had the audacity, but find my mum instead with eyes brimming with tears.

I'd forgotten she was here.

That both my parents traveled back to help us with the ceremony. My beast recognizes her and settles enough for me to grit out, "Mum, I need to find her. Head to—"

"Son, your father found something in a prisoner's cell."

Alpha
XADIEL

Kissing my mum on the cheek, I leave her with Faith and head straight for my dungeons. The entry is already open when I arrive, and the first thing that hits me is her scent. She's been here; there's no mistaking the floral scent of jasmine uniquely hers among the filth of our prisoners.

Yet the lower the level, the stronger it becomes until it overpowers everything else.

That's where I find my father. Pacing. Angry.

"What did you…" I trail off as my eyes shift to the fae prisoner. "How the bloody fuck?"

"Alpha, please watch the video. You'll see."

Nodding, I pull out my mobile and open the Messenger app. Grady's text is the last one, and the clip in question is of this area. Right at this cell, and it shows my mate on a rampage.

Motherfuck, she's glorious in her anger. Even my father chuckles beside me as we watch her ask him a question and how afraid he becomes the longer she meets his stare. Gaston scrambles back, yanking on his shackles while her hand rises and toys with the remains on the floor.

Those infected wolves have dissolved into nothing but sparse fur, toxic decomposition, and bones—bones she lifts and snaps before throwing them as daggers. Her powers have grown as of late, her emotions providing the incentive to unleash what she's kept under lock and key.

Out of fear. Worry.

Some days my female still believes people will turn on her.

And that's on me and the wolves we govern. They once saw her as a despicable being, blaming her for something that never happened, and it seems I've done a shitty job of erasing.

I will prove you otherwise, my love. You couldn't be more perfect.

He's stabbed by various sharp bones, piercing his skin and the solid rock behind him that slowly bled him to death. The largest wound is across his chest, as if she dragged the jagged edge from right to left before piercing his heart.

He's been dripping for hours. Whimpering and begging for help for just as long.

Yet what stands out the most is the way she daggered a piece of paper to the wall before stepping through a portal, her lips mouthing the words *come find me*.

I enter the domain to detach it from the wall. It's a thick paper, the ink a deep indigo blue, but the writing isn't one I'm familiar with. Ancient and not wolfen; I'm going to need help deciphering it.

Moreover, as I rub the edge, the scent of jasmine hits me once again and I close my eyes for a second. The bond inside me throbs, needing her touch. To have her safe and back in my arms.

"Double the guards, and no lapse in shift changes. Not a bloody fucking second unattended, do you understand." The men nod while my father scratches his jaw, coming to stand beside me while eyeing the script. "Have you seen this before?"

This time, he's the one who nods. "It's Wiccan. Very Old."

"Where did you put Diego?"

"A cell down the hall."

"Wait for me here." Without pause or giving a single blue fuck, I find him inside the cell and crook a finger over. He comes to me, careful to avoid the solid silver bars, but I reach a hand through and press his face against them, enjoying the way they burn his skin. It sizzles and stinks, but I don't ease up, nor do I care about my flesh being damaged. "Where are they?"

Struggling, he tries to scratch at my arm holding him in place. Whimpers in pain. "I don't know what you're talking about."

"Diego, I won't ask you again." Using my foot as leverage, I yank harder, causing the flesh of his cheeks and jaw to melt off. He's stuck. His eyes bulge out while his screams of pain reverberate throughout the floor. No one comes to check or help him, and the screams become pleading, which aggravates me. "Where did she go to find Larue?"

It then dawns on him, and the idiot tries to smile. "Release me and I'll tell you."

"Last chance."

"Canada's too big. You'll never—" Before he can finish, I've unsheathed my claws and ripped out his throat. There's a gaping hole where the vocal cords once were, and he bleeds out in minutes, drenching my white vest in the process.

I'll send an apology to Eloisa and her son after I find my female.

I hope the Moon Goddess took mercy on her and the pain felt during his death was mild, if not non-existent.

IT'S BEEN three days without word or sight of Isabella.

I've combed every inch of our lands, looking for anything we might've missed while trying to subdue the rage nearly controlling me. I'm volatile, short-tempered, and stay away from my people for their own safety. And the only thing helping right now is the note she left behind in her elegant handwriting, down to the small and cute hearts on either side of my name. I'm going out of my mind with concern.

"When I find you, I'm going to spank that arse red and fuck you into the ground, Isa. You will pay for putting yourself in harm's way." Picking up the gin atop my desk, I sit back and take a pull straight from the bottle. My eyes read the note once again, even though I've memorized every line.

It's my lifeline. What I cling to as I board my private plane heading to Seattle.

I need to find her sister. Neither Leo nor Gabriella have returned any of my calls, and my gut tells me something is wrong. Has to be. Because if something happens to my wife and they ignored my call for help, I will forget we're family.

No one is spared from my wrath. Not even those she loves.

Closing my eyes for the first time since she disappeared, I give in to my exhaustion while reciting her heartfelt words in my head once again.

My Dearest Werewolf,

If you're reading this, I am gone, and it will be some time before we're reunited.

Please trust in me that I'll return to you, that my love for you knows no bounds, and I will move heaven and earth to always make it so. King Larue is after me. The threats have risen in the last few months, and I accept it's my turn to sacrifice.

There is no other choice for us. Not if our future is to be bright.

You are my heart, Xadiel.

My reason for getting up each morning, and so is our future pup. I've seen him many times, my love. He will be strong, a warrior like you, but to save him I must first play a role.

Yours always,
Little Moon

It doesn't take long for me to fall asleep, listening to her gentle tone read her letter. My body and mind need to recharge, to think clearly, but I'm glad I do because her lovely face appears as soon as it all fades. Yet when I come to, we're back in our lake in England.

Same place we met. Where I marked her as mine.

"*Mate.*"

THE ASTORS ARE HOLDING a private showing of Gabriella's latest art collection tonight. We'd been invited, had plans to spend a week here in the new home Isabella has no idea I purchased for us. An anniversary gift I'd failed to give her after spending a beautiful night outside in the wild, knot buried deep in her warmth.

The place is packed as I search the lower level for familiar faces, but the only thing I notice is the vampiric emblem on the guard's uniform and the back of Meera's head when she disappears through an employee-only door.

The soldier closest to me flares his nostrils and turns his head in my direction, bowing his head in greeting. "King Evergreen, please follow me. We were instructed to escort you and Luna Isabella if you made it."

His eyes shift behind me looking for Isa, and I swallow hard, sadness piercing through my chest.

In my dream, we'd spoken.

She promised to send me signs and asked me to take care of two things before we meet:

The blade in Theo's possession needs to be returned, and the uniting of our nations.

We need each other, my love. Those above and below.

"It's just me tonight."

"Of course, sir. Right, this way." We ascend the large and opulent stairs to the overcrowded second level where a live show seems to be the main attraction. Two snakes, each digesting a meal that I know is human—can see it clearly through the near dark they've set up as mood lighting. Tero and Marcia, Gabriella's guards, are being rewarded—the shifters each huge and under the appearance of containment inside of a thick glass enclosure.

And if I weren't here because of my female being in danger, I'd snort.

Humans can be quite morbid.

They love the rush of adrenaline from being in danger. Are curious about death—taunt it, even—yet are clueless when it comes to what a real predator looks like.

Look at their serial killers. Most are documented as nice people with good looks and charming personalities. Their neighbors think they couldn't hurt a fly while bodies are buried in backyards a dime a dozen.

No self-preservation.

Edging closer to where the hosts stands watch, I let them finish their welcoming speech and then disperse the crowd before making myself known.

"Xadiel," Gabriella calls out, voice too low for the humans to hear, but everyone else does at the surprise and is on high alert. Tero tilts his head in my direction, then looks behind me like the guard did. The question in his eyes is clear: *Where's Isabella?* "You guys didn't let us know you were coming?"

I clear my throat to respond but fail.

Looking at her is painful. She's her twin.

And I understand Theo a little more right now: how did he survive their separation? It's only been a few days, and I'm fluctuating between extreme ire and emptiness.

"Gabriella, she's…I don't—"

"Where. Is. She?" In those three words, the vampire queen emerges and blood-red eyes pierce me. Her worry for Little Moon makes the next words difficult to say.

But I do. Now isn't the time to crumble.

I can only afford to do so after she's locked on my knot. Once she's home.

"She's gone."

"Gone?" Theo pulls Gabby off the stage at once. His movements are quick—too fast—and many of the humans look over, not sure if what they saw is real. The couple now stands inches from me while Gabriella reaches for my hand, squeezing it tight in support. "Xadiel, what's going on? Whatever it is, we'll help—"

"She's gone, Gabby. Isabella disappeared, and I can't find her."

Isabella

Cold water snaps me into consciousness, shocking my system that's already rattled. I've been held in a dark and dank room, metal bindings on my arms against a wall that feels like ice on my skin. I'm still in the same clothes as the day I walked through the portal—I have no idea how many have passed in between—but I am hungry.

Thirsty too, and I lick my dry, chapped lips.

A girlish giggle greets my ears at that, and my eyes snap to the blonde female from all those years ago. The same one who infiltrated the royal house with the help of my mate's aunt and his former beta —the same woman who mourned the death of an elder fae who tried to make everyone believe he'd been sent by my mother to kill the then queen.

We met a few times back then. She ran from me each encounter, too.

"I've missed you, Luna Isabella. It's been so long," she says, her voice a little higher in pitch than I remember. "Are you finding the accommodations to your liking? Is there anything we can do to make your stay more enjoyable?"

"Yes." My grin challenges her smirk and her eyes narrow, but I keep my expression as sweet as possible. "You can drop dead." Her strike turns my head to the side, splitting my lip, which I lick as a few drops of blood pool at the cut. "Thank you, I was thirsty."

"I'm going to enjoy breaking you, Isabella Moore." A vision hits me then, of her and another man in bed while he uses her. Her emotions are clear as day; she's in love, while the male simply fucks her without care and after, kicks her out of the room with no tact. She's disposable. At first, I can't make out who he is. His back is all I see, but as the door closes and he turns—stretches while facing forward—I get a clear view of the fae prince, Larue's son. "You disgust me."

I blink and the image is gone, which is good news.

My powers have been bound since we arrived, wherever this is. As if there's a shield.

"Is it disgust? Or is it that you wish you were me?" A kick to the midsection. This knocks the air out of me, but I grit my teeth through the pain. Settle myself as I test my ability to move objects telepathically. In this room, there's a tiny window with bars and a dirty mattress on the floor I'm unable to use, which as I look at it, is a good thing. Nothing that can harm, but I want to remind her who I am. Using my shackled wrist, I bang the metal cuff against the wall until a chunk of the cold concrete falls to the ground.

It won't do much damage, but I'm able to elevate it and aim for her face, reminding her of the cut I left from chin to cheek a century ago. The scar is there, uneven and pronounced, ruining her otherwise delicate appearance.

"The fuck! Guards!" she screams, and three tall, muscular men rush inside. They're each holding a large weapon, a high-caliber rifle with a translucent bullet full of a silver-ish liquid inside of an open-view magazine.

"What happened, Lilou?" the one with a bald head and bushy eyebrows asks, his eyes darting around the room before landing on me. They narrow, while his lips thin. "Are you hurt, Soeur?"

Sister. She's his sister.

I don't call them out on this. Instead, I pretend to not understand and scrunch up my eyebrows as if lost. Like I'm trying to decipher the word, but haven't.

"I'm fine, but we might want to check on the wards. She's breaking them."

"Are you sure?"

"Oui."

"I'll contact the old mage. Her husband's been a bit unreasonable lately." They share a chuckle at his words, while the other two guards exit the room after he snaps his fingers twice. Once they're out, he turns my way and his expression becomes one of absolute loathing.

He also holds a high resemblance to the man Xadiel killed.

"Something on your mind?" He doesn't like my tone, spitting at the ground near my bare feet. The spittle bounces off the ground, and a tiny bit catches on my baby toe. My face reflects the expression of my response. "Disgusting."

"Wiccan cunt."

"Very original. That insult gets a two out of ten." I'm baiting him, want him to get close enough for me to remove a bullet. They need me alive, but that slug will come in handy.

"I should rid the world of another Moore. Your entire bloodline is garbage." Raising his gun, he aims at my chest. "You don't deserve your gifts."

"You cannot shoot her, Brice!" Pushing down on his arm, his sister tries to force the large muzzle away but he's unmovable. His finger is on the trigger—mine move, spreading wide as I prepare to remove the weapon altogether, but then he lowers it to the ground by his feet at the last second.

"You're right, but there are other ways to gift pain. I'm going to make your life hell as payment for the life your mate took." An electrical shock follows that promise. The prongs of the taser now in his hands are embedded into the skin just below my collarbone, and it unleashes a sharp voltage through my system.

It hurts. My breath catches in my throat as I bite the inside of my cheek until it bleeds so I don't scream.

The room's door swings open then, and a petite woman enters. She's young and wearing a dress that reminds me of the fashion trends used by royals when I was a child. Big and over-embellished, the design doesn't suit her.

This girl doesn't belong in a place like this.

There's a delicate nature about her that pulls me in, and more so as she places herself between the siblings and me with an angry expression on her face. "Who gave you permission to hurt her? Answer me."

Neither do, but I catch two different expressions.

Brice is worried.

Lilou dislikes this fae woman.

"Anaya, what are you doing here?" The taser is turned off, his tone gentle. Soft. "This is no place for our prin—"

"My father has asked me to take care of the prisoner as you two fail common decency." My consciousness is slipping; I blink a few times but the electrical shock has zapped me of all energy. Yet, I catch their discussion. Manage to remove a single bullet while they go back and forth, ignoring the woman slumped over who with the last of her strength, managed to hide the slug in her pants pocket. It takes everything I have left to move it; I'm fading fast right after, but I still manage to confirm her identity. "…If you have a problem with that, ask him. King Larue enjoys being questioned."

Golden eyes with identical swirls of black; a beautiful combination that calls to me.

Soft fur that shines in the moonlight.

The scent of cedar with a hint of mint that I find irresistible.

Every aspect of this wolf embeds deep, tattooing itself within every molecule of my DNA, and I can't deny him. Even without meeting the man and seeing his handsome face, I know I'll never belong to another.

Without conscious thought, I lean forward and close my eyes, placing my forehead against his lowered muzzle. I inhale deeply while that rumble deepens, while his exhalation warms my skin, and we stay this way without giving importance to time or commitment.

Quiet and without needing to fill the silence because we're content to just be. My fingers slowly stroke his fur, petting and enjoying the softness, but then bones begin to break and shift, his midnight pelt receding as a hint of skin breaks through.

My breathing accelerates.

It's want and wonder and hunger. It's excitement and acceptance and—

"I'm coming for what's mine."

"Where did you go in that mind of yours, ma sorcière?" Two male voices speak in unison, yet I hear each clearly. Can make out the honest love coming from one, while the other reeks of jealousy— so much hate and possessiveness in his tone for a man I'm meeting for the first time. "Answer me, Isabella. Don't make me hurt you."

Both are angry for different reasons, yet I don't pay heed to the man a few feet from where I sit. His stench tells me he's close, just a few feet separating us. It's a gag-inducing scent, like rotting meat, and I fight back the urge to wretch. I haven't eaten much in the last two days, per the king's instructions, and I can't afford to weaken any further.

I'd rather die than submit to these fae bastards in any way.

Anaya isn't like them. His sister is the only exception in this place. She's sweet and caring, bringing me water behind her father's back. Making sure I'm able to shower, have clean clothes, and get a piece of bread or crackers when no one is around.

It's not much, but she's doing the best she can. Showing me kindness the way only a family member would—putting herself in danger and possible trouble with her father —while keeping Brice and Lilou away.

No one has entered this bedroom but her…until now.

Her presence also serves to deepen my hope on good and honest faes existing, even if she's the first I meet. There's no decaying in her scent nor malicious intent in her actions; I believe—my theory is those poisoned by her father's grooming are all destined to die, and what others pick up on is a mark of their fate.

Opening my eyes, I stretch my neck from side to side but don't answer. I tug on the metal shackles attached to my right wrist and ankle, testing the bruising there, but don't meet Prince Larue's stare.

Not until I test out the ward they'd placed on this room. Their magic is strong, but not dulling mine enough to be worrisome. Something I keep to myself as King Larue is formidable.

He's been kept at bay all these years by force, not by choice, while his heir is pathetic at best and just another puppet. Moreover, they share a trait that will be their downfall: greed. Unadulterated and blinded by a need to amass fortune and power at all costs, yet don't take into consideration just how high some payments can be.

I know how steep the interest can be.

How much it hurts to lose what you love the most.

And yet, I'm one of the lucky ones. Given a chance to reclaim what I lost.

An annoyed huff comes from the stubborn prince, and I finally meet his eyes head-on. Something that surprises him, my defiance so clear, and a flash of trepidation sweeps across his brown eyes. It's quick, and the reaction is well hidden behind an overconfident bravado, but I catch it just the same.

I make him nervous. He wants me to be broken and mindless, easy to manipulate.

Stupid, arrogant man. "How can I help you, Prince Ruben?" Tone calm, and I keep my expression neutral.

"People have warned me of your mouth, ma sorcière."

"I'm not your little witch."

"You're very brave, Isabella Moore."

"And I'm not interested in this conversation." I wave a hand toward the door. "Finish your threat and leave; I'm tired."

"Don't test my patience," he spits out through clenched teeth, hands fisted. "Your life at my side will be one of misery."

"I'm not one to be easily controlled, Prince Larue. Don't get ahead of yourself."

"One day, I'm going to fuck the ornery out of you." Another step toward the bed I'm sitting on, stopping once he reaches the metal frame my chains are welded to. Ruben tugs on the bindings, knowing it will dig into the cuts on my leg, and then he waits for a reaction I refuse to give. "You'll beg for it, too. I'll make sure our forced binding leaves you unable to resist my call."

At his threat, I grit my teeth and smile. "You're always welcome to sit and wait for the day. It'll never come, but at the very least, you'll be comfortable."

"I'm going to revel while watching you eat every word."

"Or maybe I'll kill you. I'm not afraid of you or your father." The malice in his stare is crystal clear, as is the dark aura that surrounds him and those that follow their indoctrination. And for as long as I can remember, the Larue dynasty has been corrupted and full of bitter selfishness. Males sneer at the thought of a woman being their equal. "Rid the world of the trash currently unbalancing the natural order."

"I love your spirit, *Luna Supreme*." Mocking. A disrespect to my title, but he's not as unaffected as he wishes me to think. I unnerve him. It's there in his eyes; he hates the challenge. "It's entertaining."

Inside I bristle, a part of me that's always been there but laying low perks up and bares her teeth. I'm angry—volatile—yet get a grip and push back every emotion because I'm aware of what's happening. The changes started a few months back.

It's taken me this time by myself to realize the slight mood swings. The visceral need clawing at my skin, growing bolder—a little more noticeable with every day that passes.

My body is preparing for the next full moon. Something that should be good news for me—us—but now fills me with dread.

I can't go into my first heat here.

Xadiel has forty-eight-hours to get here at the most, or I'll have to find a way to block it for now.

Maybe Anaya can help me put a potion together. Desperate, but I'll do whatever I have to.

"And you bore me."

"Enough," his voice thunders, and a heavy set of footfalls comes inside the room. All males. All fae. These guards are willing to do anything for their king and his heir, especially Brice who wishes to gain favor. *Two siblings are in love with people who will never love them.* One because of greed, the other because her life is destined to intertwine with her mate very soon. "Who did you contact? What made you smile like that?"

When I don't respond, Ruben grows livid.

He doesn't like to be challenged. Abhors me for embarrassing him in front of his men.

Then, there's the way each word is brimming with a fit of territorial jealousy that throws me off for a second. Not because he cares for me, or I him, but because this man believes he has the right to feel so. Because like his father, this man-child spits higher than he should.

The audacity is astounding, yes, but this time it works in my favor and will buy me some time.

Timing is everything right now. My sacrifice can't be in vain.

I can't lose him again.

"Fuck. You." No sooner has the insult passed through my lips than Ruben is in my face with his hand wrapped around my throat.

Hold tight and is painful, he cuts off my air supply while my body can't help but fight the lack of oxygen. Thrashing. Coughing. I'm losing consciousness and can't do anything but take it.

No one can know that my powers aren't bound.

No one can attack those I love until the final piece has been moved into place.

And as my mind shuts down and Ruben becomes fuzzy, I remember my beast's promise. A recurring dream since arriving— every time I close my eyes—it's a promise and memory of the night I got my wolf's tattoo.

The words are different now, from how our reality began, but I cling to them anyway. To him.

My alpha king soothes me as I lose consciousness.

"I'm coming for what's mine."

Alpha
XADIEL

"You're going to find her, Xadiel," my father says, taking a seat beside me on the grass while not far from us, a group of teenagers takes a training class with Cain. He's running them through drills and stamina training, starting with cardio. "She's smart and capable, stubborn like her father…" he chuckles at that, and a small smile tugs at my lips "…no one can stop Isabella when her mind is set on something."

"No. No one can." Maybe it's the circumstances, but I can't help the direction my thoughts travel to. After all this time, I still have a hard time with how things unfolded after I took over as king, and while I let it go back then, I don't want to now. "Did you know she was planning this all along?"

If he's surprised by my mistrust, my father doesn't show it. He just looks down for a second and then meets my stare. Unwavering. "No. I didn't."

"Did she ever mention any of this happening? Her fear of King Larue?"

"No."

"Don't lie to me." It's a low growl. A command from his king. "If she did, I need to know. Every bit of information helps."

At the moment, I'm not talking to him as a son would a father. Familial ties hold no weight over the bond I hold with Isabella.

She comes first. I would never make the same mistake twice.

In the distance, I make out the figure of Leo rushing through on his way toward my home. He teleported before we arrived from Seattle, waiting for us on the tarmac with a book on ancient translations and the opal dagger I'd given him over a century ago.

The Wiccan king had missed my call with good reason, although he was apologetic. Their aunt is missing, too, having disappeared a day before Isa without leaving a single trace behind.

He wants to believe they're not connected. The rest of us don't think as he does.

Yet the focus right now is Isabella, especially after the two notes were fully translated. Larue hit her in the chest with those threats, and it's a cruel shot to manipulate her into doing what he wants: being his.

It's something I'll never allow as long as breath fills my lungs. It's why Theo left to handle the Stygian blade and Tero is helping Grady comb my forest for the grimoire her father left her.

It's one she treasures. Uses the most.

Both Moore siblings have taken over my office while trying to locate where Isabella is being held. They've been scribing—going through old books and notes—my wife left behind for us to use, but nothing we've learned so far leads me to her, and this separation is becoming near maddening.

I want to be her happiness and shelter, who Isa comes to in her time of need. It's not healthy for a person to walk around with so much weighing them down.

"You don't trust me." Not a question, and I don't deny it. "I'd never hide something like this from you, Xadiel. Isa is like a daughter to your mother and me; what happened when you met wasn't done on purpose on my end."

"I almost rejected her because of your silence." My words are laced with venom. Feelings I've kept tucked away because, at the time, he'd lost my mother. We—I—thought her dead, while he silently looked for her. Their bond was alive, but he didn't bother to share his mistrust over the accusations thrown at Isabella's mum. "Don't hide things from me. This time I won't—"

"You're right, and I'm sorry." His rough exhale is full of regret and self-reproach. "I should've told you. I should've trusted your judgment as our king to handle things correctly, instead of working and shouldering the weight of finding your mum on my own. The time wasted and the misunderstandings are on me, but I swear this time I truly do not know. We're just as desperate to find her as you."

"Okay. I'm choosing to believe you, but lie to me, and I'll forget you're my father."

"Thank you, Son." We're both quiet for a few minutes before he asks, "Have you found anything new?"

"No, and that's what makes this worse. Our bond is frantic inside me, demanding I find her, but her end is shielding itself from me." Running a tired hand down my face, I stand before cracking my stiff neck. "The tether that connects us isn't leading the way but it is a rather chaotic ball of string that doesn't want to give and unravel. I'm left with a hunt, but no scent to trail."

However, what she's left behind does teach us a few things:

How long she knew that one day she'd leave.

The pressure on her shoulders.

The feelings of guilt and distress over keeping everyone safe.

Her pack. Her family. Me.

Because I'm the biggest of her worries.

The mere thought of losing me breaks her.

I'm so sorry, Little Moon. I've been so blind.

"Then hunt, Xadiel. It's the one thing under your control." Dad stands, too. His gaze shifts to those running drills not far from us. "Give in to your animal instincts and let the beast take control. He's as desperate as you are to find her. Let him do so."

"You know she won't show me the way until it's time."

It's the reasons every one of fighting age is training in shifts. Some will go with us, and others will be tasked with the safety of our people. Everyone is ready to do their part, and lay their lives on the line for their queen who sacrificed herself so we had time to prepare.

Something we could've been doing all along, but when it comes to Isabella, I trust her reasoning even if I hate it at the moment. Fate has a way of moving pieces as she chooses and Little Moon will not disrupt the order of things, especially if it comes with the price tag of a loved one's life.

Needing a break to clear my head, I give his shoulder a squeeze and head toward Cain, who's leading a class for recently shifted wolves who need help controlling their animals. It's not a mixed-sex class as is the norm; females are sometimes better fighters than males as they strategize whereas men rely on brute strength, but this bunch of overconfident boys requires a more direct lesson.

Because these beasts are us—a part of our being—but still ruled by instinct, and without harmony between the two forms it can lead to dangerous situations. They need to submit and respect those of a higher rank very early on, or you'll have teenagers challenging their superiors.

In a normal society, that would be defined as normal. The know-it-all git with a smart mouth you just ground as punishment, but insubordination isn't permitted within pack life. You either respect your leader or are forced to, and the latter is never done through a peaceful conversation.

It's done through pain and broken limbs before you're sent to the infirmary to be patched up.

Most of the time, their human understands this right away and the animal recognizes it after. Wolves are pack animals by nature and need a leader they can rely on; someone to keep the peace and rule with a firm hand. And I demand that loyalty not because I'm an arsehole who's led by his ego, but because it's a show of respect and a vow of trust.

An instinctual knowledge that I will always protect and provide for my people while their queen nurtures and gives advice. We're two halves of a whole who live to serve our kingdom with honor and love.

The pack needs her. I can't live without her.

"Alpha," the pups, varying in ages of adolescence, say in unison the moment I cross the field. They're paired up at the moment, fighting in their skin and ready to shift when the command is given. They've also bared their necks, their wolves rumbling lowly in their chests in a greeting for their alpha.

I nod at them, pleased with the respectful acknowledgment, but I'm not fooled. "Carry on."

I can sense their sudden unease at being in the presence of a dominant wolf. The curiosity and *what if* of an unspoken challenge, but instead, they retake their stances and begin a set of boxing combinations. One throws a punch, while their partner evades, working on the defense aspect as they're ambushed by jabs and hooks with an uppercut added here and there.

It's rapid, unapologetically a provocation, and done at full force with the aid of their wolf.

"Shift!" Cain calls out once I'm at the front with him. The command is sharp, pushing those participating to grunt in acquiescence before the sound of ripping clothes and bones snapping fills the afternoon air. It's painful; I remember those early days as fur sprouted and features elongated to reshape my skull and jaw.

Where nail beds tear, bleeding as claws emerge. Where gums ache as teeth become fangs.

Where each voice becomes a howl and their call is heard and felt by me.

These young warriors are the future defense for our pack. Some might even reach elite status and replace the older members when the time for retirement comes. In our society, you receive your wolf—can shift for the first time after the age of fifteen—and then find your mate as early as eighteen.

Unlike humans, we don't believe in divorces or accept cheating. You treasure your other half; are faithful and supportive because it's a privilege to be mated. Those are lessons given to us from a young age.

Some wolves find them right away. Some never do; a meeting in this life is never guaranteed.

It's also why my reaction when I met Isabella still haunts me; I almost lost her then.

Why her absence now feels like a punishment for the pain I put her through then.

"How's it looking?" I ask Cain after clearing my throat, surveying the group of twelve. Most are keeping track of me, fumbling through their pinning exercise while I fight back a grin. *Bloody pups never change.* "Anyone with promise?"

"A few." Ticking his jaw, he narrows his eyes toward a pair to my left. Out of the group, their animosity—desire to hurt each other—is escalating. "Faith says there are two she-males in her class with great poise and promise. Elton's pups are just like their Father.

"He's an honorable wolf and loyal elite."

"He also trained the twins himself before their shift."

"Good. Nothing makes me prouder than knowing our young can protect themselves."

An angry snarl rips through the clearing and I find the same two, no older than sixteen, snapping at each other. Teeth click and fur bristles. The sounds are menacing, a warning, and I hold a hand up when Cain steps forward to separate them.

This is a lesson best taught by me.

The larger of the two is a deep brown color, his untrained muscles holding strong but not for long, and I notice the small tremble in his right shoulder immediately. His grey counterpart also has mass, but there's a small limp to his gait from not being used to the shift. If the body isn't trained to sustain the switch and land correctly on those paws, you can and will be injured.

Do we heal fast? Yes. But like athletes, you have to learn and develop the ability to be one with your beast. One part is nature and the other is practice.

"Cody and Edwin are late shifters, correct?"

"Yes, Alpha." *Go easy on the lads. They're fighting over a mutual high school crush.*

Chuckling, I pull off my shirt and hand it to my beta. I stretch my neck from side to side, watching the two circle each other before the grey wolf lunges for the brown's tweaked leg. He misses and eats dirt while the attacked becomes the aggressor, biting the flank of his brethren.

Blood seeps from the wound, and I unleash a growl that forces every wolf to submit. The ground shakes beneath our feet as heavy, furry bodies fall flat with their heads turned, showing me their necks. Then there's the sound of wolves coming from every corner of our lands, young and old—the entire pack responds to my ire.

They submit, whimpering and understanding who the real threat is.

That I am their leader. The strongest beast here.

And a man who's lost his luna isn't one to cross.

Fur sprouts across my arms and chest; the bulging of muscles stretches my trousers and tears the seams, but the fabric stays put. My claws drop and my fangs break through the gums; I taste the blood before it drips down my neck and chest.

I don't fully turn, but the alpha wolf lets his presence be known as I make my way between the two disruptors. Those on the ground rub paws over their faces while Cain kneels behind me in a show of respect, yet my attention is on Cody and Edwin who cry in pitiful yips.

"We don't fight each other out of anger. We protect and respect. We teach and help your fellow pack members grow," I say, voice thundering across the field as I grab a scruff in each hand and lift them off the ground. My claws nip their hides, the gouges only deep enough to damage the outer layer. "Pack is family. Pack is sacred."

"Yes, Alpha."

Tightening my hold, I force them to look the other in the face. "Repeat that."

"Pack is family. Pack is sacred."

"Bloody fucking louder."

"PACK IS FAMILY. PACK IS SACRED."

"Never forget that." One flick of each wrist and their heads collide, knocking foreheads and creating an identical laceration. Blood spills from the cuts and they whine in pain, but I'm not moved as I drop them. Instead, I'm disappointed in their lack of respect for our goddess-given laws and responsibilities. "Keep those hands to yourself unless you're training, and no more bullshit aggressiveness. Is that understood?" Both heads nod, shying away from meeting my eyes. "Good. Now shift back, while someone finds you a pair of trousers." They do as I ask, changing and dressing immediately, but they're still arguing. "Enough."

"Alpha, he kissed my mate."

"She is *my* mate. Not yours, dickhead."

"I said bloody fucking enough," I snap, and the two whimper again, shrinking back. "Neither of you is old enough to have recognized your mate and know better than to claim a she-wolf like this. What you're doing is a disservice to her, to your future female, and to this pack. To the teachings of past generations and the blessings our goddess bestowed upon us."

Edwin and Cody lower their heads in shame, while their brethren yip in agreement. The other wolves watch me with admiration and acceptance of my role in this pack. My rules.

Without another word, I turn and walk back to Cain, who stands with a look of pride on his face. Neither of us say anything. We let the pups stew in their alpha's reproach before I send out a single command through the mind link to the others still in their wolf skin.

Shift.

And as they morph back, realigning and welcoming their human side with the help of Cain, who coaches a few strugglers, I hear Gabriella call my name. She's running at top speed, her eyes blood red and her smile wide as she reaches me.

The pups don't react, and I'm proud they're learning acceptance. Where vampires were once our enemies, they are family now.

Disrespecting her would be a slap in the face to the woman they call their queen.

"Everything okay, Gabby?"

"It is now, Xadiel. I know where she is."

Isabella

"I'll see you soon, my king. It's time you come find me." A deep and satisfied purr builds in his chest, one I feel against my lips when he takes them in a quick and sensual claim. It's fast and sweet, and I melt against him, blessed to be loved so deeply. He breaks the kiss after a few minutes but doesn't pull back. Instead, we share the same breath. Enjoy the connection, and it's all I will ever need. "I've missed you."

Just him.

His touch. His giving heart.

"I've never stopped, Little Moon. My world revolves around you."

"Then I'll be waiting, Xadiel. Go to my favorite place and find the book...it's the key."

A cold hand on my forehead snaps me out of my daydream and my eyes snap open, meeting the ones of a man I loathe. Yet he's smiling at me, sweeping those icy, long fingers from temple to temple as if taking my temperature. "Your body seems to be heating up quite nicely, Isabella. Are you feeling all right?"

"Don't touch me."

"Such horrible manners." It's a tsk. His touch becomes more aggressive as he drags a sharp nail down my face before his hand wraps around my throat. "My son warned me you were ungrateful, mon cherie, and I don't tolerate insolence."

This is where Ruben's condescension comes from. The belittling and narcissistic tendencies.

King Larue is an abuser that once forced the true ruler, his wife, to a lesser and unnatural role within their kingdom until she took her life. It's what they want from me. To take my powers, old and new, and use me to help them attain what they'll never accomplish.

Control over all above and below the dirt we stand upon.

I never met the queen, but know the story well as my mother was once her friend.

Long before she met this man and took him as her chosen mate. He was never her fated.

Another set of footsteps reaches my bed and the body sits beside mine, his hands settling on my knee. Not higher or moving, but as a presence. "The little witch is brave, Father."

"However, not untamable." The glint in the king's eyes is pure evil. There is no light in him, yet I notice right away that his scent is blocked. Doesn't smell like anything at all. "She isn't the first or last woman I break during my reign."

"But she is *my* first. Besides, you're stepping down soon—"

"I'm not abandoning my throne. Ask me again, and I'll take her as my bride and not a simple concubine I let you use as a trophy." Using the area just below my neck for support, Larue leans his body weight over me to get in his son's face. Each adds pressure—tightening their hold and exerting force—while the sharp spikes of the metal around his finger break my skin. It hurts like hell, too. *What kind of ring is that?* "Is that understood, Ruben? I decide what to do with the witch, not you."

"Oui, Father." Spit out. Angry.

"Good. Now find your sister and ask her to assist Isabella with a bath and a meal." At the mention of food, my stomach growls loudly, much to both their amusements. I've been kept here with barely any sustenance and the little provided was all Anaya's doing. "We show her just how well she'll be treated if she complies and behaves like an obedient witch."

"Father, are you sure that's—"

"Never question me again. Go and do as I said." After Ruben exits, Larue smiles at me as if we were friends but doesn't move away. Instead, his face gets a little closer to mine. "Children nowadays have no vision for the future. They rely on the elders to make all decisions and reap the rewards with little effort put in. He wants you, young one, but what has he done to deserve such a coveted prize?" It's a question with a response that will anger him, and I choose to pick my battles. I need food in me. I'm weakened in this state and don't trust either of them to not force themselves on me. "But you, Isabella…there's so much intelligence in your eyes. I'm no fool, but I do enjoy your fire."

"My mother taught me well." That comment irks him. I see it in the tightening around his mouth and eyes, but technically it's not disrespectful. It's a mere homage to my upbringing with a strong woman.

"Smart, indeed."

His daughter chooses that moment to enter and he stands, moving his body away from mine. She's wearing another ostentatious gown. This one is poufy and matches the color of her irises, which are red-rimmed while there's a handprint on her right cheek. Its size is large, encompassing nearly half of her face, and fury builds within me.

"Who hit you?" The words are out of my mouth before I reel my ire in. There's power in my tone, so much that for a moment, Larue takes a step back. It's minute but he changes his lax posture from a moment ago while he studies me, head tilted to the side.

"It was nothing. A simple misunderstanding."

"She asked you a question, Anaya." Yet he's looking at me. Not the least bit concerned with her being abused. "Who hit you?"

"It was Ruben."

"Why?" Unmoved by his son doing this. Just watches my reactions.

"Because I said I didn't wish to marry Brice."

Now his eyes cut her way, a sneer on his face. "No one asked you for your opinion on the matter, Daughter. He's served the crown well and you will do as you're told."

Before she can answer, I raise a brow with my own scornful expression. "So what you're saying is you don't believe in finding your mate or marrying for love."

Larue scoffs. "Those things are a hindrance."

"And you also believe in women being abused."

"Discipline isn't abuse, young one. It's a tool to correct un-useful behaviors."

"So should I correct your son for putting his hands on someone young and defenseless?"

I expect him to lash out or say something cutting. Instead, the fae king throws his head back and laughs. Deep and loud, his chuckles reverberate with an eerie echo. "You amuse me, indeed. Our life will never be dull, Isabella."

I'M NOT FEELING WELL.

It's hot, and the clothes they chose for me are uncomfortable. A scratchy fabric clings to my body and it's short, with a scoop neckline that makes my breasts look great. Xadiel would love this, but I don't want to wear it here. Not with so many disrespectful and entitled men walking these halls, the worst of which are the fae king and his heir.

Anaya scrunches up her tiny nose. "You look like you're going to a nightclub."

"Who gave this to you again?" I ask, and her face says it all without words. This is her father's doing. *Sick bastard.* "Jesus, it's hot in here. Has the heater been turned on?"

"Not at all. I'm actually cold." She's been rubbing her hands together for a while now. Her arms, too. "When will your mate come for you, Isa? Something isn't right, and I have a bad…"

I understand a second later why Anaya trails off as Lilou walks in with a tray in hand. Her haughty expression tightens at the sight of me dressed in so little; I'm a threat to the future she's clinging to without an anchor.

Ruben doesn't want her. Neither does his father.

Both men use her to get off and nothing more. Yet having the title of concubine doesn't truly bother her; she craves males with power.

"Here's your lunch." She drops the tray unceremoniously atop the bedside table, causing a bit of the hot tea to spill onto the thick cut of bread beside a beef-based stew. Without a fake apology or even a *whoops*, Lilou turns around and walks away, but pauses just inside the doorway. Her face turns in our direction, gaze set on the princess. "My brother made the tea just for you. Be grateful and drink it; that's all your getting today. Deny him again in any way, and I'll personally see to him delivering the whipping you deserve, bitch."

Anaya's bottom lip trembles, but she doesn't fight back.

Yet I do as I'm no longer shackled. I'm quick to grab the fork and throw it at her head, wishing it was the bullet I'd confiscated, but Anaya had taken away with my dirty clothes without knowing. The pronged end hits her cheek, though, right where I damaged her face and she screeches, launching herself at me but is caught midair by another royal guard. "Let me go! She must pay!"

"King Larue made his stance on her very specific. No one touches a hair on her head."

"You're lying." The implication makes her go from red in the face to pallid in the blink of an eye, her body going slack in the man's grip. "He doesn't defend—"

"Go ask him."

"Yes. Please do so, Lilou," I taunt, waving at her. "I'd love for him to treat you as the opportunistic whore you are."

"You little—"

"Guard, please remove her from my room."

"Yes, Miss." He takes her out without fuss, not giving in to her thrashing or complaints. The sight causes Anaya to giggle, and the sound makes me happy. I'm protective of her, and the reasons why are so obvious.

She's going to complete our family.

THE ACHY FEELING has only gotten worse as the hours pass.

I'm sweaty and cranky, feeling as though I've caught something while my head is foggy. I keep seeing my male arrive, my visions flickering in and out of focus. It's the anticipation coupled with the sweltering fire growing under my skin that has me throwing my legs over the bed in search of the bathroom.

Maybe a cool shower will help. My first step is unsteady, though, making me grab onto the bedding for support as I try to head in the right direction. It lasts all of fifteen seconds before I'm sitting again and grabbing my head. *Need Anaya to help me make a suppressant sooner than I thought.* "What's wrong with me?" I'm so lost in the fogginess that I don't realize someone's in the room until the sound of ice clinking in a glass meets my ears. My reaction time is slow, my entire body lethargic yet needy. "What are you doing in here?"

"Just came to check how the heat activators are working. I wouldn't want you to find a way to stop your heat from commencing." King Larue's tone is husky. Nearly a groan. "I must say you smell divine, young one. Better than any woman I've ever bed."

"Get. Out."

"We've spoken about being ungrateful, Isabella. Disrespect me again, and I will take my anger out on Anaya." He takes another sip, savoring before swallowing. "It's been a while since I've whipped anyone."

"Don't touch her."

"Then behave." Standing, he walks over and brings a hand to my face. Runs the pads of two fingers down my cheek before stopping at the corner of my lips. "I've chosen to keep you for myself, Isabella. You should count yourself blessed." Now a tap. His touch and proximity almost make me gag; it takes everything in me to hold it in. I don't want her hurt. "I'll also share a little secret with you since we're engaged now. Your uncle didn't betray you or your family, mon cherie. It was your aunt, and his imprisonment here has always been part of the deal."

"Why?" I hiss as a wave of pain settles in my stomach. I'm going to be sick.

"Because she's my half-sister."

"No. No, that can't be."

"Silla has been my spy for many years, little Luna, but now she's home." That feeling of being burned alive becomes dormant for a moment. Literally stops dead, and I look up to find a surprise on Larue's face. "What the—"

Isabella

Alarms wail throughout the floor right as I'm about to unleash my pent-up wrath. It's loud and ear-splitting, causing the man before me to take my wrist and yank me out of the room. Men in heavy artillery are rushing past us, heading in the direction of whatever is going on, while two stay behind and flank their leader as he leads us to an elevator.

With the three of them, we're cramped inside; I'm disgusted by their proximity and it shows clear as day. One tries to wink at me, but his ruler doesn't like it and shows me a taste of his powers as the orb used swells and pushes out of the socket, popping as it dangles from the attached ligament.

Cannot submit to heat. Focus on my anger.

He doesn't scream. He doesn't so much as make a sound just turns around and continues to guard our front as the doors open into a large and semi-furnished space without windows. *It's a panic room.* Lilou and Ruben are already here, the latter of which is pacing and wringing his hands together as an explosion rattles the floor we stand on. Then another. Everything shifts in the aftermath. The walls become littered with cracks and the crystal décor crashes to the ground, leaving large shards of glass everywhere.

The tension in the room mounts.

Where are Anaya and Brice?

Glances are exchanged. The scent of fear, this one I enjoy, fills the space while I keep my eyes on my biggest threat. "What the fuck is going on down there? Who's responsible?"

The same guard that removed Lilou from the room earlier shifts nervously, tapping on some kind of tablet and pulling up a feed. Outside, hundreds of people have arrived. They're not wolves, vampires, or witches, but they do attack the entrance.

In their hands are Molotov cocktails, one after another aimed at the main-floor windows of this building. These are the faes who've been hiding while protesting however they can—trying to fight back against a power that's murdered his people. Anyone who's risen against King Larue was dubbed a traitor to the crown and has been dealt with as such.

He's a dictator, not a savior. The darkness in his, and his followers' hearts are reflected outward by their stench.

I'm coming for what's mine.

Relief floods every molecule of my system then at the rich sound of his voice in my mind. Goosebumps rise across my skin. It shakes me from head to toe, causing the lick of heat in my belly to flare up, but I focus on my hatred for this group of people to combat the aching need growing.

Just until I'm back in his arms. He'll take care of me; I refuse to fall into my first heat without my male and his protection. No other will ever taint what is rightfully his.

We're on the eighth floor. Larue is keeping a close eye on me.

His possessive growl at that almost makes me giggle. Once

again, it's hard to swallow back what is a natural response, but I do. ***Please remain calm.***

Little Moon, that's a promise I cannot keep. I'm here for what's mine.

I'm about to respond when the sound of heavy gunfire erupts from the tablet and everyone around me starts to speak in French. From the king to his minions, all begin shooting off exchanges, except for the man holding the device broadcasting what's happening.

From the security feed, we watch the front doors get demolished by a large delivery truck, ramming through and leaving a wide-open gateway for people to enter. There's some shouting and crying, the sound of a horde—but then I see him.

Tall and proud; my male stands with my family at the back, watching. They're allowing Larue's subjugated people a chance at retribution before he hunts.

Moreover, I'm not the only one who notices as all eyes shift my way. There's some surprise and a lot of resentment, but it's Ruben who attempts to strike.

"You knew!" He rushes at me, arm cocked back to land a punch but never makes it. The sound of a gun cocking forces him back as the quiet guard takes his place beside me, pointing at the arsehole who will never measure up to my king. "Who do you think you are to point that at me? I'll have you—" Every bit of light goes out in the windowless room. The tablet gets turned off and tossed aside.

This is my Xadiel's doing. I saw it in his stance earlier.

Proud. Hungry. A beast.

And he's mine.

"Someone shine a flashlight," King Larue snaps, but the only thing available are those attached to phones. They work, but only two people are carrying a mobile and only one turns it on, even though it appears his battery is low. The other hands his device over to me as we take a step back, his weapon still drawn.

"Isabella, come to me right now. Put an end to this, and your family will live."

My smile in the dark widens as the scents of my siblings infiltrate my senses. Gabriella is to my left while Leo is right behind them, using his ability to become invisible and knocking out the guard with the two good eyes.

"Beg me, Larue. Beg, and maybe you will live."

XADIEL

WHILE HER SIBLINGS disappear through the back, I take the front with Cain and my army behind me. We overwhelm them in sheer numbers, dealing with the sector where the scents of my people are captive.

I no longer see people but obstacles as the sight of wolves in shackles with tubes and needles piercing their hides enrages my wolf. The shift takes seconds, but I plow through the first guard, ripping out his throat before tossing him aside and unleashing a howl those that call me king respond to.

Snarls fill the space as bodies are ripped apart and blood paints the walls. My coat is filthy, the remnants of a few organs sticking to me as I hunt down the monster in charge of this.

He's in a lab coat and stumbling back, whimpering as a stalk him slowly. A bullet whizzes by me and I snap my head in the direction of the shooter, a young man who's shaking. He's no older than sixteen at the most and scared out of his mind.

"Leave!" I thunder in my wolf's garbled tone, causing those not infected to shift in their restraints. Some of them smell like regular rogues while others as if they belong to a pack, and I unleash another growl, demanding they wake up. That they shift.

As they do, thrashing in their bonds, the young man drops his weapon and makes a run for it, untouched by every wolf under my command. I do not kill innocents, and that kid reeked of forced labor.

Now, the scientist? Him, I want.

Cain, you and Grady kill anything that resembles a dirty fae. I want their bodies in a pile and ready to burn when I return with my queen.

His bow is deep and maw dripping blood, the scalp of the enemy stuck between his teeth. Finding out what happened to his pups and about the danger Isabella put herself in after saving the pack, he's full of a deep-rooted need for revenge that mimics my own.

Please bring her home, Alpha. She belongs with her family.

I nod once and with a slow gait, walk toward the fae who's pissed himself, deepening his acrid scent. He's standing behind two guards, big and burly with matching tattoos of the royal crest on their wrists.

Each carries the same caliber weapon as the other soldiers, but I can tell they're trained both in magic and combat, but I'm not here to play. Testing their knowledge isn't on my agenda and I launch myself, tackling the one on the right while digging my claws into his chest and crushing his heart from within, the useless organ becoming mush in my grip.

I chuck the remainder at his comrade. Right across his horrified face, an expression that leaves just as quickly as it arrives.

And for every step he now takes back, I follow.

For every shot aimed my way, I dodge while a warning growl builds and unleashes as the last shot in his magazine grazes my flank. Not deep. It's a mere scratch that begins to heal automatically, yet my ire makes everyone in the room stop.

Wolf, witch, and vampire. Even the fae fighting to stay alive take heed.

All except the two who now push a tiny woman my way to use as a shield.

"Please don't kill me," she shouts, catching herself a few steps from me, but I'm taken in by the scent of jasmine on her. That, and the lack of decay in her natural odor. Everything about her is different than the others here, and I bypass her, gripping the tail end of the lab coat before it disappears through a hidden stairwell.

The other man is long gone. *Fucking pussy.*

However, the scientist I drag with me before dropping him between the girl and me. Immediately he focuses on her, and his tone isn't gentle when he speaks. It's an intimidation tactic. "Don't say a fucking word, Princess. Your father, King Larue, is—"

"That man stopped being my father the day he drove my mother to an early grave." For a sprite, she's full of venom. Shares the sentiment as so many here do, and I half-shift back to retain a few of my human traits. Grady is nearest to me and tosses a pair of pants my way, a little tight and drenched in blood, but they'll have to do for now.

I still have my pelt and claws. It's my fangs she's currently focused on.

I'm dirty. Angry. But she smiles and for some reason, I feel protective over her.

Not romantically. More like she's meant to be family.

"Do you know where my female is…" I trail off, a clawed foot pinning the male between us down, my talons breaking the skin of his back. "I'm—"

"I know who you are, Alpha King Xadiel. She's been waiting for you."

"Has she, now?"

"Yes, and the name's Anaya. Please kill him, so I can take you to her."

"As you wish." It takes no effort at all to drive my foot clean through his flesh. I destroy his organs, ripping through his spine and flesh until I once again touch the concrete floor below him. "Now let's go find Little Moon. I've missed her."

The words inside the grimoire I found in her favorite tree not only confirmed her location—she'd left behind a special map to locate her through scribing—but below was a warning of her upcoming heat.

It was close, and she was alone.

Without my protection or knot to satisfy and ease her pain.

ISABELLA

"I WILL NEVER BEG A WHO—" He doesn't get to finish as we attack, incapacitating the guard with the good eyes, but then the room is filled with more of his soldiers. They pour in from different entry points with Brice at the head, his shirt ripped and marked with blood tinged with dark blue.

They see us and pause, eyes bouncing between their king and our side before drawing their weapons and pointing at us. Cockiness fills their bravado, a false manhood that glitches quickly when Leo hides again. The groups shift and take their eyes off Gabriella and me long enough that I'm able to lift every piece of glass off the ground with ease, letting go of everything around me but the feel and weight of each shard and hold them high while Gabriella toys with the life force of Brice and his sister. She's bending their blood while creating havoc on their nervous system.

They're frozen where they stand, slowly being drained as panic sweeps across the room. It's a dangerous thing. Blinding and torturing; it showcases what isn't there while hiding the threat mere steps away. While they move around their king, shielding him from us, three entities fill the room.

As it should be. Two males and one female, the latter of which causes Leo's molecular structure to glitch and reveal his identity. It lasts only a second, but it's enough that multiple rounds are aimed where he once stood but they find no one there. Instead, he appears near Xadiel who senses my brother before sending our bond a playful tug.

His playfulness causes me to smirk at King and Prince Larue. "You have until the count of five to drop to your knees."

"You're outnumbered, Isabella. You and your siblings should've been eradicated long ago—you're not worthy of what you possess."

"I'm getting tired of greedy scum saying that, Ruben." Cutting my eyes, I bring down every sharp piece of glass over his guard's heads, cutting and ripping through their muscles. They scream, not understanding how this is happening while Theo and Xadiel make their presence known. One by one, they begin to take out the fae army, slashing throats and ripping off heads, not stopping until all that remain are four horrified assholes.

Three men. One woman.

Two of which can't break the hold my sister has on them, and when the king realizes this, he tries to retreat. Grabbing the nearest gun, he pulls his son with him toward the exit, and all the while we inch closer. He's all but forgotten about the faithful siblings that carried out his every whim.

He ignores his daughter. He doesn't truly care for his son.

I've been the center of his universe for so long that he pulls the trigger with the aim at my chest. "If I can't have you, no one will."

Every person reacts differently. Leo and Gabriella freeze, stopping what they're doing as my male shouts my name, seconds from reaching me, while a dominant presence appears out of thin air, grabbing King Larue by the neck. His back is to us, but an aura like his I've only encountered with Thanatos. *Is this a god?*

Tall and imposing, his dominance outranks every person in this room.

The bullet never reaches me, though, and my view is blocked as Theo stands in front of me, shielding my body before I can react. He's smiling at me, not at all bothered by the casing that sharply bounces off his back. "You okay, little sister?"

"I am now, big brother." Emotions nearly choke me. He cares. It's the first time he's truly looked at me with open kindness in so long.

"Good." He steps aside with a wink as our mates rush to our sides, Gabriella thanking him while Xadiel breathes me in. My male places his hand against his brother-in-law's chest, a silent show of gratitude that Theo returns with a nod as a garbled scream rends the air.

"Aries." One word, and the God of War chuckles, reveling at the way fear laces every pore of the man who once thought it possible to kill him. "How?"

"Didn't you call upon me?" Aries's voice is deep, a thunderbolt of power in each syllable, and I watch from the corner of my eye as Brice and Ruben slink away. Slowly, they're heading toward Anaya who stands off to the side, in shock and unaware. "Didn't you think yourself better than a god? Named yourself my killer?"

They enter her space but don't get close as Leo appears in front of her. Her brother and Brice startle at this but fall back when they realize the guard who helped me earlier is also there, his finger on the trigger and set on Prince Ruben.

Not that they get far. Both men freeze when their mighty leader begs for mercy.

"My Lord, please. It's not—"

"Silence." That's all he says. One word, and then he's driving the Stygian blade deep into King Larue's stomach, driving it deep and then up until pulling it out just below his jaw. There's no surviving that. There's not even the chance to utter a single sound as the second Aries holds the now blood-drenched sword between them, and he swings it across and chops his head clean off.

Each piece falls in a different direction, flayed open while the head will forever hold a horrified expression.

"I will take my leave now, Theo. I'll be seeing you again soon."

"I'll await your call."

Their exchange is quick and a bit cold, but I don't see the God of War as a man who could ever be soft. Don't think that's built into him, but then I'm no longer paying attention as I notice the semi-conscious woman on the floor looking around her for help that will never come.

Her lover and brother will be incarcerated.

Her king is dead.

Lilou is alone without the backup she's always hidden behind. A nobody trying to be a somebody by deception and greed, not caring about who she hurts on the way to the top.

"I warned you." Her lips part, the beginning of the word *please* on her lips, but I ignore it. Instead, I choose to do what I'd thought of doing the day she woke me up with a cold bucket of water to the body. "This will hurt."

The pretty bullet sits alone on the floor near her now-dead king's body. It must've slipped from the magazine when it fell from his grip, rolling a tiny bit away before stopping. Shiny and new, I lift it with ease and up high over Lilou's body—hovering as she shakes.

"No."

"Rot in the underworld." It comes down, and I take pleasure in watching it pierce her skull, the force shattering it upon impact. This causes an implosion that spreads brain matter around the room, the two faes on the floor now drenched in her.

Alpha
XADIEL

"You're a wicked witch, Little Moon," I whisper in her ear a second before wrapping my arms around her, locking them tight and with no plans of letting go. She's warm to the touch and pliant, every bit of worry draining from her body as she relaxes against me. "Such a perfect luna."

"You came for me." Her voice is small and hesitant, but the needy whine is unmistakable. So is the rich scent of her arousal, thicker in the air the longer we touch. "You're not mad?"

"Oh, I'm very angry, sweetheart." Whirling her around, I cup her cheek while my other hand runs down her back and sides, everywhere my hands can reach. Needing to make sure she's unharmed, that nothing marred her flawless skin, and as the bloodlust recedes, I'm starting to take in other things.

How she's dressed.

The slight change in her eye color.

A subtle lengthening of her canines.

How are you feeling, love?

"Earlier I felt hot, but this is so much worse." The fact she's answering me verbally instead of through our mind link is also alarming. "He drugged me."

"Who did, baby?"

"Larue. To force my heat, but this feels so much stronger."

"I'm sorry, Little Moon. Please forgive me for not getting here sooner." I'm trying to keep my voice calm, not relaying the animalistic urges to kill and fuck that want to take control. Rationality isn't conducive to these emotions as I know the fae fuck is dead, but I still want to piss on his corpse and then bend her over in the same breath.

It's instinctual. Built into all wolves.

"Not your fault." A hiss, her nails digging into my back and these cut the skin there.

"Isabella, can you look at me?" Gabriella calls out, but my mate simply buries her face in my chest and shakes her head—scenting me with a desperation that tugs at my cock. "Xadiel, what's wrong with her? Is she hurt?"

"No. She's fine," I manage to grit out through clenching teeth as she drags her own newly sharp ones down the side of my neck. Just the thought of her bite has me throbbing with drops of pre-come rolling down the shaft. "We need to leave, though. Can you handle this?"

Before she can respond, Theo places a hand over her mouth. "Get out of here. We'll handle everything, including the jailing of those two." His wife protests, grumbling under his palm but quiets the moment he lowers his mouth down to her ear and whispers the word: *heat.*

"Thank you." Wrapping her legs around my waist, I head for the door I'd used earlier with Anaya, but Isabella puts her hand on the doorframe, pausing us. She looks up from her position, face buried in my neck, and tilts her head to the side with a slightly out-of-focus look. We're facing away from them so they can't see her dress riding up, or how my fingers have a tight hold on her right arsecheek, but the curl of her lip tells me she likes it. "Did you forget something, Little Moon?"

"Somewhere in this building is Uncle Roberto. He never betrayed us." Taking in a deep breath, a low purr begins in her chest, and the sound is hypnotic. I want more of it, but she shakes her head to regain focus. "Silla was Larue's half-sister. He confessed this minutes before the first explosion."

"Are you sure?" Leo asks, his expression heartbroken. He's lived with her all these years, and in a way, she's like a mother to him.

"Yes. Please find Uncle and take him home." As soon as she's done, Isa grips my face with one hand and bends low so our lips skim. "Now let's go home, Xadiel. I need your knot."

I leave without looking back at our family. My goal is to reach the outside and I do in record time, taking in the pitch-black night sky, but when I try to place her down so I can shift, Little Moon shakes her head. Her grip is tight and her skin flushed; her pussy is wet and staining the trousers I'd borrowed earlier.

We're a mess, and she's never looked more beautiful to me.

"I have enough energy to get us back, Xadiel."

"My female, I don't want you overexerting yourself. We can find somewhere nearby to—"

"I want my nest." No words could sound sweeter from her lips. Our place in the woods that I built with our relaxation and love in mind, where I hammered every nail in place with the image of her one day round with my child.

"Then let's go to your nest, Isa. I got you."

"And I love you." The portal opens without any use of powders, herbs, or stones. It's a little weak and unstable but holds as I walk through with her in my arms and enter our glass-ceiling dome.

Her scent is faint. As if she's been here recently, and I see why almost immediately.

It's clean and the bedding washed, sitting at the edge of our mattress waiting for her to accommodate however she chooses.

Which she does the moment we step inside, squirming in my hold to be let down while she places every piece to her choosing. Sheets and pillows and an extra heavy comforter along with her favorite soft blankets that I stole to make this place cozier.

It all works together right now, and my chest fills with so much pride as she readies this for us. *Such a perfect little mate. Worth everything.*

Occasionally she looks up at me, giving me a bashful grin as excitement blooms in our bond. Coming back here was the right decision, where we're meant to be, and as I look up and find the full moon shining down on us, I know I'm blessed.

She home. Safe. And the gods have given us the opportunity we've been longing for.

"Come, my male. We need a shower." Isabella stands not far from me, her hand extended out toward me. She's naked now, and I admire her every curve in the low lighting. Nothing but the sky illuminates us as nature intended. Like packs did in the past when fire and caves were used to provide shelter.

Taking her much smaller hand, I let her guide me inside and turn the water on. It heats after a few seconds, steam billowing and filling the space as she steps under the shower head. Blood drips down onto the floor, cleansing her small frame while I run my fingers through her soft hair.

Beyond the sex and our bond, she's my dream come true. Intelligent. Thoughtful. Beautiful inside and out; I waste no time in pressing my front to her back. I cover her as the yearning to be closer crashes into me with the weight of a freight train. It reminds me of what she did for everyone.

What she wrote in her journals.

The love note left behind is a testament to her honest love for me. Because in a moment when her world seemed to shut down around her, Isabella's focus was making sure I understood she'd always be mine. Forever.

Grabbing the shampoo bottle, I pour some into my hands and

lather her from hair to toes. The more my fingers knead and massage, the purr she released for me in Larue's building builds and I respond with one of my own, memorizing her freckles and the cupid's bow of her lips as she tilts her head back and lets me rinse her off with her eyes closed.

Later we'll take care of the conditioning and moisturizing, but right now, I hunger for her.

She's calling out to me with each vibration. "Will my male let me wash him?"

"Later." Gruff. Voice deeper than normal, I soap myself before grabbing the removable shower head and rinsing myself off. She turns to watch with a pout. Follows the reddish suds slide down my body and into the drain. "Turn around, Little Moon."

"That's not fair." Her lilt is coquettish now while her lashes flutter, but she follows my command like a good girl. There's also the way she arches her back to present her chest. "I'm all clean now."

"And you want to be dirty, Little Moon?"

"Yes. Your dirty girl." Four words and they snap the last of my resistance. I'm taking a firm hold of her hip and lifting, pressing my front against her back while impaling her on my cock. She's suspended and mewling, wetness dripping down my knot as I bounce her with no gentleness or the care she needs after a traumatic few days.

I don't care for towels or being dry.

Don't give a bloody fuck about the mess left behind or the trail of water on the floors.

My destination is clear, and I fuck her through every step until her body is pressed against the glass of the nearest window overlooking the forest. I take ownership of my soulmate before the gods and nature, giving in to my baser instinct as my senses become sharper. Heat licks at my skin. It prickles and ignites where we touch, but it's the sudden clutch of her walls as an orgasm rips from her— how she thrashes in my hold and releases her claws for the first time —that sends me into a rut.

"I love you, Isabella Evergreen," I hiss out, loving the way they bite into my skin. How each break leaves behind the perfect imprint of a black-tipped claw. "There's nothing in this world more important than you."

"And I live for you, my king. My world." Her declaration is followed by a little shiver, and I fuck Little Moon through each one, giving her no time to catch her breath or moan. Everything she is and will ever be is mine. Her cunt. Her womb. Her heart. The way she tries to match my thrust with a push of her arse back which I find utterly adorable. "Please give me your knot. Take away the ache only you can."

Wetness drips from her at a steadier pace now; the slickness needed through a heat will help her take me over and over and over again until the fever breaks—

"Motherfuck, beautiful." Bending, she uses the window as leverage and cups my balls. Isabella is nearly folded in half, sitting on my dick as I see fit, while her tiny hand squeezes to just shy of pain. It's a heady feeling. I'm losing myself more and more to this feeling and when she skims a single finger down to my perineum, I snap my hips hard and fast, locking her on my knot. "Such a good girl for her mate. Knowing what he loves."

Not that she could do anything but accept it, and I kiss the back of her neck before walking us over to the bed. I crawl in with us on our sides and one of her legs raised high so I can continue to thrust slowly, shallowly, while the expanded base pulses inside of her.

Rope after rope of my spend fills her womb, and it calms my blind need for the time being. Not gone, but enough that I focus all my energy on her, catching some of our overflowing, combined releases and using two fingers to massage it over her clit. That's how I get her to come again. Tight, rough circles using my come and hers in between sharp smacks on her mound, the pads of my fingers barely grazing where she's swollen the most.

"Again, baby. Give me one more." Her responses are no longer words. Just whines and low growls with an occasional low purr that answers my call every time I push in a little deeper.

And once she's somewhat sleepy and completely sated, I'm able to pull one of the softer blankets over her and settle down. My knot hasn't let go and my cock is hard—throbbing—while nice and warm inside her walls where they'll remain until I can put the last few days out of my mind.

"You will never put yourself in danger, Little Moon." My tone is stern, a little of the anger at her I've kept at bay coming through in the demand. Not that she seems to mind, though. Her body just burrows deeper into the warm heat of my chest and the blanket. "Don't do that again."

"I promise." A whisper followed by a deep yawn. "It's too much work, anyway."

"Is it, now?"

"Yeah. Next time, you kick their arses."

Her response pleases this man and beast very much. It's my honor to fight all her battles, even if every time she tries to mimic my British accent, she butchers it.

EPILOGUE #1
Isabella

FOUR MONTHS LATER...

"Are you ready, Isabella?" Leo asks, extending his elbow for me to slip my hand through, careful not to ruin the lovely bouquet of lilies and roses my male chose for this date. He didn't have many stipulations, only caring about my comfort in a simple satin spaghetti-strapped dress in white that perfectly molds across my baby bump. Then, there are the flowers. A hand-picked arrangement he chose from the same garden the ceremony is taking place in.

This softness—the flowers, garden, and dressing up—are a complete contrast to the last few months. We've spent our time searching and curing wolves, hunting down those too late to save and giving their beast a dignified ending. We're lucky those instances weren't the majority, and most are now recuperating and regaining their normal lives.

"I am. More than." My other hand goes to the baby bump that's already showing; the pup's been fluttering all day, and I tell myself he's just as excited as I am. That our little heir is sensing the pride and joy radiating over the people he will one day lead. "Just don't let me trip."

"Never, Isa." His tone is serious, and I look over, meeting his eyes. My brother hesitates for a second. He wants to say something, and right when I think he won't, Leo bends down and places his forehead on mine—shares his emotions with me. They're beautiful and full of a filial respect that causes my breath to stutter in my chest. "If I don't say it enough, I want to thank you for all you've done. You and Xadiel mean more to me than just a brother or brother-in-law relationship. You gave me the parents I didn't have. Stepped in when you didn't need to, but did so out of love."

"You suck, kid. So much right now." Of course, they're happy tears. A little embarrassing and totally hormonal, but his words touch my soul. "I never wanted you to be without. Even if I couldn't be there every day, I tried to make you miss the painful parts a little less."

"And you did."

"That's just what a sister—"

"No, Isa. That's what someone with a generous heart does." Shaking his head, he smiles and reaches for my belly, placing his hand atop it. Our baby greets him with a little push. "This little one's going to be so spoiled in the best of ways. I'm going to take my annoying uncle duties to the extreme."

"I'd kick your ass if you didn't." More tears, and my bottom lip trembles.

Pulling back, Leo wipes under my eyes. "Let's get you re-lunafied, big sis."

"Okay." Inhaling deeply, I gather myself. It takes a few minutes, the tug at my end of the bond lets me know Xadiel's getting impatient, but my grin is wide and matches Leo's. "Let's do this thing."

As soon as we reach the ceremony trail, Leo takes off his shoes to match me. The trek to the stage is just as I remembered it, but this time the atmosphere is festive. Our pack, family, and friends—vampire, wolf, and one fae—are all here. Something I love, as we make it a third of the way and find Gabriella waiting for us.

She quickly intertwines her fingers with mine as we continue to walk; the wedding song plays in the background. It's a soft piano rendition of a popular pop song I fell in love with after finding out we were becoming a family of three. It speaks of finding each other through the storm, never letting go because nothing could feel better than waking up to each other.

Halfway up, I'm greeted by the vampire king who holds out a blood-red rose. Theodore smirks, and unapologetically sneaks it into my bouquet; a representation of who he and my sister are. A lovely gesture I accept with love by crooking a finger and placing a tiny kiss on his cheek before he and Gabriella fall into step behind us.

My next stop is Xadiel's parents, who I give a kiss and hug to before walking up the stage alone to reunite with the man who holds my heart.

The Alpha King's grin matches mine. It's been a long time coming, and it's only sweeter when he places his hand over our future king inside my womb. Recognizing his father, our baby moves a little, enough to say hello while the crowd watches on with grins.

England has always felt like home, and I couldn't be happier to move back. This is where our future lies. And while Alaska remains tied to us, run by us—this place is the right fit for us—our baby.

He will be born in our nest, though. It's a desire my mate is aware of and has promised to fulfill; I want him to come into this world in our little oasis where he was conceived with love, before being shown to his people for the first time on our royal lands. Xadiel's family and mine understand this, even if it's going to make things difficult as we bounce back and forth between continents, but my heart is set on this. *This is home, but that dome is special.*

The Astor's have also returned to their land in Italy. To be closer to us. So our children can grow up on the lands, they will one day rule, even if we do own homes not far from each other in Seattle and now Alaska, the latter of which was a gift from Xadiel to my sister and her vampire.

Everywhere we go, we will always be near. My male made sure of that with my anniversary gift; a deed to a property in Seattle given to me after my first heat subsided.

Then there's Leo and Anaya. They're working on ways to unite their kingdoms while ridding themselves off the trash left behind by her father. Some are fighting to retain control, to claim the for-now-abandoned throne, but none of us will allow it. Each monarchy has sent out a few of their most trusted to keep the peace, while protecting what belongs by birth to the fae princess.

Not even Silla, who remains in hiding, will be given a say. Her fate will cross with death, by my hand or the devil himself. Her path and ending don't matter as long as the vision remains the same, especially after all the damage she's caused.

To her family. To her coven. To her mate.

My eyes scan the crowd and fall on Uncle Roberto for a minute. He's mute now. They cut off his tongue years ago to keep him quiet about Larue's and Silla's dirty deeds, and it's there his hatred began. It'll take some time for him to see not all mated relationships are like his toxic one with Silla, and that's okay. Beside him, Anaya sits looking healthier and happy, wearing a pretty lavender dress from this century as she smiles at me.

Our beta and gamma couple, too.

Everyone I love is here as an elder wolf asks me to pledge myself to the Evergreen Royal pack.

"I, Isabella Evergreen, vow to be the best queen and luna for this pack. To love and care and help nurture the future generations while being a pillar of strength to our current members. I will always put the well-being of my wolves before the selfish calling of the outside world. By blood and pact."

"We are one," the crowd responds.

Because of my pregnancy, they don't cut my palm again. This is more of a renewal, but with one special surprise. There's one thing in our relationship Xadiel has always wanted—craved all these years.

"Kiss me, my king."

"My pleasure, my queen." His golden eyes with swirls of black become hooded the closer to my mouth he gets. The rumble in his chest, a sweet purr for his mate that I respond to with pure desire.

My small fangs drop, and he barely catches a glimpse before I latch onto the edge of his jaw, breaking the skin and giving him my mark: a symbol of our union and love for the world to see.

"Son of a—" I wave a finger up high so he sees. ***There are kids present. Don't you dare!*** "Fudge ice cream. Son of a fudge ice cream that's…" he trails off while the adults chuckle, some snorting at his save, while I lick and tend to the perfect imprint of my teeth.

It's pretty. So perfect. "That's lovely."

"You're feeling mighty proud of yourself through the bond, Isa."

"I know. No shame either."

You're going to pay for that, you cheeky minx. Throwing his head back, I admire the way he laughs and allows himself to feel every emotion. The good. The bad. The Ugly. Xadiel doesn't shy away, and this is one of those moments. He shows me through our bond just how happy I've made him, while the outside world witnesses the devotion of a good male pulling his mate close while caressing the round bump carrying his firstborn. His love shows no bounds or limits, and I will work every day to return the deep affection he so freely gives.

"You could always return the favor."

For a second, those orbs I adore flash fully black, and his wolf's growl is salacious. "Never doubt that, Little Moon. I'm going to eat you whole."

"I'm counting on it."

This time, he chooses to nuzzle his nose with mine and then pecks my lips. "Tomorrow and always."

"And every day that follows."

Because life isn't always easy, yet there's no doubt in my mind this is where I'll always belong.

With him. Our family. In every reincarnation.

Every bite fate gifts us, this man is my home.

Epilogue #2
XADIEL

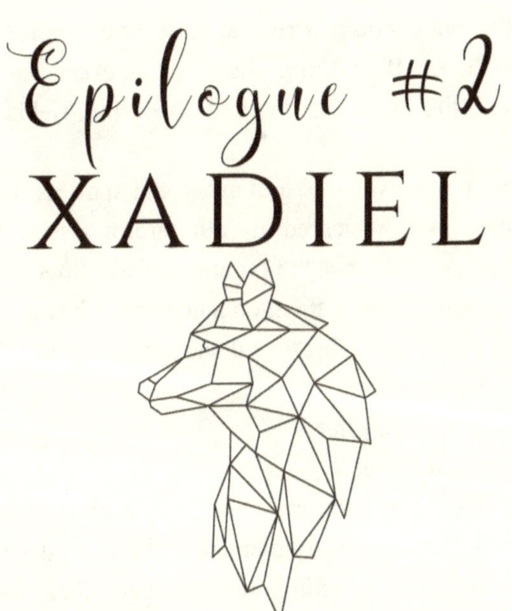

HAPPY BIRTHDAY, LITTLE ONE…

"Get up," I growl, prowling the edge of the makeshift ring set up for their disciplinary action. "Don't make me repeat myself."

The man currently on the floor, dragging his beat-up body toward the border across from me is the last of the fights today. I'd taken on all but two alphas, yet I feel refreshed, the beast inside me showing through our half-shift—a symbiotic merging of man and beast that many here are afraid of.

All but her. My queen.

Little Moon isn't afraid. She's watching with a smirk on her face, hand over her swollen belly while sitting in a comfortable chair far enough from the sidelines that I'm not worried. Not that she's alone. Faith, Grady, and her doctor are there.

At a little over eight months pregnant, our wolfen OBGYN has warned us the baby could arrive at any given moment…yet she refuses to stay home. If anything, she's nesting *everywhere*:

Our home, the pack house, and even the fields where our warriors train.

Everything must always be put away and spotless, no exception, and I'm amused by how scared my elite are of pissing her off. Not that she's mean or yells, but the bursting of tears does them in, and I'm called in a panic to *save* them on a near-daily basis.

Looking over, I raise a brow and she shrugs. **Same, Xadiel. He's comfy, and I'm hungry.**

Foot rubs and pizza after?

Fuck, how I love you.

It's hard, but I bite back my chuckle at how adorable and easy she is to please. Yet the amusement dies the second I eye the men nursing their wounds, groaning, while one of their lot was taken straight to the infirmary after I dislocated his jaw and he passed out.

That asshole lost his title, but I was kind enough to let his nephew take over as the former has no children. The new alpha has already sworn his allegiance to Isabella and me, grateful for the opportunity to work with the crown and take his people out of the depleted position they are in.

Because Diego did more than lie—fill their heads with utter rubbish—the man cleaned out their financial reserves. Most of these packs are near bankrupt, something their leaders will atone for with hard labor and sacrifices, the first being their opulent comforts.

Pack is family. Pack is sacred.

"Please, my king," the man, a wolf deep into his two hundred years walking the earth, pleads from his position on the ground. And while he's closer to my age than a few of the other idiots, he looks a mess. Unkept and thin, as if he's been denying himself sustenance, but I'm still not moved enough to pity him.

Not when I remember how they rebuked my female.

A queen who gave herself—put herself in a position to be hurt— to save those she loves.

My beast closes the gap between us, the ground ripping beneath the power of my claws. "Get. Up." The command is met with a whine, but compliance. He teeters a bit, already nursing a swollen eye and the marks of my claws digging into his shoulder—bleeding from the latter. Each drop staining the ground serves as a reminder that while I am an understanding king, Isabella is my weakness.

Who I will kill for time and time again if she so much as frowns.

"Alpha Xadiel, I was wrong. Please take mercy on me."

"Where was your mercy when you were willing to let my mate suffer?" Each word drips with venom, my fangs dropping a little lower as the angry rumble in my chest grows. While the pelt of my animal bristles in annoyance over his pathetic attempt to sway me. "What was it that your brethren said? Asking you to sacrifice yourselves for her is a crime?"

"I'm—" He doesn't get to finish. In a few short steps, I reach him and lift him clear off the ground by my grip on his neck. It would be so easy to snap it, to be done with this and take my female home, but I made a promise and I am a wolf of my word.

They each had to last ten minutes, and he still has four on the clock.

Fucking pathetic pussy. A flick of my wrist and he slams into a large tree a few dozen feet away, splitting the trunk. It doesn't fall over, still firm in its stance, but the wolf's eyes roll back for a second. His body slumps a bit, too, but I'm not done with him and let my animal take over.

Dropping to all fours, I give in to my wolf and recede back so he's in control.

Seeing this, he panics, eyes flashing wide and body trembling with fear. "I'm sorry! So sorry!"

"You will be," leaves my maw on a thunderous roar, and he struggles to move away, nearly crawling backward. He doesn't make it far, though. Before he can clear a few feet of distance, I've tackled him and opened my jaw over his neck, teeth poised to bite down.

Everything they said. The lack of respect.

All of it goes through my mind, but just as I'm set to discipline him—tear a chunk of flesh—a presence stops me. This is someone I know and trust, but it doesn't stop me from lifting my head and bearing my teeth while a front paw presses the weak alpha into the ground.

It's time, Xadiel. They took her to the birthing room. Cain's in his wolf's skin and giving me the equivalent of a wolfish grin. ***You shifted, and her water broke. Faith left with her.***

I've already taken off before he's done speaking, tearing through the field on my way to the nest we had converted into her delivery room. This meant a lot to her. To be where he was conceived, and as I reach the edge of the clearing, I throw back a ***break his leg*** before disappearing.

It's not long before the sound of a pain-filled scream rends the forest, chasing away some of the wildlife brave enough to investigate. Those in attendance cheer at the sound, their rage over the arrogance of these men still very pronounced.

Pack Evergreen loves Isabella. Adore my little witch and call her our blessing.

It takes me a few minutes to reach our nest, and I find movement inside, yet the moment I enter the glass dome, nothing else matters. Little Moon's in her birthing tub already in nothing but a sports bra, hair pulled up into a messy bun, while gritting her teeth and gripping the edge of the tub with both hands.

Her knuckles are white; she's already sweaty as I kneel before her while candles are lit and a bit of sage is burned.

"I'm here, Isa," my gravelly voice fills the space and she shivers, lifting her head long enough for me to find her wobbly grin. "What can I do to make this better, my love?"

"Hold me." That's all she asks. Nothing else, and I'm inside sans shirt within seconds. I sit against the tub and place her between my legs, giving her my warmth while gripping one of her hands the way I've seen Gabriella do a hundred times. The touching of the palms and fingertips soothes her, she draws from me—feeds off my essence as another contraction hits—and I'm surprised by how fast they seem to be coming.

It was mere minutes ago that Cain told me. My eyes snap toward the doctor, finding her already looking our way. "Is she okay?"

"She'd started experiencing minor labor pains earlier today, but kept quiet." There's a hint of reproach that Isa responds to with a huff, then a small yelp as every muscle in her body clenches tight. With my other hand, I massage her from hip to shoulder and back down again, trying to ease even a little of her pain. I don't like seeing her this way. "We've checked her, Your Highness, and our Luna is not under any distress. Pain, yes, but that's something we can't help with as she's chosen to do a natural birth."

"Thank you."

"I hate you all right now," Isa groans, the long and drawn-out sound full of discomfort. I know her words are her way of trying to crack a joke, but I don't laugh. Not when her face is pinched tight and cheeks red—when tears gather at the corner of her eyes. With Little Moon's body against mine, I monitor each rough ripple. "This hurts so much."

Each contraction that follows are close together and her whimpers break my heart. One comes and wrecks her—then mellows out —before another slams into her tiny body. This pregnancy hasn't been too rough on Little Moon, but the size of her belly compared to her stature has been a worry for me and the pack. Our family.

Not for Isabella, though. This woman has been a pillar of strength and calm. Only smiling and telling me to *chill out* whenever I raise a concern.

Gods, I love her so much. "You're doing so well, Isa," I whisper, nuzzling the side of her temple before dropping a kiss there. "Our baby is blessed to have such a wonderful woman as his mother."

"And you as a father…oh *fuck*!" she screams, the guttural sound ripping through her chest as I growl at the doctor who's already reaching to check her dilation progress. There's a smile on the woman's face, excitement, and I begin to purr for my female. Her beast sings for her as we're told it's time to push, giving her his comfort and showing his love through our bond.

A bond that at the moment is vibrating with so many different emotions, but love is the predominant one. Where it all begins and ends.

"Just a little more, sweetheart. He's almost here."

"Breathe, Luna. You are doing so well." Her doctor's words go in through one ear and out the other; the only thing my female can focus on is the purr in my chest. This brings her warmth—helps to soothe some of the wracking tightness across her abdomen and lower back. "On the count of five, I need you to push for me."

The doctor begins and I tap each count, but at four Isabella suddenly stands and turns to face me. Her hands grip my shoulders while I try to steady her, but she simply shakes her head while ignoring what everyone—the medical staff—says.

Grab him, my male. He's ready to say hello.

I'm not sure what to say. It takes me a moment to understand, but then I watch in total love and awe as my mate grits her teeth and pushes. Her claws unsheathe and tiny fangs drop, cutting her bottom lip as she embeds those nails deep into my skin.

And I'm with her through each painful cry. Through each nerve-wracking moment as she brings our little prince into this world.

Moreover, the moment I hold him, my world changes.

The love I have for this tiny pup cannot be measured or contained, but can be shown. He's the perfect mix of his mother and me. With her reddish hair but my eyes—even at this age, the golden tone is unmistakable—he has the sign of a royal wolf.

Tiny and barely taking his first few breaths, the presence of his animal is there and my wolf rumbles with happiness. We kiss our pup's head and breathe him in before placing his tiny body against his mother's chest; Isa's slumped against the tub's edge and weak, but her smile is wide as she traces a finger down his downy hair and soft cheeks.

His subtle scent of oranges and pine make me smile. "He's perfect, my love."

"I know." There's a bit of cockiness in her tone and I look up, finding narrowed blue eyes trained on me. "I'm also going to kick you in the balls after I heal a bit, Xadiel. You deserve to be in as much pain as I've been put through."

A frown creases my brow. "Does this mean you don't want any more kids?"

"No." A small pang rips through me. I'd love nothing more than a huge family with her, but I don't voice this. "I want at the very least six, but prepare yourself for sore testicles right after. It's your penance for knocking me up."

"Yeah?" Now I'm smirking. "Because I'll take one for the team without a bloody complaint."

"Yeah." Little Moon looks down at our handsome prince and tiredly shakes her head, a little giggle slipping out. "Atticus Paolo Evergreen is going to need a little sister to bug the hell out of him, and soon."

THE END FOR NOW…
UP NEXT IS OMISSION
LEO & ANAYA'S STORY

SERIES ORDER:
LITTLE LIES
LITTLE MATE
HALF TRUTHS: THEN
HALF TRUTHS: NOW
OMISSION PART ONE
OMISSION PART TWO

SPIN-OFFS:
COME TO ME
THE HUNT

The Beautiful Sinner Series are all interconnected standalones full of suspense and romance and an OTT alpha willing to burn the world to the ground for the woman he loves! It's sexy and has an edge of darkness that will leave you breathless! #MAFIAROMANCE

Now Live!
SIN #1
COVET #2
MINE #3
YOURS #4
RISQUE #5
OWN #6

Beautiful Sinner Spin-Off:
CORRUPT
MY SINFUL VALENTINE
SAVAGE KISS
ONE RULE

ABOUT THE AUTHOR

Elena M. Reyes is the epitome of a Floridian and if she could live in her beloved flip-flops, she would.

As a small child, she was always intrigued by all forms of art: whether it was dancing to island rhythms, or painting with any medium she could get her hands on. Her passion for reading over the years has amassed her with hours of pleasure, but it wasn't until she stumbled upon fanfiction that her thirst to write overtook her world.

She's a short and sassy Latina with an adorable pup, a kiddo that keeps her on her toes, and a husband who claims she'll cause him to go bald prematurely. Lol

Want to keep up to date with Elena's crazy book life?

Follow here:

Website:
https://www.elenamreyes.com/

Find My Books Here:
https://www.bookbub.com/authors/elena-m-reyes

Email:
Reyes139ff@gmail.com

FB Reader Group:
Elena's Marked Girls. Come join the naughty fun.
Link: https://www.facebook.com/groups/1710869452526025/

facebook.com/AuthorElenaMReyes
x.com/ElenaMReyes
instagram.com/elenar139
amazon.com/Elena-M-
Reyes/e/B00E3E26X8/ref=dp_byline_cont_pop_ebooks_1
bookbub.com/authors/elena-m-reyes
tiktok.com/@elenamreyes

Each book is a standalone.

SIN (#1)
COVET (#2)
MINE (#3)
YOURS (#4)
RISQUE #5
OWN #6

BEAUTIFUL SINNER SPIN-OFFS

CORRUPT
SAVAGE KISS
ONE RULE

MARKED SERIES

Marking Her #1
Marking Him #2
Scars #2.5
Marked #3

I SAW YOU SERIES

I Saw You
I Love You #1.5

TEASING HANDS DUET

Teasing Hands #1
Taunting Lips #2

SAFE ROMANCE:

ALSO, BY ELENA M. REYES

Taste Of You
Doctor's Orders
Back To You

<u>STANDALONES:</u>

Craving Sugar
Stolen Kisses